the
fall
UP

ALY MARTINEZ

Editor: Mickey Reed
Cover Designer: Hang Le of By Hang Le
Interior design and formatting: Stacey Blake of Champagne Formats

ISBN-13:978-1518711398
ISBN-10:1518711391

dedication

To my husband:
No hero ever written could do you justice.
Not even the ones who are six foot five.
You were, after all, the original "badass."
I love you even when I hate you.
And that's a lot.

the
fall
UP

1 (800) 273-8255

National Suicide Prevention Lifeline

www.suicidepreventionlifeline.org

chapter one

Levee

It was raining. Isn't that the way all great love stories start? And also usually end? The midnight air was cool against my skin as I stared off that bridge. My blond wig was secured in place by a headband, and chunky sunglasses covered my whiskey-colored eyes. I didn't look like myself any more than I felt it. Bruises from the night before painted my legs while fresh scabs covered my knees, but it was the hollowness in my chest that hurt the most.

Yep. Still me.

Which was exactly why I was standing on that bridge, wishing for the mental fortitude to hurl myself off.

A man's voice interrupted my thoughts. "You finally gonna do it tonight?"

I instinctually smoothed my fake hair down and pressed the bridge of my glasses closer to my face, sealing out any possible glance he could

1

catch. I stared ahead as I snapped, "Excuse me?"

"I've seen you here three nights in a row now. I was just wondering if tonight was going to be the night you finally jump."

My eyes flashed wide, but since they were covered by the dark glasses, my reaction remained hidden. "I just like the view. That's all." *What a load of shit.*

I watched him nod out of the corner of my eye. "Yeah me too. It's gorgeous up here."

Shuffling my feet to the side, I attempted to slip away as he pulled a pack of cigarettes from his pocket and offered it my way.

"You want one?"

I shook my head and then crept down a few inches to put distance between us.

"Suit yourself." He used a hand to shield the lighter from the wind, but the constant sprinkle of rain made his task impossible. "Damn it," he cursed with the cigarette tucked between his lips. "Little help?" he asked, swinging his gaze to mine.

Arching an eyebrow, I asked, "With what?"

"It's raining…and windy…and I'm trying to burn one." He tilted his head, equally as incredulous.

"You want me to call God? We had a bad breakup recently, but he might be willing to do me one last favor."

He breathed an exaggerated sigh of relief. "That would be *fantastic*. What's the big guy's response time like these days? Last time we spoke, it was"—he paused to look at his watch—"oh, twenty-seven years."

A soft laugh bubbled from my throat, and one side of his mouth lifted in a gorgeous grin.

"I'm not exactly in the mood to wait that long, so maybe you could just block the wind with your body?" His smile spread as he stepped toward me, forcing my gaze to nervously bounce away.

"Sorry. Can't help you there. Lung cancer and I broke up too." After gathering the back of my wig into a ponytail, I pulled it over my shoulder and turned away from him. The chill of the wind blasted my face and roared over my ears as it rushed past me.

I went back to staring out at the dark, choppy water, becoming lost in the idea of how cold it might be.

Is tonight the night?

No.

My feet would more than likely never leave the edge of that bridge, but there was a definite reason why I was imagining ending it all. Exactly zero other people in the world would understand why. I had it all, and I dreamed about losing it all—more often than I would ever admit, even to myself.

After stepping out of my heels, I slipped my foot between the bars on the railing. The wind slammed my bruised leg against the metal. "Shit," I hissed as pain shot through me.

"You think that hurts? Imagine falling twenty-five stories then crashing into the water, which might as well be concrete, at speeds upward of seventy miles per hour," the man said, leaning on the metal railing next to me.

"Wow. Someone's done some research," I said sarcastically, barely sparing him a glance.

"Daily," he responded frankly, causing my surprised gaze to swing to his. Simply shrugging at my reaction, he turned his back to the railing and propped himself up on his colorfully tattooed forearms. "You forget I've been here the last three nights in a row too." He smirked, lifting the cigarette up to his lips for a deep inhale.

"Listen, I'm not going to jump if you're some kind of caped crusader on a mission. I just needed some fresh air." I pointedly glanced at his cigarette.

A laugh escaped his mouth in a grey puff. "Fresh air is overrated. Especially given the reason you're standing here." He knowingly arched a dark-brown eyebrow.

"Riiiiight," I drawled, rolling my eyes behind my glasses. "Okay, well, I was just heading out anyway."

"Then my work here is done." He bowed, and the corner of my

mouth lifted in a smile as I stepped back into my shoes and walked away.

I shook my head at the random stranger. Then, a thought struck me, stopping me only a few feet away. Spinning back to face him, I asked, "Wait. Were you reaching out to me as a cry for help?"

"Oh look. Designer Shoes has a conscience!" He dropped his cigarette to the damp ground, stepping on it with the toe of his well-worn, black boots. Bending over, he picked the butt up and tucked it in his pocket.

At least he didn't litter.

"Oh look. Tattooed Stalker has jokes!" I smarted back.

He smiled, pulling another cigarette from his pocket and then pausing just before guiding it between his lips. "Were you judging me based on my tattoos? I'm offended." He feigned anguish then laughed while lifting his lighter to once again battle the wind for a nicotine fix.

I wanted to walk away, but he wasn't wrong. I did have a conscience, and right then, I was worried that it might really be his night to make good on his apparent numerous visits to the bridge.

With a huff, I headed back toward him, praying that I could wrap it up as quickly as possible then head back to my house for a few hours of sleep. Or, more likely, lie awake while staring at the ceiling and crying.

"Are you planning to jump for real?" I asked.

His smile fell as he focused on the water. "Nah. I don't have the balls to do something like that. Talking to you wasn't a plea for help or anything. You just look worse than usual tonight." His gaze slid down to my battered legs.

"Oh!" I exclaimed in understanding. "That's not at all what you're thinking. I fell down some stairs."

He quirked his lips in disbelief.

"I'm serious!"

"I'm sure you are," he told the wind. "You can go. I'm good."

I could have walked away, but for some reason, I pulled my jacket tighter around my shoulders and silently stood there while he finished his cigarette.

After a final deep inhale, he flicked it over the railing of the bridge. *Apparently, he does litter.*

Turning to me, his face became serious. "You need to call the cops before he makes the decision to end it all for you."

"Who?" I asked, watching the burning ember hit the metal column then explode in a million different sparks before disappearing down to the water below.

Lucky cigarette.

"The stairs...and whatever inanimate object you're blaming for those bruises you're hiding behind sunglasses at one in the morning. You should call the cops before..." His voice trailed off, but his dark gaze narrowed on mine. His eyes bored into my hidden stare, combining with the rain and wind to send chills down my spine.

I took the moment to secretly assess him. He was insanely sexy, but nothing like the men I was accustomed to. His chin was the kind of scruffy that made women weak, but it was obvious he didn't pay four hundred dollars for his personal hairstylist to shape it. Judging by his shaggy, brown hair that begged for me to thread my fingers in it, I wasn't sure he was even a barbershop kind of guy. He stood a few inches taller than I was in heels, so I pegged him at around six one. And while his tattooed forearms were deliciously sculpted and his shoulders were notably defined, his body didn't appear to be swollen with muscles from hours spent at the gym. By the aura of *bad boy* he gave off, I would have expected him to be a self-consumed, arrogant prick.

He wasn't though.

He was just an average guy worrying about the well-being of an average girl.

Only he couldn't have been more wrong, and a pang of guilt hit me hard.

Just not hard enough for me to do anything to correct his assumptions about who I was.

Very softly, I attempted to put his fears to rest. "I promise it's not what you're thinking."

"Okay," he responded, unconvinced. He nodded to himself before dragging another cigarette from his pocket.

I watched him struggle for a second before I scooted towards him, using my body to block the wind.

Biting the cigarette between his straight, white teeth, he smiled devilishly around it. "Thanks." Flicking the flame to life, he hunched over until a stream of smoke swirled up from the red tip.

"You should stop smoking."

"Noted." He exhaled through his nose.

We went back to silently staring over the side of the bridge. The familiar lights of the San Francisco skyline danced all around us. And, even as tourists and locals alike passed by us, I felt an odd, and unbelievably *comfortable,* isolation standing there with him.

When my teeth began to chatter, his attention was drawn my way. "I'm not here to jump. You really can go."

I nodded but didn't move away.

He chuckled, crossing his arms over his chest and rubbing his biceps for warmth.

"How are you not frozen?" I asked, taking in his thin Henley for the first time since we met.

Shrugging, he dropped his cigarette, answering as he bent to retrieve it. "Thick skin? I'm used to it? I come here a lot? I'm half Eskimo?"

I eyed him suspiciously. "You're cold, aren't you?"

"Fucking. Freezing," he admitted, tucking his arms close to his body and blowing into his hands. "I just came up here for one smoke. Then I saw you. Now, come on. Be a lady and loan a man a jacket," he joked, tugging on the edge of my coat.

I laughed, hugging it even tighter around my body and stepping out of his reach. "How about we both just leave? Then neither of us have to worry about the other plummeting to their death."

"Sounds like an amazing plan." He shoved his hands into the pockets of the tattered jeans riding low on his hips. As we began the hike back down to the foot of the bridge, he asked, "You have a name, Designer Shoes?"

I smiled and shook my head, not willing to lie—or divulge the truth.

"Yeah. Me either," he replied.

I bit my bottom lip to suppress a laugh.

Side by side, we trudged the rest of the way in silence.

When we got to the foot of the bridge, he turned to face me and sighed. "Well, I genuinely hope I never see you again."

My head snapped back in shock, and maybe a little hurt.

But he quickly corrected himself. "No! I just mean... Shit." He ran a nervous hand through his hair while I watched, amused. "I just mean, given the way we met... I...um. I hope you never have a reason to go back up there."

I teasingly tipped my head to the side. "But I really like the view."

He cleared his throat. "Right. Of course, the view. Okay, well, have a good night."

"You too." I smiled tightly, but my feet didn't budge. I told myself that it was because I didn't want him to see my car or the bodyguard waiting for me behind the wheel. But, in reality, I just wasn't ready to leave. Home wasn't where I wanted to be. I didn't actually want *to be* anywhere.

Not even standing at the foot of a bridge, talking to a witty and sexy man.

Okay, maybe I wanted that a little bit.

"Yep. Have a good night," he repeated, shoving his hands inside his pockets and slowly backing away.

I gave him a quick wave, which he returned before he jogged in the other direction.

I smiled to myself, shaking my head at the entire interaction—secretly lamenting that it hadn't been longer.

chapter two

Levee

The next day...

"You have to come with me, Miss Williams," Devon, my bodyguard, said, pressing his finger against the small speaker in his ear.

"No. I really don't." I glanced back at the line of young girls. Lifting a finger in their direction, I signaled for a second. Dropping my voice to an angry whisper, I snapped, "I don't care what Stewart told you. I'm not leaving." I flashed the girls another smile before watching him repeat my words into the microphone on the sleeve of his suit coat.

Devon extended a ringing phone in my direction, but I quickly pressed end, knowing that my manager, Stewart, was on the other end.

"Tell him to get his ass down here if he wants me to cut this short."

"Yes, ma'am," Devon replied.

I turned my attention back to the line of girls freaking out and furiously snapping pictures of me with their cell phones.

"Hey, sweetheart," I cooed, walking in the direction of a little girl no older than eight. Tears were streaming down her face as I took in her bald head, which was wrapped in a Levee Williams bandana, and a slew of wires and tubes dangling from her frail body.

"Thank you so much for doing this," a woman, who I assumed was her mother, said with red-rimmed eyes while snapping pictures.

"No. Thank *you*." I hugged the woman before squatting down to the little girl for a huge embrace I wasn't nearly prepared for.

As her tiny body slammed into mine, I was rocked off my heels, falling backwards with her still in my arms. Security, doctors, and parents all tried to catch me, but my ass found the tile floor first.

"Oh my God!" the little girl gasped, tears of embarrassment welling in her eyes. "I'm so sorry." She frantically scrambled to her feet, continuously apologizing.

My expression mirrored hers. "Oh my God. Are you okay?" I patted down her small shoulders and straightened the oxygen cannula in her nose. "Did I hurt you?"

She shook her head and rushed to her mother.

"I'm so sorry," I apologized, feeling like a clumsy-ass for having made such a sick little girl cry.

Her mother shook her head, dismissing my apology, and mouthed to me, "She's just embarrassed."

"*I'm* embarrassed," I mouthed back.

Stewart suddenly appeared at my side. "Levee, what the—"

I snapped twice and lifted a finger over his mouth, silencing him midsentence. "What's her name?" I asked.

"Morgan," the woman replied with a kind smile.

"Hey, Morgan." I approached her, dropping to my knees. "I'm really sorry about that. I'm such a klutz sometimes." I lifted the edge of my maxi dress, revealing one of my legs. "Look." I pointed to the bruises and scrapes on my legs. "I even fell down the stairs at a rehearsal the other night." I rubbed her back, and she peeked over her shoulder, flashing me a smile that relieved the tension in my shoulders.

"I know. I saw it on YouTube."

I returned her grin. "Ah, yes. My dear friend YouTube. Always there when I need it," I teased.

She began giggling at my joke.

"So, what do you say? Can we maybe try that hug again?" I reached down and made a show of pulling my heels off and dropping them one by one to the ground beside me. Squatting down like a baseball catcher, I motioned for her to come at me. I braced myself as she rushed in my direction then slammed into my arms a second time. I took a deep breath, holding her tight as she giggled.

Stewart's loafers moved into my periphery. "Levee, we need to go," he ordered.

Morgan began to release me at his words, but I squeezed her even tighter. "Nope. Not done yet."

She was amused by my joke, but I was pissed the hell off that Stewart had had the audacity to interrupt that moment.

"Guess what? I think I have some special surprises in the back."

Her eyes lit up.

"Can you give me, like, one minute? I'll see if I can find them." I gently guided her away while I pushed myself upright.

She nodded excitedly, backing to her mother.

I followed Stewart toward the room the hospital had set up for us. Loud groans of disappointment started to rumble through the crowd as I left.

"I'll be right back. I promise," I announced, which earned me a loud cheer from the group.

"You won't be right back! You're already three hours late," Stewart grumbled.

"Well, I'm going to be a hell of a lot later than that too, because I'm not leaving here until I've seen everyone," I whispered out of the side of my mouth. I gave the group one more wave as Devon ushered me into the room, closing the door behind us.

"Come on, Levee. Don't make me the bad guy. In less than an hour, you have a VIP meet-and-greet. I understand your dedication to being here, and it's great. Good for your heart, good publicity. Win. Win."

I rolled my eyes. I wasn't there because of publicity. I had plenty of that.

I was there because it was what I did.

Where I felt comfortable.

Where I was happy.

Where I had once been crushed.

But, ultimately, the only place I felt like I needed to be.

"Levee, you have hundreds of fans who paid for the VIP treatment. If you aren't there, it's not exactly VIP, now is it?"

"You know I can't leave," I snarled.

I hated Stewart, but it wasn't because he was an asshole. He was just doing his job. I paid him thousands of dollars to make sure my life ran smoothly. And for all intents and purposes, he was good at what he did.

But that didn't mean I liked having absolutely zero control over my life, including something as simple as time.

"Levee, what about all the people who waited in line for hours to meet you? What about the parents who've scrounged and saved in order to buy the four-hundred-and-fifty-dollar tickets? That's not exactly pocket change. What about the guy who's planning to propose? All of that has been set up way in advance. I get it. I swear to Christ I do. I let you stay an extra three hours, but if someone doesn't show up at that venue in the next hour, it's going to be a mess."

I nervously chewed on my bottom lip. He wasn't telling me anything I didn't know. I'd signed the contracts for three concerts and three meet-and-greets. It had been heavily promoted as my big homecoming since I hadn't been back to perform in San Francisco in over three years. It was my last stop before closing out my tour with a live television event in Los Angeles the following week.

I'd known ahead of time that a man had paid a large chunk of money in order to surprise his (hopefully) soon-to-be bride by proposing beside her favorite singer. And then there was the little girl with leukemia waiting there as well. I had personally sent her tickets the month before. There was also the Olympic gold medal swim team that had recently suffered the loss of one of their teammates. They'd used my song "The Belief" as her dedication on social media. I'd mailed those tickets as well.

They were all there.

Waiting.

Guilt overwhelmed me. Regardless of how hard I tried, I couldn't be everywhere.

And, *God*, did I try.

"Okay, how many are left out there?" I asked, trying to get my head on straight.

"At least a dozen more kids. Then their siblings, and parents...as well as a handful of doctors and their families, nurses—"

"Okay, okay. I got it." I sighed, pinching the bridge of my nose.

"Levee," Stewart breathed, walking up behind me and squeezing my shoulder. "I'll tell them. Maybe I can set up something for next month. You can come back, specifically for those you missed. We'll block out an entire day."

A month.

Lizzy hadn't lasted a month.

How many won't be here when I get back?

I shook his hand off. "I can't leave. I'm sorry."

He groaned behind me as I started to open the door. I froze when an idea hit me.

"Hey! What about Henry?" I twisted to face him.

"What about him?"

"He's in town. If I can get him to go over to the venue first, it will buy me some extra time here, and it will be like a double treat for the VIPs. Everyone loves Henry!"

Stewart didn't. So he rolled his eyes. "It's not a good idea, Levee."

I rushed to my bag in the corner and pulled my cell phone out. "Bullshit. It's a fantastic idea."

Another groan came from Stewart's direction, but I was too busy dialing Henry's number to pay it any attention.

He answered on the first ring. "There she is! What's up, beautiful?"

"I need a favor." There was no reason to bother with pleasantries. Not with Henry.

"Mmmm, I like the sound of this. What kind of favor?"

I could envision his flirty smile as he patted his purposely messy blond hair. "I have a meet-and-greet for my VIPs in an hour."

"Okaaay?" he drawled.

"You're in town, right?" I chewed at my freshly manicured nails.

"Levee," he warned.

This wouldn't be the first time I'd asked Henry for a favor. He wasn't exactly shy about asking me for them, either. And he always had the same answer I had for him.

I lowered my voice and said softly, "I'm at the children's hospital."

"Jesus, babe," he breathed.

I love him.

"There's still a line. I can't leave. But I'm supposed to be at the arena in an hour."

"I'll go," he said, quickly answering the unspoken question.

And he loves me.

Henry Alexander was the biggest name in music. Well…besides mine. He'd started off songwriting, the same way I had, which was how we'd initially met. We'd become fast friends. He helped me with the music, and I helped him with the lyrics. We brainstormed, jammed, and eventually moved in together. We sold more songs than any two twenty-one-year-old kids could have fathomed. But it wasn't enough. Selling songs was one thing. Selling yourself as the singer was something totally different.

But we both had dreams.

Huge ones.

Thanks to YouTube, we had accrued a massive following. We wanted to be individual artists but realized quickly that cross promotion and appearing in each other's videos every few weeks earned us the most views. People loved Levee and Henry together, but his gruff, sultry R&B voice didn't mesh well with my soulful-pop feel. A duo was out, but our fans began to expect us as a team. So we did what we always did: We got creative.

At twenty-three years old, we released our dual debut album. Fans went nuts. We threw our hearts and souls into that project, spending day and night in the studio to make it cohesive but different enough that people saw us as solo artists. *Dichotomy* ended up being six of his songs, six of mine, and two together. But, oddly enough, those weren't what people fell in love with.

My first single, "Isolation," hit number one on the charts almost immediately, while Henry sat at number two with "Belonging." Three months later, his single "That Night" took the top spot, while mine, "Another Day," sat right beneath it.

Less than a year later, Henry held me on his arm as we swept nearly every category we had been nominated for at the Grammys. It was the same night we made the announcement that, from that point on, we were strictly solo artists. We expected backlash, but if there was any, we didn't feel it. Both of our sophomore albums were certified diamond, securing our spot not just in the music industry, but at the forefront of it all.

Henry was my best friend for a ton of reasons, only one of them being his agreeing to go to the VIP meet-and-greet without even needing an explanation.

"Do you have Carter with you? Or do you need me to send Devon for security?" I asked.

"I'm good. Don't worry about me, sweetheart," he replied warmly.

With a huge smile, I gave Stewart a thumbs-up. His reply was a string of expletives.

"I owe you. You want to go out tonight after the concert?"

"Nah. But you can pay me back in other ways," he murmured suggestively.

"How's that?" I whispered, playing along.

He cleared his throat dramatically. "Don't play games. You know what I want."

"No. I'm honestly clueless." I walked over to the mirror, scrunching my long, brown curls back into shape then adding more makeup to cover the dark circles under my eyes.

"Levee," he scoffed before blurting out, "Let me fuck your bass player."

I burst out laughing. "Henry! He's straight."

"So? I thought I was straight once too."

"You are such a liar. You were never straight."

"This is probably true, but come on, Levee. Just tell me I can try," he pleaded.

There was no point in telling him no.

"Sure. By all means...go for it. Make sure you say hello to his fiancée first though," I teased.

Henry didn't find it humorous. "Damn it. Why is heterosexuality such a cock block?"

"It really is."

And it *really* was for Henry. He was tall, with a lean, muscular body that even I couldn't help but notice on occasion. Women adored him even though he was openly gay. However, Henry's biggest problem in the love department was his obsession with straight men. I couldn't even count the number of times Henry's heart had been broken by a guy who he'd convinced to give him a chance but ultimately went right back to women.

"All right, babe. I need to get dressed. Tell Stewy I'll meet him at the venue in an hour. Ask him if he wants a little action during the show tonight."

I smiled before calling over my shoulder, "Hey, Stewart. Henry wants to know if you want some man-loving?"

It was supposed to be a joke, but Stewart took an angry step forward, his eyes boiling with rage. "I swear to God! I'm a married man. He starts spreading that shit around…" He paused to run a hand through his thinning hair.

Still holding my phone to my ear, I gasped. "Oh God, please tell me you didn't really hook up with Stewart."

Henry burst into laughter. "Fuck no! But he hates me already, so I figure why not pretend? Drives him fucking nuts."

It was my turn to laugh. Stewart continued to fume.

"Okay, go get dressed. I'll see you in a few hours," I told him while straightening my long dress and preparing to go back out.

Henry's gentle voice caught me before I hung up. "Hey, Levee. Do me a favor. Take it easy, okay? You've got a show tonight. I know you want to be there…but don't get lost in the past. They aren't Lizzy."

He was wrong.

They were.

Every single one of them.

I didn't tell him that though. Instead, I replied, "Thank you."

He sighed at my non-answer. "See you tonight, babe."

"Yeah. Tonight." I dropped my phone into my bag and began rummaging through the boxes of CDs and T-shirts we'd brought to give away. "Are we out of the copies of *Dichotomy* that Henry signed?" I asked.

"Yep. We're out of damn near everything, Levee. Yet another reason you should come back another day."

"Oh, shove off!" I called as I headed to the door. With the VIPs sorted, I had a little girl named Morgan to properly apologize to.

chapter three

Sam

At least it wasn't raining. That had to be a good sign, right? Turning my back to the wind, I lit a cigarette. I was staring off the bridge just as I had done every night for months. The chill was still in the air, but thankfully, the depressing, grey clouds had moved out of the bay overnight. Some people loved a good thunderstorm, but to me, the dreariness that accompanied them was stifling. I was already grappling to find the light in the whole struggle known as life; I didn't need the weather making it that much dimmer.

"Shit," I cursed to myself when the gauze I had wrapped around my palm unfurled. Biting the cigarette between my lips, I quickly rolled the bandage back around my hand. I attempted to secure it in place with the worn-out tape but ended up tucking the edge under when it refused to stick.

I was such a pussy.

The moment that splintered wood had sliced my palm open, the whole world had begun to spin. It was a miracle I'd even stayed upright as the sight of the blood dripping from my hand had forced my ass to the dusty floor of my workshop.

Slitting my wrist was officially never going to happen.

But killing myself was never going to happen, either. With my luck, Hell was real and I'd only end up spending an eternity longing for the emptiness my life was already full of.

My life was fine. My job was fine. My house was fine. My love life was fine. My friends were fine. God, I was sick of fucking *fine*. I needed something—anything—to be *great*.

Why I thought death might be that, I wasn't sure.

But it had worked for *them*.

Most recently, it had worked for *her*.

Plus, I'd tried everything else. Over a hundred hours in the tattoo chair, skydiving, base-jumping, bungee-jumping, gliding. You name it, I'd tried it. And, while those brief moments had given me the highest of highs, the low on the other side fucking sucked. I hated every single minute of fine. There had to be more out there. There had to be a *great* lurking in the shadows.

I groaned.

My mind swirled with inner ramblings that had me rolling my eyes at myself. Even my emotions were logical and average. I couldn't even be extraordinarily irrational. That would have at least been exciting.

After dropping the butt of my cigarette to the ground, I snuffed it out with my boot. As I leaned over to retrieve it, I caught sight of a pair of heels I knew had cost a fucking fortune.

What the hell is she doing back?

She was not supposed to be there, despite how much I'd secretly hoped she would be.

Heading in her direction, I allowed my eyes to flash to her legs, but any possible new injuries were covered by a long, black dress.

"So we meet again," I said, dragging a new cigarette from my pack as I tucked away the old butt.

She pressed her sunglasses up her nose before stating the obvious. "You own a coat."

"Yeah. My doctor made me get it after I recovered from a bout of hypothermia last night."

Her painted-red lips parted in a smile. She was absolutely gorgeous—at least from the nose down. Who knew what the hell she was concealing underneath that silly wig and shades though. Or, better yet, why the hell she thought she needed them. Sunglasses, fine. But a wig? Who was she hiding from?

"Hypothermia. Ha! You're the wimpiest half Eskimo I've ever met," she said, compelling my mouth to mirror hers.

"This is probably true." I took a drag off my cigarette, then switched it to the hand farthest away from her when she started waving away the smoke.

After gathering the back of her wig, she pulled the hair over her shoulder. "But I don't know any others, so that also makes you the toughest."

"Awesome. Winner by default." I smirked. "I'll take it."

"What are you doing back up here tonight?" she asked absently.

I took a drag. "The view."

"Me too," she whispered. "Hey, can I bum a smoke?"

My eyebrows shot up in surprise. "I thought you broke up with lung cancer?" I pulled my smokes from my pocket, offering it forward.

"Everyone has the occasional one-night stand with the ex."

I laughed as she took the pack from my hand only to be silenced when she hurled it off the bridge.

"What the fuck?" I shouted.

She shrieked, repeating my curse when the wind caught the cigarettes, whipping it back at her. She ducked right before it sailed over her head and into the traffic behind us. I watched with a curled lip as numerous cars destroyed it.

"Well, I guess that works too," she said, straightening her jacket and proudly dusting her hands off.

"Note to self: Designer Shoes does not like one-night stands," I informed my only remaining cigarette, clamped between my fingers.

She quietly giggled, drawing my attention back to her.

Biting my lip, I noticed that her wig had slipped, revealing curly, brown hair hidden underneath.

"What?" she asked, reading my expression.

I lifted a hand to tuck the rogue hairs away but quickly dropped it back to my side. "Um… It's just…" I secured the smoke between my lips and pointed at her head. "Your, um…*roots* are showing."

Her face paled as her hands flew up to right her failed disguise. "You didn't see that."

"See what?" I answered then smirked tightly.

"Don't look at me like that," she snapped, nervously looking around to see if anyone else noticed her hairpiece malfunction.

"Like what?" I asked, feigning innocence. After inhaling a lungful of nicotine, I held it in a desperate attempt to keep my laughter hidden.

"Oh, for fuck's sake. Just laugh."

That was all it took for smoke to bellow from my mouth, followed by a hearty fit of laughter. I bent over, alternating between coughing and laughing, as she scowled at me, but her lips twitched, exposing her amusement. She fought a good fight, but eventually, she lost her battle and joined me, all the while smoothing her wig down.

By the time we both sobered, my last cigarette had burned out. Lifting the butt in her direction, I glanced over to where my pack lay mutilated in the middle of the road.

"That was fucked up."

"You're welcome," she smarted, dabbing at her lipstick with her manicured fingernails, drawing my attention to her mouth.

Shit. I swallowed hard, flashing my eyes over her body, cursing the chill in the air for forcing her to cover her every curve. From her expensive shades down to her designer clothes, she appeared high maintenance as fuck, but the stark contrast of her down-to-earth demeanor interested me the most. And since I was a nice guy who was strictly interested in her mental well-being, there was no harm in allowing myself an extra minute to check her out—while secretly hoping for a wardrobe malfunction as well.

Nothing like perving on a woman in her darkest hour. Go me!

When I made it back to her glasses, I found her watching me with a knowing grin.

Time to deflect.

"I hope you're proud of yourself. I'm going to die of nicotine withdrawal now. I've been smoking for so long that, the first time I tried to quit, I was hospitalized for a week. My heart couldn't take it, and I coded twice."

I couldn't see her eyes, but her eyebrows popped in surprise.

"No fucking way," she whispered.

I shrugged. "A heart attack can't be all that bad. I can think of worse ways to die." I tipped my head between her and the side of the bridge before flicking the butt of the cigarette over the railing.

She turned to face me, concern painting her flawless skin. "You're kidding, right?"

"About what part?" I asked, settling my gaze on her hidden eyes. I had a sudden urge to see what exactly was behind those glasses.

"All of it."

"No. Jumping off a bridge sounds terrible," I confirmed, shoving my hands into my jacket pockets, trying to pack down the emotions that were predictably stirring from my honest answer.

"And the withdrawal thing?"

"Totally serious." I cleared my throat, pushing all things *Anne* out of my head.

Her body stiffened as she covered her mouth. "Shit, I'm sorry. I was trying to help." Her nose scrunched adorably as she repeated, "I'm sorry."

She was really fucking cute.

I scrubbed the stubble on my chin. "Or maybe that was an episode of *Grey's Anatomy*. I honestly can't remember."

Her mouth gaped open. "You jerk!" she exclaimed, slapping my arm.

"Shit. Calm down." I threw my hands up in defense.

She shook her head and once again adjusted her wig, making sure it was still securely in place. I chuckled, quieting when she pursed her lips in what I assumed was an unimpressed glare.

I, on the other hand, was impressed.

That conversation with her had awakened something inside me that I hadn't been able to achieve in months.

Distraction.

She didn't utter another word as we stood silently, side by side, focused on the murky water below. After a few moments, her nails began to tap a vaguely familiar rhythm against the railing. I couldn't quite make it out and eventually gave up trying.

When the silence became awkward, I decided to make it even worse and blurted, "My name's Sam."

"Good to know," she replied dismissively.

Ouch.

On second thought, maybe the distraction wasn't worth it. Dismissed might just be a good thing. The fact that she was covered in bruises, wearing shades and a long dress to cover them, made it clear she had a ton of issues in her own life. Lord knows I did. The main one at the moment being that I was out of cigarettes—and suddenly interested in a suicidal woman.

Besides, she seemed somewhat stable. I could go. No worries.

Right?

"I should probably go. Can you promise me that you won't jump? You know, ease my conscience and all that."

"Just go," she whispered.

"That's not an answer."

Her tongue snaked out, nervously licking her lips. "I'm fine."

Fuck.

That warranted all the worries.

Fine was my specialty.

And I knew firsthand that fine was never truly *fine*.

"Look, I don't know you. But I think we've really bonded over the last two nights." I bumped her shoulder with mine. "Sure, I may have lived up to the title 'Tattooed Stalker' at first, but I didn't follow you home or anything." I grinned, and she offered me a courteous chuckle. "I mean, that has to say something about me, right? I'm a decent guy, I swear. How about we grab a cup of coffee"—cough—"and a carton of cigarettes"—cough—"and talk for a little while." I ended with a grin, giving it every ounce of charm I possessed.

"Sam, I'm serious. I'm really okay," she assured, but it was a weak attempt.

"Now, that's just not fair. I don't know your name. So it's really difficult for me to sound convincing like that."

"I'm not telling you my name."

"Okay, what if I guess?"

She shook her head but said, "Sure. Go for it."

I stepped away, dragging my eyes up and down her body (only partly to check her out again.) Then I framed my hands and pretended to be a photographer looking for just the right lighting as I walked around to her other side.

She didn't acknowledge my attempted humor, but when I leaned on the rail next to her, the slightest bit of amusement crept across her beautiful mouth.

"Bianca," I guessed.

She gasped and her hands flew to her mouth.

"Oh my God. That's it, isn't it?" I threw a fist pump in the air.

"That was incredible," she praised from behind her hands.

I blew on my nails then polished them on my shoulder. "What can I say, Bianca? I'm awesome."

I wasn't.

But watching her subtle reactions made me feel awesome. I guessed that was close enough.

"Incredible and *wrong*," she amended dryly.

My puffed chest deflated. "Yeah, I figured. Who's really named Bianca anyway? Hello, snob!"

"My mother."

Right.

Of course.

I scratched the back of my neck. "Well, it is a beautiful name." I tossed her an awkward smile, waiting for a laugh that never came.

Instead, something strange passed over the little bit of her face I could see. There was no doubting that the air around us had changed.

It was suffocating.

At least for her.

I was breathing clean air for the first time in a long time.

And that was suffocating for me.

Fuck, I need a smoke.

I didn't know her. I couldn't have even picked her out of a lineup without shades and a wig. But I knew for certain I couldn't leave her there.

"Please come with me." I lifted my hands pleadingly. "I can feel the heart attack approaching, and there was this nameless woman on the bridge tonight who fed my life source to traffic."

She flashed me a forced smile. "Thanks, but I think I'm just going home."

"Good." I breathed in relief—and disappointment.

"Have a good night, Sam."

"You too..." I paused. "Uh...Bianca's daughter."

Shaking her head, she walked away.

I stayed for a minute longer so I wouldn't really look like a stalker following her. After bumming a cigarette from a stranger walking by, I filled my lungs with the sweet poison and imagined a specific night just over four months ago.

A night where I hadn't been standing on that bridge but would have given absolutely anything to be able to change that fact.

A night where there hadn't been a beautiful woman in a blond wig as a distraction.

Or Anne would have still been there.

"I've got to quit," I whispered to myself, lifting the cigarette to my mouth for another drag. "Tomorrow," I promised myself.

But every day was yet another tomorrow.

chapter four

Levee

The next day...

After a thirty-minute conversation with Morgan the day before, she'd admitted that I was actually number two in her book. Not surprisingly, Henry Alexander was number one. The way she'd giggled as I'd told her embarrassing stories about him had touched me so deeply that I'd spent all day mourning the moment the world would lose such a sweet soul. In a fit of guilt that I couldn't do more, I'd forced Henry to sign nearly every piece of merchandise he had. I didn't have to hand-deliver it, nor did I have to make a special trip up there at nearly midnight after a show. It wasn't like she would have even been awake. But the sooner I dropped it off with her nurses, the sooner I'd feel better.

Hopefully.

With the second sold-out concert in San Francisco under my belt, I was struggling even more than usual. I was exhausted from back-to-back shows, not to mention the fact that I had another one the following night. But I found myself utterly unable to shut down. My mind raced with things I could—*should*—have been doing. Sleeping in a plush bed helped no one. Not even me. I was well aware that I was running myself into the ground. I just couldn't figure out how to stop. Which was ultimately how I ended up staring at the ceiling from the floor in front of the nurses' station at the children's hospital.

After stripping the oxygen mask off my face, I raced out the side door where Devon had parked. My chest was tight, and my voice had all but given out. The night air was cold, but my lungs burned for a completely different reason.

"Levee, wait!" Henry shouted, chasing after me.

"You didn't have to come," I squeaked, drying the steady stream of tears on the sleeves of my sweater.

"Yes, I did. And Devon was right to call me too. So don't you dare give him any shit." He threw his arms around my shoulders and pulled me into his chest.

"I'm…" My voice trailed off for a second before I finished the thought. "I'm fine."

Nothing in my life is fine.

"You have to stop coming here," he whispered, rubbing his hands up and down my back.

"I-I had to bring her that stuff," I stuttered, desperately trying to get my emotions under control—and failing miserably.

Blowing out a hard breath, he kissed the top of my head. "You have to stop this. All of it. You're not Mother Teresa, Lev. You can't take on the world."

My hands trembled at my side, and he reached down, moving them between us.

"Especially when it affects you like this."

"I'm okay," I assured him with more lies.

Leaning away, he tipped my head back to catch my eyes. "You just passed out in the middle of a hospital. I don't give a damn what you say—you're *not* okay."

"I am. I'm great." I forced a smile, but my traitorous chin quivered. I quickly buried my face in his chest. If I cried, there would be no way to keep the façade up. Not with Henry.

I swallowed hard.

I could fake it all with a smile.

I was good at that.

A fucking professional.

No tears.

Stepping away, I plastered on my stage face. *I really should have been an actress.*

Henry's expression disagreed.

Narrowing his eyes, he put his hands on his hips and asked, "When was the last time you ate?"

Food?

A little girl was about to lose the battle of her life and he wanted to talk about *food*?

"Who the hell cares about me. *She's going to die!*" I yelled.

He grabbed my shoulders and gave me a quick shake. "I care! Jesus Christ, Levee. Half the fucking world cares. It seems you're the only one who doesn't."

If only he knew how true that statement really was.

But I wasn't about to inform him of that.

Devon's voice caught both of our attentions as he leaned against my black SUV. "Everything okay?"

"I'm going to need help getting her in the car!" Henry called back to him.

"What?" I immediately backed out of his reach. "No! I have to go back inside." My eyes anxiously flashed between Henry and Devon as they both approached. "I told the nurse I'd take a picture for her niece."

"Then have Stewart send her an e-mail, because I'm taking you home, and you're not leaving until the concert tomorrow night."

"You are not my father, Henry. You don't get to make decisions for me," I snapped.

Leaning into my face, he bit right back, "Well, until you start taking care of yourself, it's obvious someone needs to. Food and sleep are not optional."

He forced me toward the car while Devon watched uncomfortably.

"You know I'm the one who signs your checks, right?" I spat the words at Devon as I attempted to shake Henry's arm off. "Let. Me. Go."

Henry let out a huff and loosened his grip on my elbow. I started to step away but then lost the ground beneath my feet.

"Not this time," Henry gritted out, throwing me over his shoulder. "I've let you do this bullshit for the last three years. I'm done, Levee. And so are you. Just because you're helping people doesn't mean you aren't hurting yourself."

"Get your hands off me!" I screamed, but he marched to the SUV and less-than-gracefully deposited me onto the black leather backseat.

Just as I began to scramble toward the other door, a bright flash illuminated the inside of the SUV.

"Shit," I breathed as Devon quickly circled around to the driver's side.

"Back up," he ordered as numerous flashes fired off. "I said, 'Back. Up.'"

Henry groaned before straightening his shirt, pasting on a smile, and climbing in beside me. Tossing his arm around my seat back, he asked, "You done yet?"

I shook my head.

"Well, pretend you are. And put your head down. Your makeup looks like shit." Dropping his arm around my shoulders, he curled me into his side.

And just like so many times before, I hid my emotions in his chest as our car pulled away.

"Let me carry her up." Devon's voice woke me from my sleep.

"I've got her," Henry replied. "Shhhh," he whispered into my hair as I began to stir. "Lock up when you leave," he told Devon as he started up the winding stairs with me securely cradled in his arms.

"I'll feel better if I stay for a little while. Make sure she's okay and everything. I can drive you home later," Devon replied.

Henry brushed the idea off. "Thanks, but I think I'm gonna spend the night. I'll call Carter if I need a ride. You can go."

Devon growled in frustration but finally relented. "Yeah. Okay, I'll lock up."

As Henry lowered me onto my bed, I heard the beeps of my alarm being set.

Lifting my feet, he pulled off my heels.

"Slumber party?" I asked sleepily.

He chuckled, collapsing into bed next me. "It's a shame you don't have a dick. Because, for as much as I put up with from you, I should at least be getting laid tonight."

I laughed, scooting into his side, all of my earlier anger muted by sheer exhaustion.

He let out a sigh as he wrapped an arm around my shoulders.

"I'm worried about you," he whispered.

I didn't reply.

I was starting to worry too.

"You're overdoing it, Lev. I know this job isn't exactly nine-to-five, but it's not twenty-four-seven, either. You have to stop being Levee Williams all the time and just be *you*."

"I know," I responded.

I didn't though. I felt like a robot parading around in a lost woman's body.

Smile.

Pose.

Turn.

Toss in the occasional song.

Repeat.

What little time I did manage to carve out for myself was spent at various children's hospitals across the country.

Smile.

Pose.

Turn.

Watch a child die.

Repeat.

With every day that passed, the smile became less and less genuine, the pose more and more forced, and the turn took me further and further away from who I really was.

My career was soaring while, personally, I was plummeting. Every single day felt like a terrifying free fall in no particular direction. I was stuck in the middle with no way up—or down.

"You remember that girl, right?" Henry asked, tucking a hair behind my ear.

I nodded.

I did remember her. She was fun and carefree. She loved going out and dancing at nightclubs until the very last song played. She slept until noon if she could. Then, fueled by coffee alone, she'd spend the day with a guitar strapped around her neck and a notepad at her side. She had a huge heart, but she knew her limitations.

Oh, I remembered that girl. I just couldn't figure out how to get back to her.

"You have one more show here tomorrow night. Then one in LA next week. After that, cancel New York. Stay here and rest up," he urged.

I suddenly sat up. "I can't cancel!"

"Yes, you can. It's a stupid award show. I'll accept whatever you win on your behalf."

"I'm supposed to perform." I sighed, flopping back down.

I couldn't say that his idea didn't sound appealing. Without New York, I'd have two glorious weeks off.

Which would leave me a full fourteen days to sit in a children's hospital. My gut wrenched at the idea.

"You need a break, Lev. It's not a concert. I'm not suggesting you let down thousands of paying fans. It's one song…at an award show. You'll be missed, but they'll find someone to fill your spot. I swear."

Not wanting to continue the conversation any longer, I simply nodded in agreement. I didn't know what the hell I was going to do. After that night's little fainting episode, I couldn't argue that I needed a break. My mind and conscience just wouldn't allow me to take one.

"Get some sleep, Levee." He kissed the top of my head.

I lay there for several minutes as Henry's breathing evened out. From my position on the bed, I could make out the dancing lights of the San Francisco skyline outside my balcony doors. I'd bought the house for that view, but as I stared at the bridge in the distance, my mind drifted to a completely different view altogether.

One of the tattooed variety.

chapter five

Sam

I **went through both** packs of cigarettes I'd brought to the bridge with me that night, but six hours of pacing later, my Designer Shoes still hadn't showed. To say it scared the shit out of me was an understatement. I was a swinging pendulum of emotions as I walked that side of the bridge more times than any smoker should be allowed. On one extreme, I was freaking the fuck out that maybe she'd actually jumped at some point before I'd gotten there, but on the other end, I was celebrating the fact that she had found other ways to cope with her issues and didn't need to go up there anymore. In between those two polar-opposite options, I chastised myself for being such a mental case, freaking out over a woman I hardly knew.

Then her smile would pop into my mind and sling me right back into a panicked state again.

By the time I left, the sun was peeking over the horizon and a slew of what-ifs were running rampant through my mind. None of which were good, and all of which ended with Anne.

I was a disaster.

With exactly zero hours of sleep under my belt, I started the next morning in the shittiest of shit moods.

And that was only the beginning of it.

"What do you want?" I greeted my visitor around a mouth full of apple as I opened my front door.

"Are you avoiding me?" Lexi asked, sliding past me.

"Well, come on in."

I didn't linger in the doorway. If Lexi was showing up at my door, she had something to say, and knowing her, she wouldn't be letting it go until she said it—probably multiple times.

The clip of her heels followed me to the kitchen, where I was cooking my breakfast.

"You know, this really isn't fair to me," she said, stopping beside the 1970s barstools I had just finished refurbishing the day before. "Are these new?"

"New? No. New to me? Very. Now, cut the bullshit and tell me what exactly is not fair so we can get this over with. I need to eat and get to work." I nabbed my spatula and flipped two eggs frying in a pan before setting it back down.

"Becky told me that she saw you at a bar with a woman last week."

Crossing my arms over my chest, I cocked my head to the side as I propped a hip against the counter. "I'm not sure you can consider a party at Quint's a bar." I shrugged nonchalantly.

I knew what was coming.

Three, two, one...

"You're making me look like an idiot!" she screeched, throwing her hands up in the air.

With her outburst, Sampson came barreling down the stairs only to come to a screeching halt when he caught sight of Lexi. He was a dog, but his disappointment was palpable. I couldn't help but laugh; I shared those exact feelings.

"Stop laughing!" Lexi snapped.

My already-thin and sleep-deprived patience disappeared. I could've pretended that I didn't have the time or energy to deal with her bullshit, but quite honestly, I just had no desire.

"Get out of my house," I ordered, going back to cooking my eggs.

"Stop. You need to stop being stubborn and give us another chance. I know you're pissed. I screwed up, and I've apologized at least a dozen times. But, Sam, we can't just throw away what we had."

"Excuse me?" I spun to face her, shocked by her nerve.

"You're making me look like an idiot in front of our friends. When we get back together—"

I abruptly cut her off. "We are *never* getting back together."

"Sam, I love—" She took a step toward me, but I pushed a hand out to halt her.

"I'm going to stop you right there. Listen up, because you obviously need to hear this—*again*." I quirked an eyebrow. "I do *not* love you. I have *never* loved you. I will *never* love you."

Her head jerked to the side as if I'd physically slapped her. Sure, it was harsh. But she clearly hadn't heard me each time I had uttered those words over the last two months. Lexi Prior was a nice enough girl, or at least she had pretended to be for the six months we were dating. She was also gorgeous and used to getting exactly what—or, in this case, who she wanted.

But so was I.

And Lexi was no longer who I wanted in any regard.

"You need to take a step back and let this really sink in, Lex. This crazy-ex-girlfriend bit you have going on is not a good look for you." Never tearing my eyes off her, I blindly found my coffee on the counter and calmly tipped it to my lips.

Unfortunately, Lexi was also determined. "Don't act like that. You know you didn't give us a fair shot. After Anne—"

Like an electrical shock, anger radiated through my body before finally firing from my mouth. "Get out!" I dropped my coffee cup in the sink and stormed to my front door, yanking it open.

"See! This is the problem. You lose your fucking mind at the mere mention of her name."

"No. I lose my fucking mind when *you* mention her name. Big difference." I snapped my fingers then pointed out the door.

Her eyes softened, and a tear escaped from the corner. "I apologized about that."

My mouth gaped. Apparently, the crazy-ex-girlfriend thing wasn't an act at all.

"You apologized? Ha!" Closing my eyes, I dug in my pocket for a cigarette. I didn't usually smoke in my house, but it was either that or allow my head to explode. "You apologized?" I repeated to myself as I lit the end. Inhaling a long drag, I held it as long as possible, but the calming effect I was so desperately seeking never came.

I scrubbed a hand over my jaw, reminding myself that she wasn't even worth my anger. After the shit we'd been through, I should have been awarded a medal for even allowing her in my house at all. Just because I didn't hold grudges didn't mean I had to put up with her shit though.

Sucking in a deep breath, I found a very fake version of my inner calm. "Lexi, if I ever see you again, I'm going to do far more than embarrass you in front of our friends. You can spout whatever you want about us falling apart because I withdrew from our relationship. I won't even bother lying and telling you that it's not the absolute fucking truth. But I need you to listen closely right now, because I'm *not* doing this with you again. I'm done here, Lex. And, judging by the fact that you spent the morning before Anne's funeral with your mouth wrapped around your personal trainer's cock, you were done even before I was. Now, get the fuck out of my house, lose my number, and forget I exist. Because I sure as fuck have forgotten you."

My smoke detector chose that moment to start blaring. Whether it was my cigarette or the eggs that had started to burn on the stove,

I wasn't sure. My only focus was on the woman unmoving across the room. She opened her mouth several times, but each time, I shushed her with a pointed glare. Finally, she gave up and stomped out. I was positive she wasn't giving up though.

Christ!

I pinched the bridge of my nose and stared down at the floor. Sampson came over and nuzzled his thanks for getting rid of her against my leg—or maybe he just wanted his ears scratched. After snubbing my cigarette out on the sole of my boot, I headed to the kitchen to trash my breakfast, cursing Lexi for having trashed my morning.

And I did it worrying about a blond wig and shades that had trashed my night as well.

Two hours later, Henry Alexander's latest album was blaring from the speakers in my workshop, until the room suddenly fell silent.

"Why do you listen to that shit?" Ryan asked, snatching up my iPod and scrolling through before landing on The Smashing Pumpkins.

After flipping my safety glasses off, I dropped the angle grinder into the claw-foot bathtub I was working on. "I like one song. Fuck off."

"Bullshit. You love that crap. You're such a bitch." He walked toward me, dragging his hand over the smoothed edges of the porcelain.

"Says the man wearing a pastel-pink tie."

He groaned. "Jen bought it for me. It's hideous, but the first rule in attempting to sleep with your administrative assistant is: If she bought it, wear it."

Lighting a cigarette, I asked, "What's the second rule?"

He blew out a loud, frustrated breath. "I have no fucking clue. Covering my body in fucking tattoos and shoving a needle through the head of my cock? You prick."

"Hey! She doesn't know about that."

"She better not!" Smoothing a hand over his short, brown hair, he mumbled in defeat, "I have no idea what to do with that woman. Any thoughts?"

"See, I thought the first rule of sleeping with your assistant is: Don't. So I'm probably pretty worthless on the second."

"Come on. It's *Jen.*"

"Oh, I get it." I tossed him a wink that he returned with an all-too-familiar glare.

Ryan had been obsessing over Jennifer Jensen since she'd walked into his office holding her résumé six months earlier. He was right—it was *Jen,* and she was fucking gorgeous. And, for that reason alone, I hadn't immediately turned her down when she'd all but sexually assaulted me in the kitchen at Ryan's office Christmas party. Ryan had been pissed when I'd told him later that night that she and I had shared a kiss (and a few gropes I'd purposely omitted from my confession). He'd blamed it on the tattoos and banned me from all future social gatherings.

Within twenty-four hours, he'd gotten over it and was back on the chase after Jen.

He turned his attention back to the tub. "What's this going to be?"

"A loveseat," I answered on a puff of smoke.

"No shit?" he breathed, notably impressed.

"Well, once I manage to get the front off. After that, I have to smooth everything out, resurface the outside, then upholster it. I got this incredible chocolate leather. Cost me a fucking mint, but it's unbelievable."

"How much?" he asked, squatting down in front of it and running his hand over the guidelines I had etched into the side.

"More than you can afford."

He arched an eyebrow. "Try me."

Ryan Meeks had the money. I knew that much.

I'd known Ryan since we were scrawny kids playing basketball in middle school. We were two unathletic losers who merged a friendship during one season riding the pine. We remained tight through high school and eventually shared a dorm at college. For as many years as we had been best friends, we couldn't have been more different. I considered myself the beauty in our duo, but there was no doubting that he was the brain. While I spent my days covered in dust with at least one power tool in my hand, Ryan was a criminal defense attorney at one of the biggest law firms in San Francisco. He was still making a name for himself, but his six figures were nothing to sneeze at.

However, neither were my prices.

When I had gone off to college, I'd originally planned to major in architecture, but Christ, that shit was boring. I quickly switched to graphic design and fell in love. I dabbled in the corporate advertising world for a year or two after graduation, but ultimately, I hated that life. One random Wednesday afternoon, as I stood staring at my office door, overwhelming dread filled my gut and bile rose in my throat. It spoke wonders to me that I'd become physically ill at just the idea of doing my job. I couldn't imagine how that shit would affect me mentally over the course of the years. So, without another thought, I marched to my boss's office and quit.

In retrospect, it might not have been the smartest decision I'd ever made. The nausea I'd thought was overwhelming dread turned out to be the stomach flu. However, when I finally quit puking three days later, I couldn't even bring myself to regret my choice. I'd finally discovered my true calling.

I'd always loved working with my hands; it had been ingrained in me at a young age. My parents hadn't been rich by any means, but they hadn't been destitute, either. My dad had a series of mental health issues, but even in his darkest hours, he could've been found locked in his shop, repairing something. He'd been a firm believer that you used everything until you couldn't possibly use it anymore. My parents' microwave had to have been at least twenty years old, but my father had refused to replace it. He'd fixed that thing on a daily basis for almost five years. The amount of money he'd spent on parts and the time researching how to make the repairs was insane. But, as far as he'd been concerned, you didn't throw anything away *ever*.

Even after he died, it was a lesson I applied to my adult life as well. So, faced with my newfound unemployment, I tried to figure out some way to put to use my love for graphic design and my experience in repairing and repurposing. I came up with the dream of opening an up-cycle furniture store.

One month after I'd quit my job, I opened rePURPOSEd.

I had exactly one piece to show people when I opened the doors. I also had exactly one customer that first month. I just couldn't gamble on the time and money it took to make a piece that may or may not sell. I did, after all, have to eat. And buy smokes.

Luckily, creativity wasn't a problem for me, so I developed a plan. I closed the store for a week and settled behind my laptop. Over those five days, hopped up on coffee and cigarettes, I designed over a hundred unique pieces. I had a college buddy help me with the website, and by the following week, Virtually rePURPOSEd was born.

And it exploded.

Suddenly, I had orders flooding in from all around the world. They were far more than I'd have ever been able to fulfill on my own, so I hired two unbelievably talented carpenters, Shane and Travis, to breathe life into my designs. They were a godsend, but they were also expensive as fuck. The first month they were employed at the shop, I had to sign over half of my savings account in order to pay them. But, with my designs and their craftsmanship, we had no problem moving furniture for a hefty profit.

Shane and Travis eventually took over running the physical store, and my time was mostly spent designing on the computer or at the shop behind my house, building whatever project was calling to me at the time.

On this particular day, it was an old claw-foot bathtub I'd found at a thrift shop and was determined to convert into an art-deco loveseat—a project that would easily sell for over ten thousand dollars.

So, while I knew that Ryan could afford it, I couldn't afford to give him my usual friends and family discount—free.

"Forty grand," I lied so he'd drop the topic.

"Jesus Christ. That's it. Next time we go out, you're paying for drinks. I'm not buying the poor-struggling-artist angle anymore."

I snuffed my cigarette out in my overflowing ashtray. "Don't even try that bullshit. How many times have you accidentally-on-purpose left your wallet home in the last month?" I mocked his voice as I slid my safety glasses back on. "'It's in my other suit, Sam. I swear.'"

"One time. That happened one time, and I've never heard the end of it."

"One time my ass," I said as I picked my angle grinder up, preparing to get back to work. "Did you need something?"

"Actually, I need a big favor."

I motioned for him to fill in the blank.

"Okay. First off, my mom wants you to come to dinner tonight as a thank-you for making Morgan that bookshelf."

I eyed him even more warily. He knew as well as I did that eating his mom's cooking wasn't exactly a hardship. "Okaaay," I drawled suspiciously.

"And secondly, I need you to come fix the drawer on my filing cabinet," he rushed out in embarrassment.

"I'm sorry. What?"

"I can't get that son of a bitch open to save my life. I have a big meeting at three, and if I have to hire a goddamn repair man to come in there to open it, I'm going to look like a dumbass in front of the entire office."

My lips twitched as I crossed my arms over my chest.

Ryan was three inches taller than I was, and while I worked with my hands to keep in shape, he visited the law firm's private gym on a daily basis. He had me by at least twenty pounds—all of which were muscle. He looked like the clichéd all-American, even as he stood in front of me sporting a pink tie.

I couldn't even pretend to stifle the laugh that escaped my mouth.

"You can't get your filing cabinet open?" I confirmed incredulously.

His shoulders fell in relief even though I hadn't agreed to go yet. "Shut it, asshole, and just help me out."

I continued to laugh as I, once again, dragged my glasses off. "You think me walking in there with a bag of tools is going to look any less conspicuous than hiring a handyman?"

He curled his lip in disappointment. "What a fucking novice." Chuckling, he steepled his fingers under his chin like the evil genius he so obviously thought he was. "So here's the plan. No tools. Just pretend you're coming to say what's up. They all know you." Pausing, he narrowed his eyes and pointed an angry finger in my direction. "Stay the fuck away from Jen."

"Right. How exactly am I supposed to fix this with no tools?"

"I snuck a hammer, screwdriver, a pair of clamps—"

My eyebrows shot up. "Clamps?"

He tipped his head and lifted his fingers to mimic a pinching motion. "You know, the little things you use to grab stuff or pull it off."

"Pliers?" I asked in disbelief.

He tapped the tip of his nose. "Bingo. Anyway, I snuck them all into the office this morning. They didn't work for me, but I have faith in you."

I stared at him for several beats. "How the fuck are we best friends?"

"No clue. Now, put on a long-sleeve shirt to cover the ink and get your ass in my car."

"Right," I smarted, but I said it as I dragged my jacket off the chair and headed to his car.

One hour later, I pried my best friend's filing cabinet open so he wouldn't look like the bitch he really was.

Then I parked my ass at his mother's dinner table for the best home-cooked meal I'd ever had. Well, since the last time I'd eaten there. All the while I was counting down the hours until I could head back up to the bridge—hoping and praying that it wasn't too late for the designer shoes I couldn't seem to stop thinking about.

chapter six

Sam

"**O**h, thank God." My heart jumped with relief when I saw her standing on the bridge. I dragged a cigarette from my pocket and headed in her direction. "I hope you know you scared the piss out of me last night," I said when I got close.

Her hidden gaze flicked to mine, but her lips didn't pull up at the corners like they usually did when she saw me. "I'm not in the mood tonight, Sam."

"If I had a dollar for every time a woman told me that." I smiled, but it fell flat as tears rolled from under her dark sunglasses. My breath painfully stilled as my mind raced. "What's going on? Did something happen? Did he—"

"Oh God. There is no him!" she yelled. "I don't have an abusive boyfriend. So please just stop with that and leave me alone."

I was shocked by her outburst, but her reaction secured the fact that I wouldn't be leaving her alone at all. I didn't give one fuck that it made me creepy as hell. I could live with that—as long as she *lived* too.

I didn't reply, nor did I move away. I simply focused my attention on the water below—which meant I was secretly studying her out of the corner of my eye.

She nervously adjusted her hair at least a dozen times while I finished my cigarette. She even scooted down the rail a few feet, and much to her dismay, I slid down with her.

"You aren't going to leave, are you?" She sniffled.

"No."

"Sam, I'm—"

I pushed off the rail and spun to face her. "Don't say *fine*. Whatever word you're planning to finish with, don't let it be *fine*." I huffed and shoved a rough hand through my hair. I was probably overreacting, but I couldn't risk that I wasn't. "I get it. You don't know me, but in some ways, that makes me the perfect person to talk to. So, please, I'm begging you. Tell me what's going on with you. Just give me your story. I'm not here to judge."

"I can't," she said, swiping two fingers under her glasses to dry the tears.

I would have given anything to be able to see her eyes—get a real read on her. Her mouth and her body language only gave away so much, but I needed *more*.

"Well, then. I'm sorry if me being here bothers you, but I can't walk away. You don't have to talk, but you're stuck with me until you walk down off this bridge."

Tilting her head up to the sky, she sucked in deep breath. "You don't have to babysit me."

"Fine. Then you stand there and babysit me. Last night was shitty for me." I pointedly lifted my eyebrows at her. "And this morning wasn't any better. I could use a babysitter." I blew out a breath, trying to check my attitude.

She didn't deserve it. She obviously had enough going on without some stranger blowing up at her too.

Humor. I can do that.

"And, as my babysitter, if you're fighting the urge to pat my ass and tell me that it's all going to be okay, I definitely wouldn't stop you." I flashed her a grin that I knew would go unanswered. I was okay with that though, because she stopped moving away.

Her chin quivered as she chewed on her bottom lip.

I fucking hated seeing her like that and had to ball my fists at my sides to keep from reaching out to touch her. I was desperate to console her, but I was already forcing my company on her. I wasn't going to do it physically, too.

That wasn't what she needed.

What does she need?

I swallowed hard when her shoulders began to shake as sobs ricocheted inside her chest, seemingly unable to find a way out.

Fuck it. Maybe just a little touch.

I slid a hand down the rail to cover hers.

It was a simple gesture, but it was easily the *greatest* decision I'd ever made.

That one touched destroyed a wall.

I wasn't even sure whose wall it had been to begin with—hers or mine.

But I would have spent my entire life tearing it down if I could have only predicted what was on the other side.

Spinning, she threw her arms around my neck. Caught off guard, I stumbled back a step before steadying us both. Folding my arms around her waist, I pulled her flush against me. Sobs ravaged her, but I held her as though I could siphon them away.

I couldn't, but just trying returned to me far more than I was giving her.

And, for that alone, I squeezed her even tighter.

Tourists bustled by us, probably staring as they passed. But only one person on that bridge mattered.

It wasn't me.

And, for once, it wasn't even Anne.

I actually didn't know her name at all.

"I'm sorry… I'm…" She continued to cry into my neck.

"Don't be sorry," I croaked around a lump in my throat.

Nothing else was said for several minutes as she wept in my arms. I didn't whisper soothing words. I just stroked her back and allowed her time to collect herself.

What would I have I said anyway? Why she was crying in the first place was a mystery to me, but it was one I was determined to solve.

Finally, she stepped out of my grasp and began frantically drying her eyes. "I need to go. I'm really sorry about that."

I immediately wanted her back.

Safe.

In my arms.

To keep my hands busy, I dragged a cigarette out. "Please don't go," I whispered as I lifted it to my mouth.

"I have to get off this bridge," she replied.

I quickly nodded in understanding. I wanted her off that bridge too.

"Thanks for… Shit. I'm so sorry. Let me get that dry-cleaned for you." She motioned to the tears and black makeup smudges staining my shoulder.

I chuckled. "I'll be okay. Besides, I can't give it up. It's my only coat."

Her face paled. "Oh God. That's even worse. I'll buy you a new one."

"I'm kidding. I have a whole closet full. I swear." I made a cross over my heart. "But don't worry about getting it dry-cleaned. Really, it's not that nice. I can just toss it in the wash when I get home."

"I can tell you from experience that mascara isn't going to come off in the wash. Just let me—"

"Seriously, it's just a jacket. If you are hell-bent on making it up to me, then tell me your name."

Her chin snapped to the ground. "Uhhh…"

"Right," I said, more than just a little put off.

"It's just…"

I shoved the unlit cigarette back in the pack then tilted my head toward the way down. "Come on. I'm ready to go home."

She didn't move. "Sam, I… I mean…"

I forced a smile. "Don't worry about it."

Resting a hand on the small of her back, I ushered her down the bridge. She went willingly, but her eyes were aimed at the ground as she nervously knotted her fingers in front of her.

When we reached the bottom, she stopped and lifted her gaze to mine. "About that little freak-out on the bridge… I'm… I shouldn't have put you in that position. I mean, you—"

She could have apologized all she wanted, but I wasn't interested in the least. Pulling a yellow piece of paper from my pocket, I cut her off. "Take this. I completely understand that you don't want to talk or tell me your name. But, last night, I was freaking out that…" I paused to think of how to gently phrase it, but I came up empty. *It is what it is.* "I thought you jumped."

"Sam—"

"No. Just hear me out. That's my number. You seem to get here no earlier than eleven every night. So I'll be here tomorrow and every night after that by ten thirty. But if, for some reason, you feel the need to come earlier, use that and I'll be here."

Her face softened as she took a step toward me. "Sam—"

I scrubbed a hand over my chin and continued to talk over her. "And if, for some reason, you don't feel like coming up here, can you at least put me out of my misery and shoot me a text or something?"

"Sam, stop." She inched even closer and rested her hands on my chest.

"I get it. You're clearly a private person. Feel free to block your number and sign the text 'Designer Shoes' or, really, not at all. I'll know who it's from," I nervously rambled. It wasn't because she was suddenly touching me or the fact that heat might as well have been radiating from her hands for the way it made my chest feel, but rather because I wanted to touch her too.

But I *really* just wanted to throw her in the back of my car and force her into some kind of therapy so I could stop obsessing about her—and then maybe touch her in a different way.

I didn't think kidnapping would go over well, but instead of acting like a normal person and offering to get her help, I looped an arm around her waist and shifted her even closer against my body.

"I think you're right. I really might be a tattooed stalker."

She smiled. "I'm not going to jump," she whispered.

God, I want to believe her.

"Take your glasses off," I whispered back, tipping my head down so I was only a breath away from her mouth.

Her tongue darted out and dampened her red lips.

I needed to see her fucking eyes. And then taste her mouth.

Then kidnap her.

I decided to take matters into my own hands. After slowly reaching up, I pinched a corner of her glasses. I didn't remove them, but I made my intentions clear.

"Please let me see you."

She didn't move away, nor did she agree. So I stood there with my hand on her glasses, pleading with my eyes for a single glimpse of hers.

She did something better.

Her tongue made an encore against her lips—just before it ruined me for life.

She pushed my hands away then sealed her mouth over mine.

My eyes popped open in shock for only the briefest of seconds. Then a moan rumbled in my chest as she opened her mouth and twisted her tongue with mine.

She tasted like mangos, and I fucking devoured her like a man starved.

For as many cigarettes as I'd smoked while waiting for her, I probably tasted like an ashtray. But I could apologize for that later. I wasn't stopping any time soon.

Her tongue swirled as I took the kiss deeper.

Suddenly, she pushed off my chest and took a step away. "Fuck. Shit. I can't believe I did that. What the fuck is wrong with me?"

My head was spinning, and her words sounded a whole lot like insults, but I still followed her forward.

"I'm standing right here," I reminded her. "Can you possibly check the freak-out for after you sleep with me on our first date?"

"Oh God," she groaned.

I tugged her back against me. I wasn't letting go no matter what her reaction might be. Not after that small sampling.

"I'm kidding! Jesus, lighten up."

"I'm sorry. About…" She dropped her head to my shoulder.

"Stop apologizing and grab a drink with me. I'll even find a place with really bright lights so you won't even have to take the shades off," I joked, and she rewarded my efforts with quiet giggle.

At the sound, an unfamiliar high whirled through my mind. It rivaled anything tobacco could ever give me.

"Sam, I need to go. But I promise I'll be here tomorrow night. Okay?"

It was my turn to groan.

No name.

No eyes.

Just a promise I didn't want her to keep.

I wanted her to be absolutely anywhere but on that bridge tomorrow night.

But I also just wanted her to be with me.

"Okay," I replied, begrudgingly releasing her.

She began backing away, and I could feel her hidden gaze locked on me.

"Thanks for tonight," she said. "Let me know if you change your mind about the dry-cleaning."

"How about this? I'll trade you my jacket for your wig and sunglasses!" I yelled as she got farther away.

A smile lifted one corner of her mouth. A mouth I now knew and desperately wanted to taste again.

"Goodnight, Sam." She waved her hand before heading to a parked black SUV and climbing into…the backseat?

Interesting.

"Goodnight, Designer Shoes," I whispered to myself as her vehicle left the parking area with the silhouette of a man behind the wheel.

An unnatural rage flooded my veins.

What the fuck?

chapter seven

Levee

What the fuck had I done? Oh, that's right. I'd kissed Sam.

A freaking stranger.

Who was suicidal!

While standing on a bridge.

While he'd thought I was suicidal as well.

But, worse than all of that, I couldn't stop thinking about it.

I'd replayed it in my mind at least a thousand times since I'd walked away from him.

I'd made poor choices with men in the past. I was far from the angel the media portrayed me as. But I had a sneaking suspicion that, if the news outlets got ahold of this little story, it wouldn't have the romantic spin my stomach took every time I thought about the moment his lips had touched mine.

My steps were a little lighter that night while I was performing for thousands on stage. My thoughts weren't filled with dread and guilt. Instead, they were focused on the top of that bridge, waiting for the moment I could return.

To Sam.

The show was entirely too long, but I snuck out of the backstage after party about thirty excruciating seconds after it'd started. Like a Freudian slip, I left my wig at home. I should have stopped to pick it up or at least checked to see if my stylist had something I could borrow, but after the concert that night, I just wanted some fresh air and a few moments alone.

And, by that, I meant a cloud of smoke and the sexy and intriguing man who accompanied it.

"You look better as a brunette," Sam announced as he sauntered up next to me with a cigarette hanging from his lips.

A smile pulled at one side of my mouth.

He was wearing jeans and a black, long-sleeve button-down shirt. His sleeves were rolled up, which drew my eyes down to the colored inked on his arms, and I wondered what they meant. But, seeing as my heart was racing and I couldn't figure why I was suddenly nervous around this man, I decided to give up on the deeper meaning behind his tattoos and worry about covering my clammy palms instead.

"No jacket again?" I asked, pulling the beanie low over my curls.

"Any chance tomorrow night you're going to lose the shades?" he replied, ignoring my question.

"Not likely."

"Your legs are healing up well," he stated, leaning on the railing beside me.

"They looked a lot worse than they were."

"Right." He rolled his eyes, which I noticed were the most amazing shade of gold. Not quite hazel, but definitely not brown.

Damn it! Stop ogling the hot, suicidal man!

I flipped my gaze back to the water. "Your hand looks better to-night."

He paused just before he got the cigarette to his mouth. "You noticed? I was worried you were gonna stop checking me out after you drove off with another man last night," he said roughly, causing me to swing my head to face him. "Is he the one who gave you the bruises?"

Ugh!

"What? No! Besides, I told you there is no *him*. I fell down the stairs."

"Whatever." He brushed my honest answer off, but thankfully, his attitude also seemed to disappear. "So, you feeling better tonight?"

"Actually, yes. Now, let me see your hand."

He twisted his lips, but he lifted it for me to inspect his cut.

"What'd you do?"

"Splintered it on a guitar."

Now that perked my attention. "You're a musician?" I asked as the idea of Sam strumming beside me made my cheeks heat.

I tried to hide my face by refocusing on his palm, even though I had no idea what I was looking at. I just wasn't ready to drop his hand yet.

"Not in the least. I tore it apart to make a bookshelf."

My gaze snapped to his. "A bookshelf?"

"Yeah. Just cut off the front and then added shelves." He pulled his phone from his back pocket and started scrolling through pictures. It took him a minute to find the image he wanted, and it wasn't lost on me that he did it one-handed.

What the fuck am I doing?

Again.

After dropping his hand, I tugged my beanie down as he thrust his phone in my face.

Sure enough, there was an acoustic guitar with the front cut off and three wooden shelves running horizontal inside the body.

"It's for kids books, but I guess you could use it for spices or something too. They'd have to be short though." He sidled up beside me so we could look at the picture together. "Or maybe some little knickknacks?

I don't know."

"Wow," I breathed. "You made that?" While he was close, I stole a deep breath of the musky scent of Sam's cologne. He shouldn't have smelled that good—not while smoking a cigarette. But he absolutely did, so I took another not-so-conspicuous whiff.

"Yep," he boasted proudly, flashing me a megawatt grin my hidden gaze lingered on a little too long.

Okay, that's a bit of an understatement. I stared.

And his smile grew as he stared at me…staring at him.

And it continued.

For entirely too long.

But not nearly long enough.

"Why are you looking at me like that?" he finally asked, snapping me out of my stupor.

"It's just…" *You're sexy.* "I mean…" *And funny.* "I, uh…" *And happy.* I suddenly got my thoughts together and shook off whatever hypnotic trance the memories of his mouth against mine had put me in. "You just don't strike me as someone who would want to kill himself," I announced.

His smile instantly disappeared and his eyes jumped to the ground as his black Converse nervously tapped against the railing. "Not everyone does."

I should have been a decent human being and not watched such an obviously overwhelming moment for him, but the pain that had appeared on his face rendered me unable to look away. Frankly, in *that* moment, he more than looked the part of a man who wanted to end it all, and it scared the hell out of me.

I might have been up there too, but I knew what was going on in my head. I wasn't going to jump off that bridge, but suddenly, I worried that Sam couldn't honestly say the same.

My pulse spiked as he struggled to force down the demon my innocent observation had somehow unleashed. I wanted to help, but I had no idea what the hell to do. I was clueless as to the war he was waging behind those golden eyes. I barely knew the man breaking down in front of me, much less how to comfort him—or if he even wanted to be comforted.

The only thing I knew for sure was that I had to get him off that bridge.

"I'm… Hey, I'm sorry. Listen, I'm starving. Any chance you want to go grab a bite to eat?"

He swallowed hard then asked the ground, "You asking me out?" The question was teasing, but his voice was gravelly and packed with unshed emotion.

Mine wasn't much better, breaking as I nervously replied, "I really just want to get off this bridge right now."

His head popped up, and I offered him a tight smile he seemed to accept as my answer. As he focused on me, the color began to slide back into his face.

"Okay," he agreed.

I breathed a sigh of relief and nodded entirely too many times. Dropping his cigarette to the ground, he took a step in my direction. He soothingly rubbed my arm, and I couldn't pretend that it didn't help calm my nerves, but that wasn't the only reason I leaned into his touch.

A gentle smile played on his lips as he brushed the curls off my neck and whispered, "I know a little Puerto Rican restaurant that's open until two. You good with that?"

"That works," I mumbled.

His eyes studied my face as he asked, "You okay?"

"Are *you*?" I countered.

He didn't bother with a response. Resting a hand on the small of my back, he guided me toward the foot of the bridge.

We didn't chat on the way down. Only a few stolen glances and shy smiles were exchanged. I hated feeling awkward with Sam, but judging by the way he watched me out of the corner of his eye, he didn't like it much, either.

"You want to ride with me?" he asked, spinning a keychain around his finger when we got to the parking area. All signs of his earlier distress had surprisingly vanished.

"Umm…" I stalled, not wanting to acknowledge my driver waiting for me in the car. However, I was fearful that Devon's forehead vein would rupture if I disappeared with a random guy—even if Sam was only random to him. "I, uh… I'm not sure. Maybe I can just meet you there or something."

He lifted a finger and tapped on the bridge of my glasses. "You gonna wear those all night?"

"I haven't made it that far." I smiled tightly.

"Well, how about this? Let's start with you telling me your name. Then we'll deal with the carpool and sunglasses. After you accosted me with your mouth last night, we're practically dating. I should probably know your name so I can go ahead and buy our matching airbrushed license plates."

I threw four fingers up. "Four-eva."

He drew in a sharp breath. "The fact that you got that joke is so fucking sexy."

My cheeks heated as I attempted to cover with more humor. "Besides, I owe you nothing. If I remember correctly, you seemed to enjoy that accosting. Wait. How did it go?" I stopped to tap on my chin then gave a breathy moan, mimicking his from the night before.

"Oh, come on. It was a manly moan and you know it," he flirted, flashing me a bright grin that warmed places other than just my cheeks.

The absence of that feeling in my life might have been the only reason I let my guard fall away. I couldn't restrain myself anymore. I scooted forward, and as I hoped, Sam slid his arms around my waist, tugging me against his chest.

"Is your boyfriend going to kill me for this?" He nodded to my car only a few yards away.

"He's not my boyfriend," I whispered as my breathing began to speed.

I shouldn't tell him.

I was losing my mind.

It was one kiss that probably meant nothing to him.

Maybe that was true, but in the few days since I'd gotten to know Sam, he had begun to mean a whole lot of something to me.

My heart pounded in my chest as I weighed my options.

I can't risk him telling the whole world about my dirty little bridge secret.

I should just walk away before the headline "Levee Williams is suicidal" paints the front page of nearly every tabloid imaginable.

But, for reasons that could only be explained by the safety I felt when I broke down in Sam's arms, I announced, "My name's Levee."

He tipped his head to the side in surprise. "Really? Levy, like the tax or the pop princess?"

Shit.

"Levee, like the embankment used to prevent the overflow of a river."

His head snapped back as he barked a laugh. "True story."

I didn't quite understand his reaction, but I steeled myself for worse.

Squeezing an arm between us, I pulled my sunglasses off and quietly finished, "And the pop princess."

His eyes, not surprisingly, flashed wide, but his words were not at all what I'd expected.

Cupping my jaw, his callused thumb rubbed over my cheekbone. "No bruises," he breathed, visible relief paining his face.

My mouth quirked in confusion. "What?"

Placing his other hand on my cheek, he framed my face. "Your shades—they weren't to cover bruises."

"Jesus, Sam. I told you no one was hurting me. I tripped down some stairs."

"Yeah, but everyone uses that excuse," he said through an infectious smile.

"I fell off the stage during rehearsals the other night. Some asshole leaked the video. It's probably trending right about now if you need proof."

He laughed. "That's really fucking good news. I was worried about you."

I was worried about *him*.

"Well, don't. I'm fine."

He angled his head, giving me a side-eye that told me he wasn't buying it. He was probably right, but I rolled my eyes. Once again, he laughed, but this time, he brushed his lips against mine.

"So, the guy in the car?"

I pressed to my toes and grazed my lips against his again. "Bodyguard."

Nipping at my mouth, he pulled me even tighter against his firm body. "You should fire him"—*kiss*—"for letting you go up a bridge every night alone." *Kiss.*

I smiled against his lips. "I'd fire him if he followed me."

"I follow you." He smirked. *Kiss.*

"Every celebrity needs a stalker I guess. The good news is I happen to like mine."

"That definitely makes my job that much easier." He licked his lips in a way that sent tingles over my body. A soft moan escaped my mouth when his tongue retreated.

"Kiss me," I whispered.

He stared at me for a moment, his eyes searching mine for something. There was nothing to be found except lust.

"Kiss me," I repeated.

He all-too-willingly obliged my plea and crushed his mouth to mine. It wasn't timid or laced with concern like the kiss from the night before. It was deep and filled with indescribable relief.

He was kissing *me*.

"I'm sorry I taste like smoke," he murmured against my mouth. "Damn it, I'm ruining the mango."

I giggled, sliding my hands up his sculpted back. Sam might not have been thick, but taut muscles curved his lean body.

"It's just gum," I said. "I'll give you some next time."

"Definitely." He stopped kissing me and leaned his forehead to mine. "Levee, it's really fucking good to meet you." He sighed and then punctuated it with another kiss. "Now, let me buy you some of the best rice and beans you will ever taste at midnight on a Wednesday."

"Okay," I replied, reluctantly stepping out of his embrace.

"So, how does this work?" He shoved a hand in his pocket and rocked to his toes. "Do you have an entourage or just the bodyguard you need to take with us?" He teasingly poked my ribs.

It was my turn to give him the side-eye. He was acting entirely too nonchalant about my little identity reveal.

"Did you know it was me all along?"

"What? No! I would have *immediately* tried to have sex with you if I'd known," he answered frankly.

"Great. Is that supposed to be reassuring?"

"No, it was supposed to be a joke, *princess*."

I leveled him with a glare. "Don't."

He laughed and threw his hands up in surrender. "Hey, you were trying to get in my pants way before I was trying to get in yours." Then he grinned something so beautiful that my eyes dropped to his mouth before I could even stop them.

"Can we just go eat?"

Quirking an eyebrow, he fought a smile. "Is that disappointment I sense? Levee, do you *want* me to try to sleep with you?"

"No," I scoffed, looking away.

When my gaze drifted back to his face, he was sporting another huge grin, and just like it had earlier, it did some seriously warm things to me.

"Then I won't."

"Good," I replied quickly.

"Good," he repeated, but his eyes bounced to my mouth and his smile spread confidently.

"Oh God, can we just get some food now? This is getting awkward,"

I huffed.

"More awkward than making out with your stalker?"

I swayed my head in consideration. "It's getting there."

His shoulders shook as he chuckled until something caught his attention over my shoulder. "I think you're being summoned." He pointed to the headlights flashing at us across the parking lot.

"Yeah, that's Devon, my um…bodyguard."

"Soon-to-be ex-bodyguard?"

"Uh, no. He's been with me for years. I hated him at first, but now, he comes to my house for Christmas dinner. I'm not firing him for respecting my decisions."

He huffed. "All right. All right. I get it. He's your Kevin Costner."

"Wow. You were so much more charming from behind my shades."

I actually adored that he wasn't acting stiff or freaking out on me. He was just…Sam.

"You're full of it." He winked.

I rolled my eyes. There was no use arguing with him. I really was full of it. Sam was even better now—and he was already intoxicating. Thankfully, that remained locked in my own head.

"Come on. Devon can drive."

He rested his hand on my lower back. Only, this time, I didn't even pretend not to arch into his touch as I returned his flirty wink.

Leaning forward, he brushed my hair off my shoulder and whispered, "Game on," into my ear as he slid his hand down a fraction of an inch, moving it from respectable territory to just above my ass.

But, as far as I was concerned, not nearly low enough.

chapter eight

Sam

After meeting her hulking bodyguard—who, thankfully, didn't resemble Kevin Costner in the least—he drove us both the mile and a half to Raíces. When he parked us out back, I tried to open the door to lead Levee inside, but he slammed it in my face. Levee laughed and informed me that Devon needed to "scope it out first." The man would let her wander up the side of a bridge nightly, but God forbid she walk into a tiny hole-in-the-wall restaurant where the biggest worry would be stumbling down the steps after too many sangrias.

However, I didn't argue. I assumed they had a system. And besides, Levee was curled up under my arm with her head resting on my shoulder. As far as I was concerned, we could have waited in the back of that SUV all night. During those twenty minutes, we didn't talk much. I'd drawn circles on her arm, and even though she later denied it, she'd fallen asleep at one point. I was absolutely in no rush.

When we finally made it inside, Raíces was strangely empty. The place wasn't usually packed, but it was never a ghost town. I had a sneaking suspicion Devon wasn't paying for our dinner as he stood with the owner, swiping a black American Express.

I gave Levee a suspicious glance as she peeked up at me through her lashes, embarrassed. Tossing her a reassuring smile, I kissed the top of her head. It wasn't like I was going to complain about some quiet time.

Two beers, three sangrias, and an order of mofongo and plantain chips later, I was sitting across the table from one of the biggest celebrities in the music industry.

But that wasn't why my cheeks hurt from smiling. Or why my hands itched to touch her. Or why I had forgotten about the entire world outside that restaurant.

Of course I'd been shocked when Levee had pulled her sunglasses off, but really, I'd been just so fucking relieved that her life wasn't nearly as hard as I had speculated over the last week. It was a huge burden off my shoulders for me to know that she had the money and support system in place to take care of her issues. She wasn't some lonely woman navigating life alone. Kidnapping wouldn't be necessary. I could focus on getting to know the real person behind the shades. The one I had so fiercely connected with over the last week.

"You can't hold that against me. I mean, I like your music too. I was trying to be honest." I laughed as her mouth hung open in mock horror.

Clinking her glass of sangria against my beer, she said, "I can't believe you like Henry more than me! Well, I guess the good news is that Henry would probably prefer you over me too."

"Hey! I'm not gay. I just said I like one of his songs. *One.*" I waved a single finger in her direction.

"Seriously, this is the story of my life. He's going to try to woo you."

I stabbed my thumb toward my chest. "Straight."

"Oh please. Far bigger men than you have swapped teams for Henry."

"Okay, slow down there, princess. No one is switching teams. I'm trying to woo *you* with cheap sangria right now. One step at a time, please."

"I swear to God, Sam. Stop calling me princess," she demanded, but one corner of her lips twitched. And I only noticed it because I was watching her mouth—intently.

"It's just… Designer Shoes doesn't have the same oomph to it."

"You've spent the last week trying to get my name. Use it," she snapped but hid her amusement by lifting the glass to her lips.

Reaching across the table, I pressed up on the bottom of her drink. "Clearly, with that attitude, you haven't been wooed properly. You should have more."

"Stop," she laughed, spilling the red liquid down her chin as she fought to set the glass back down.

After nabbing my napkin, I wiped it off her face while she cleaned it from her lap.

"Great," she said. "I'm a mess now."

"Well, that just makes us a matching pair." I pointed to my shirt where, earlier, she had accidently flung sauce on me.

"I told you I was sorry. That plantain chip went rogue. You can't hold me responsible for that."

I shook my head, sliding my hand across the table to intertwine our fingers.

Staring down at our joined hands, she whispered, "This is fun."

I gave her a squeeze. She wasn't wrong. It was, by far, the best night I'd had in as long as I could remember. Amazing. Yes. Surreal. Incredibly. I could easily go so far as to say *great*.

Conversation flowed easily. She made me laugh, and I made her scowl—then laugh. We didn't talk about the heavy. I didn't ask her why she was on that bridge every night, and she didn't ask me, either. We just bullshitted like old friends.

It was *great*.

She was great.

I had an overwhelming need to keep her great.

"What's your last name?" she asked, dropping her napkin on the table.

"Rivers."

"Shut up. I'm serious."

"So am I." I dragged a rePURPOSEd card from my wallet and slid it across the table. "Just think how fun your name would be if we got married." I winked.

She glared.

"What? Too soon?"

"By, like, ten years."

"Ten years? The sangria is not that bad." I feigned injury.

She barked a laugh. "So, tell me about rePURPOSEd?"

"I take junk, *repurpose* it, then sell it as new. Too easy. Rich people love it." I paused. "Present company excluded, of course."

"Guitar bookshelves?"

"Yep."

She flipped my hand over and traced a finger around the cut on my palm. Tingles radiated out from her touch. I was done keeping my hands to myself. I desperately wanted the connection the table had been denying me all night.

Pushing my chair away, I gave her hand a squeeze. "C'mere."

Her cheeks pinked as she stood and slowly closed the distance between us. With a quick tug, I pulled her off-balance and into my lap.

Tucking a stray curl behind her ear, I brushed my thumb over her bottom lip. I leaned in for a welcomed taste, and the sweet fruit from the sangria covered the mango I'd come to expect. "I want to see you again."

A shy-schoolgirl blush tinted her cheeks even darker. "We do kinda have a standing date for tomorrow night on the bridge."

"That's not what I mean." I glided a hand up her back, and as if she had been waiting for a sign, hers seductively slid under the edge of my shirt. Her smooth fingers teasing my skin stole my breath. I gasped and caught her wrist. "I want to see you again, but not on the bridge."

"Okay," she whispered, brushing her lips against mine.

She was squirming on my lap. I couldn't be responsible for the stir of my cock—or the way she seemed to approve by shifting her weight to press against it. I scanned the room, suddenly aware that I was about to maul her in public, and caught sight of Devon escorting our waitress and the owner into the kitchen.

Maybe he is good for something.

With our audience gone, I took her mouth indecently. She responded by straddling my lap, her dress inching up as she planted her core directly over my zipper. I groaned and thrust a hand into her hair, pulling her head back and moving my assault to her neck.

"You drunk?" I asked between nips.

"A little," she moaned, grinding a circle in my lap.

Fuck. Me.

"I see my wooing worked."

She turned her head to the side, encouraging me to continue.

God, did I want to continue. Just not in the middle of a restaurant with a room full of people corralled in the kitchen. But how could I get her anywhere else without looking like a jackass who was just trying to sleep with the celebrity? I knew the girl on the bridge, and everyone knew Levee Williams. But I needed her to get to know Sam Rivers... fast.

Palming each side of her face, I dropped my forehead to hers. "I'm about to make things awkward. It's kinda what I do. Just bear with me."

She licked her lips, and I was forced to kiss her again. When I finally came back up for air, I continued.

"My name is Samuel Nathan Rivers. I'm twenty-seven. Aquarius. No criminal history. I have a clean bill of health. I'm a democrat, but for God's sake, do not tell my mom. I own a furniture shop and clear six figures a year. I'm not interested in your money. I'll show you my tax return if need be. I'm also not a super-fan interested in your fame. But, for the love of all that's holy, I need *you*, Designer Shoes, to come home with me."

Her eyes lit. "Devon would have a stroke." She pushed my hands off her face in order to take my mouth again.

A frustrated growl rumbled in my chest. My cock wasn't concerned in the least about Devon's health.

"Levee," I grumbled as she folded her arms around my shoulders, pressing her chest against mine. "Devon can—"

"But you can come home with me."

God fucking bless America.

Suddenly, I rose to my feet with her still wrapped around me. "Check please," I called out loudly, digging into my back pocket for my wallet with one hand while she clung to me, giggling.

I couldn't help my smile as she buried her face in my neck and slid down to the ground.

"I'm going to the restroom. If you must, now's the time to smoke. I don't want you to have a heart attack before I get you naked." She innocently batted her eyelashes at me as if she hadn't just whispered sweet nothings directly to my cock.

I bit my lip, watching her ass sway as she walked away.

Scrubbing my face, I tried to get myself together while fighting the biggest shit-eating grin known to man. When I looked up, Devon was glowering at me with his arms crossed over his massive chest.

"Don't look at me like that," I told him as I tossed a wad of cash on the table.

"I don't fucking like this," he snarled. "She's drunk and not thinking straight."

"She's tipsy," I amended—just as much for him as for me.

She isn't really drunk. Is she?

Whatever. I was a stand-up guy. I liked her, and judging by the way she had been rolling her body against mine, she liked at least part of me, too.

"Look, man. I realize this is the first time we've met, but Levee and I have been seeing each other for the last week…. Kinda. Or…something like that." I scratched the back of my head. "You don't have to worry about me."

"Bullshit," he growled.

I pointedly lifted my eyebrows. "You know what you do need to worry about though? Her going up that bridge every night. One of these days, she's not going to come back down if you don't do something about it."

"Excuse me?" He took a menacing step in my direction.

I stole a glance around him at the empty hall Levee had disappeared down. "Look, you did not hear this from me, but I know for a fact that she's considered jumping. I'm not sure if she's suicidal or just depressed, but she needs help. I'm doing what I can to keep her walking down every night, but I need you to get word to her family or whoever she's close to that she needs serious help."

"No way," he scoffed, but I could tell his gears were spinning.

"I like her, okay? A lot. Even before I knew her name. But I don't know her like you do. I can only do so much."

He narrowed his eyes and stared at me suspiciously, but the seed had been planted.

"Do not take her back to that bridge alone anymore. If I'm there, I'll take care of her. I swear. But if I'm not, you drive her anywhere in the world but *that bridge*." I held his stare, trying to transfer the truth. He had no reason to trust me, but he also had no reason not to.

Finally, his shoulders slacked and he thrust a rough hand into his jet-black hair. "Fuck," he hissed under his breath.

I heard the door to the bathroom open, so I busied myself by digging my cigarettes out of my pocket. "She just needs help," I whispered one last time.

"I'll take care of it," he responded, still notably shocked, but my anxiety melted away.

I was going to do whatever I had to do to make sure Levee never stepped off that bridge, but it was no longer my sole responsibility. I didn't know where this thing with her was going. She could disappear on me tomorrow, but now, I could sleep easier knowing that someone else knew what was going on in her head.

I would have killed for that tip about Anne.

"Hey, beautiful," I purred as Levee rounded the corner, her eyes flashing between Devon and me.

"Everything okay?" she asked with freshly painted-red lips.

"It is now." After looping an arm around her waist, I pulled her against me and kissed her cheek, catching a whiff of fresh mango on her breath when she sighed. "I'm going to smoke. I'll meet you in the car." Tossing her a wink, I slid my hand down to her ass, giving it a gentle squeeze before sauntering out the back door.

Levee

I had no idea what the hell I was doing. I couldn't even explain it to myself. But I knew that, if I didn't strip Sam Rivers naked in the next thirty minutes, I was going to implode. I hadn't been with anyone in well over a year, and while I could easily blame my insatiable desire on being hard up, that would have been a complete and utter lie.

I'd spent the last few hours staring at various parts of his body until I had been physically unable to take it anymore. Whether it was his inked forearms, which flexed each time he lifted that beer, the way those plump lips wrapped around the mouth of the bottle, or even the way he purposely raked his teeth over his bottom lip each time he placed it back on the table, I had no idea. But watching that man drink a fucking beer, much less two of them, had been damn near excruciating. He'd talked and made jokes while I'd dreamed about his callused hands gliding over my skin. That had been the easy part though. He was rugged and gorgeous. I couldn't help but to be physically attracted to him.

The hard part was when I envisioned Sam actually wanting to stay with me once the novelty was gone. My life was chaotic, and not just because I lived it in the public eye. I brought on most of the craziness myself, exhausting myself on stage, existing on nourishment from vending machines, and fighting back tears at the bedsides of dying children.

But that night with Sam, my life didn't seem so overwhelming.

Maybe it was the sangria, but I thought it had more to do with him.

I wasn't usually the type of girl to take a man home, but Sam did things to me, most of which started with his mouth, and as I watched his lean body strolling back to my car, I hoped they all ended that way, too.

I didn't want to get laid just to share an orgasm with another warm body.

I wanted Sam.

All of him.

But I really just wanted to keep him.

"Fuck," he bit out as I slung my leg over his hips the moment his ass touched the leather seat.

I silenced him with my mouth, gliding a hand up his nape and into his hair. His dick became beautifully thick between us.

"Levee, wait," he moaned into my mouth, but he palmed my ass, rocking me forward. "Wait. Wait. Wait. Not here."

"Yeah. *Please* not here," Devon deadpanned from the front as he pulled out of the parking lot.

I laughed and rested my head on Sam's shoulder. I wasn't embarrassed. It was Devon. I'd done full wardrobe changes in the back of that SUV. He'd caught more than an eyeful of me, but never like that. When it came to transportation, though, I didn't have any options. Huffing, I cursed my lack of a driver's license and my inability to leave the house alone.

"Look at me." Sam tipped my chin up to study my eyes. "How far away is your place?"

"Twenty minutes."

"Shit," he huffed. "And, just so we're clear, we can't go back to my place? It's, like, two miles away."

I opened my mouth, but Devon got there first.

"Not a chance in hell."

Smiling, I lowered my voice to a whisper, "He has a really scary vein on his forehead that's probably twitching right about now."

Sam rolled his eyes then sighed. "Put your head in my lap."

My eyes flashed wide in surprise. And, okay fine...excitement.

"Jesus Christ. Don't look at me like that. I just mean lie down and take a nap, something—anything—that doesn't involve you straddling me. Mind if I smoke in here?"

"Yes. I do," Devon snapped.

Shaking my head, I cracked the window and reluctantly crawled into the seat beside him. "Nah. Go ahead."

I didn't take a nap, but I did lay my head in his lap. Then I watched as he chain-smoked the entire way back to my house, perhaps while dragging a fingernail up and down the seam of his jeans. Maybe.

Definitely.

chapter nine

Levee

"Thank fuck!" Sam said, swinging the door open before Devon even had the car in park.

"Oh, this isn't my place. We're just dropping Devon off. I'm about twenty minutes across town?" I tossed him a sugary smile then boldly shifted my hand into his lap, purposely brushing the bulge under his denim.

Grabbing my wrist, he narrowed his eyes and called out, "Devon, I'm gonna need to borrow a bedroom."

I burst out laughing as Devon cursed loudly.

"Fine. This is my place. No smoking inside though," I snipped as I climbed from the SUV.

"You better have some seriously exciting extracurricular activities to keep me distracted, then."

"I have Ping-Pong!"

"Not exactly what I was thinking." He mischievously cocked his head. "But I guess paddles and balls are as good a start as any." Dipping down, he hoisted me over his shoulder. "Point me to the Ping-Pong table, my lady."

I didn't. I laughed hysterically as he carried me inside. Then I directed him to my bedroom instead.

I heard Devon locking up the house as Sam deposited me on the bed.

"Jesus. This view." He pushed the curtains back. "Why the hell would you ever go up to the bridge when you have this here?"

"I don't know," I answered, pulling my earrings off and placing them on my nightstand.

Oh, but I knew. It might not have been what had originally sent me up that bridge, but it was why my feet carried me back every night. And that very reason was currently standing in front of me with entirely too much clothing on.

"You want a beer?" I asked, sliding my shoes off.

"Nah, I'm good." He faced me, and I could tell something was off with his demeanor. He didn't inch any closer. Instead, his lips were tight and his eyes uncomfortably flashed around the room.

It suddenly didn't feel like Sam standing in front of me at all.

He felt like a stranger who had just come face-to-face with *Levee Williams*.

Damn it.

"Why are you looking at me like that? Are you about to freak out?" I whispered, nervously moistening my lips.

He shoved his hands into his pockets. "I'm not really sure yet. But I'm gonna need you to stop licking your lips long enough for me to figure it out." His mouth cracked into a wide grin, and my shoulders relaxed.

Now that was a flash of my Sam.

"Want to tell me what's going on?" I asked.

"It's just… I think this is the first time I've realized that you're some big-time celebrity. I might be in over my head here, Designer Shoes."

"I just make music, Sam." I returned his smile and very slowly prowled in his direction. "Imagine how I feel though. You're Samuel Nathan Rivers. A tough, tattooed furniture designer who makes six figures a year but is too afraid to tell his mommy he votes democratic." I giggled as he frowned humorously. Stopping in front of him, I dragged a fingernail down his chest then teased the waistband of his jeans. "Have you considered that maybe I'm the one who's in over her head here?" I leaned forward to nip at his lips, but he spun us around.

"Excellent point. I'm going to need you to try really hard to keep it together, Levee. You haven't even seen my six-pack and huge cock, yet." He smirked and attempted to return my nip, but I stepped out of his reach.

"You brought beer and chicken?" I feigned excitement.

That one corny joke was all it took to bring my Sam back completely.

With a sexy smile and a coy shrug, he seductively backed me toward the bed. "What can I say? I like to be prepared."

"Clearly," I breathed.

He moved in close so his lips were only a centimeter away, but for as much as I wanted him, it was agonizing. "Clearly," he repeated, his smoky yet sweet breath breezing across my mouth.

His strong arm looped around my waist, tugging me against his chest, while I stared into his hooded eyes, eagerly waiting for him to make a move.

Any move.

Every move.

Sam

Her eyes were pleading. A plea I had every intention of answering—in time.

My time. Not hers.

After sliding my hand down the small of her back, I let it splay over her ass.

"It's hot in here. Maybe you should take this off?" I tugged at the fabric of her dress.

A laugh sprang from her mouth. "That was your line? 'It's hot in here'?"

"It wasn't a line."

"It's freezing in here. It was absolutely a line." She continued to laugh but wrapped her arms around my neck. Our breath was twisting between us in the only small gap our flush bodies had left.

"I haven't even taken them out yet and you're already busting my balls." I grazed my teeth over her bottom lip.

She lazily closed her eyes and went in for the kiss. Taking a move from her play book, I swayed out of her reach.

Groaning because of the miss, she popped her eyes open. "Sorry. It's just that you started off so strong with the huge-cock thing," she teased even further, bursting into laughter all over again.

"You seriously need to stop laughing," I replied, not even the slightest bit annoyed.

There were a ton of reasons why millions of people swooned over Levee on a daily basis, but seeing her up close as she lost herself in a snarky joke, I knew they were missing all the best parts.

I watched with a smirk as heat blazed through my veins until she finally sobered. Her smile was still filled with humor—an expression that was quickly becoming my favorite. And, like a judge and jury, my cock confirmed it by swelling between us.

Suddenly, a different smile formed, and mischief lifted the corners of her mouth.

I had been wrong. *That* one was unquestioningly better.

Fuck, I'm in trouble with this woman. Mainly because I knew the real trouble would be if I didn't get her naked—soon.

Thankfully, we shared that feeling.

She cupped my straining erection. "Then give me a reason not to laugh, Sam."

Not. A. Fucking. Problem.

With a growl, I crushed my mouth over hers and lifted her off the ground. I attempted to toss her onto the bed, but at the last second, she wrapped her legs around my hips, dragging me down on top of her. She laughed into my mouth as our teeth painfully clanked together. It transformed into a moan when my hard-on blissfully landed against her core.

"Fuck," I hissed as she rolled her hips into mine.

"What's wrong, Sam?" she asked innocently.

I would have answered, but with only two layers of clothing stopping me from planting myself to the hilt inside her, I was done talking.

Done joking.

Hell, I was even done listening to her laugh.

I was suddenly in the mood to make her come—hard.

And fast.

Then I wanted to come—slowly.

And repeatedly.

Trailing kisses up her neck and over to her ear, I tugged at the hem of her dress. "Do you want this on or off while I'm licking your pussy?"

She froze, and as I'd hoped, her laughter fell silent.

As a victorious smile spread across my mouth, she abruptly sat up and started trying to reach the zipper on the back of her dress. "Off. And, for future reference, you should have led with that instead of the 'hot in here' bullshit."

"Agreed." I nodded, yanking the zipper down and peeling the dress over her head.

In a black lace bra and a matching pair of boy shorts, she reclined back onto the bed. I didn't follow her down; I sat back on my heels and openly gawked.

Levee was thin, borderline too thin, but she was still stunning. Her flat stomach guided my gaze up to small-but-full breasts overflowing the lace. Just under the fabric, I could make out the peak of her nipples, and my mouth watered to taste them.

I brushed my fingers across the swell of her cleavage. "I'm going to detour to these first. I'll personally apologize to your pussy for the delay."

A corner of her mouth twitched. "That better be one hell of an apology."

I palmed both of her breasts. "Are you planning to stop talking any time soon?"

Arching into my touch, she gasped. "I don't know. Are you?"

I shifted one of my hands to the bed to hold my weight as I hovered on my knees above her. "Yep. Right"—I placed a damp kiss to her chest—"now."

Without any further warning, I popped her nipple from her bra and sealed my mouth around it.

"Shit," she cursed with hands flying to fist my hair and hips circling up off the bed. "Ahhh," she moaned as my tongue laved at her nipple.

Then I switched to the other before repeating the process.

Her hips continued to search the space between us for some source of friction. I could have offered her my leg, but I feared my cock would sprout arms and claw its way out of my jeans if I had to feel her riding my thigh.

With my mouth still at her breast, Levee clawed at my shirt, tugging it up my back. "Take this off."

I sat up long enough for her to tear it over my head, but when I tried to take her breast again, a hand against my chest stopped me. My gaze flipped to hers, and much to my surprise—and excitement—Levee was a gawker too.

"Fuck," she cursed, dragging a single fingernail over the ridges of my abs.

I had a torso full of tattoos I'd expected her to inspect for the first time, but as she pushed against my chest again, her eyes were glued to the outline of my hard-on in my jeans.

After licking her lips, she ordered, "Lie down."

"Funny. I was just about to tell you to do the same thing." I gently urged her down with one hand while dropping the other to the lace between her legs.

She gasped and threw her head back, grinding herself into my touch while tracing her hands up and down my stomach. "Sam," she breathed, pausing to take my mouth in a rough kiss. "Can we speed this up?"

"We can now," I mumbled into her mouth.

With one swift movement, I pushed her panties aside and pressed two fingers inside her drenched pussy. Her legs fell to the sides as she collapsed backwards on the bed.

"Yes," she hissed, fisting the sheets.

Kneeling on the edge of the bed, I stared at her hips, which were fluidly rolling against my hand. I could have watched all night, but the memory of her breasts in my mouth was still fresh.

"Take your bra off." I twisted my hand as punctuation.

She didn't delay in sitting up, sliding it down her arms, then discarding it off the side of her bed. Her eyes and her smirk were confident, but she immediately pushed her hands into her hair, forcing her breasts together like some sort of bikini model. *Fuck.* Levee's body was incredible, and the last thing I wanted was her trying to alter my view in any way.

One by one, I removed my fingers. Her mouth fell open in protest, but I tugged her hands from her hair and placed them around my neck.

"Don't do that. Not to me."

"Do what?"

I settled on my side next to her. "Try to strike a pose like I'm some cameraman looking for the perfect shot of you."

"I didn't," she huffed.

Gripping the back of her neck, I dragged her mouth up to mine and swallowed her lie. "Yes, you did, Designer Shoes. But I'm not here for a photo shoot. I'm here for the real thing."

At the familiar nickname, her eyes lit.

"I'm not perfect, and I'd really appreciate if we could pretend you aren't, either, while I have my fingers inside you."

She closed her eyes and sucked in a deep breath, holding it so long that it became unnerving. Finally, those whiskey browns opened, emanating freedom with every blink.

"Okay," she whispered, dropping her arms to the sides, revealing herself completely.

"There she is." I pecked her lips and tucked a stray curl behind her ear. "You're gorgeous, Levee. Even more right now than when you're on the cover of a magazine trying to be."

Her cheeks turned pink as she tried to fight back unshed emotion.

Even that battle was beautiful.

Several seconds later, a laugh bubbled from her chest. "That was some serious cheese dickery, Sam."

I smiled down at her. *It really was.* "It was also the truth."

"Maybe. Maybe not." She shrugged. "But I appreciate it more than you'll ever know." Her teasing gaze faded away as desire once again filled her eyes, which sent blood sprinting back to my cock. "No more talking. Touch me, Sam." She took my mouth and tried to lead my hand back between her legs, complaining as I resisted.

"Shhh," I urged between kisses.

She grumbled in frustration, "I need—"

I cut her off. Using her wrist, I guided her hand down to my denim-covered cock. "Me. You need *me*."

I only knew because I needed *her*.

And, as her face softened, the truth tumbled from her mouth. "I really do."

"Then take it."

It was just that simple. I was there to be with her. She could have me in any and every way she wanted.

Without another word, she unbuttoned my jeans and slid her hand inside, wrapping it possessively around my cock.

"Fuck," I breathed.

It was promptly followed by a curse of her own when her palm made contact with the metal of my apadravya.

I hadn't even caught my breath as her mouth collided with mine. Her hand continuously worked my cock—her thumb rolling over the metal at the tip with every upstroke. It wasn't long before a familiar sensation formed in my balls—entirely too soon.

"Levee, wait."

The words had barely cleared my lips when she pushed me off-balance and onto the bed beside her. In only a pair of panties, Levee climbed off the bed without even releasing her grip on my cock.

"Up," she ordered, standing between my legs.

"Up what?" I asked, shocked by our sudden role reversal.

I attempted to sit up only to be forced back down. Her hand fell away to shimmy the denim off my hips.

"Toe your shoes off," she ordered.

This bossy side of Levee took me aback, but she was almost naked…trying to get me naked.

I did as I'd been told.

Levee began a frenzied task of undressing me, not even glancing back up into my eyes until she was satisfied with my jeans, boxers, and socks all lying on the floor at her feet.

"God, Sam," she breathed, dropping to her knees and once again gripping my impossibly hard cock.

"Wait." I sat up and tried to pull her back to her feet. "I go first. I mean, you go… Son of a… Fuck!" I lost all conscious thought as she dipped her head and circled her tongue around the head of my cock.

"Your dick's pierced." Her hand stroked a relentless rhythm from base to tip.

"I… Fuck… Ugh." My muscles tensed as I glided through her hand. "Is it? I thought they all looked like that."

"So fucking thick." She went back down for another lick. Collapsing back on the bed, I gave up on my objections.

She could officially go first.

I continued to fire off cuss words and random thoughts as she stroked and licked my shaft, teasing the barbell that ran vertically through the head. When she finally slid my cock to the back of her throat, I came unglued.

"Shit, woman." I threaded a hand into her hair, attempting to pull her up.

Levee wasn't done yet.

But I was.

Tucking my hands under her arms, I dragged her onto the bed.

"Sam!" she squealed.

Rising to my feet, I had only one answer. "I'm fucking you."

She sucked in a sharp breath. Toying with the ends of her hair, she unnaturally pressed her perfect tits together. I quirked a pointed eyebrow in a not-so-subtle command. She promptly dropped her arms to the sides. Dragging my gaze away, I found my jeans and retrieved a condom from my wallet while silently cursing myself for not having brought a whole damn box.

Levee watched from the bed with her knees bent and wide open for me. Her hair fanned out around her as her hips squirmed from side to side.

She was showing off. And while I loved it, it wasn't enough and she knew it.

"Get rid of those." I barked, flashing my gaze down to her panties.

Her lips twisted in a smile, but she quickly obeyed, seductively sliding them down her legs. Then she twirled them on her finger before ceremoniously dropping them to the ground.

A growl rumbled my chest as she brazenly opened her legs, revealing a smooth, glistening pussy just waiting for me to drive into it.

"I'm gonna need more condoms," I announced, ripping the foil packet open.

"I have some." She guided her hand down between her legs and rubbed a circle over her clit.

Christ.

This. Woman.

"Keep going," I said as I rolled the condom on. "You ready for me?"

"You? Not even close," she whispered shyly. Then her eyes turned dark, and a sinful grin appeared on her lips. "Your dick though? Absolutely."

I swallowed hard. Suddenly, I was afraid I wasn't ready for Levee, either. But, as my pulse sped, I prowled up the bed, ready to take the risk just to feel her.

Her fingers continuously circled her clit, and I lowered my hand to join them. She was soaked and couldn't help bringing it to my lips for a taste.

"Mmmm," I purred as she lifted her wet fingers to my mouth, offering me a second course I was more than willing to accept. "I fuck you. Then we're taking a shower. Then I'm eating you until I get hard again." I glided my cock through her folds.

Her head pressed back into the pillow as she arched off the bed.

Bending down, I roughly grazed my teeth over her nipple. "Then we'll start the cycle over again."

"You'll have to smoke at some point," she taunted even as she writhed under me.

"Not if you're occupying my mouth and hands," I smarted back.

Then, without warning, I drove hard inside her.

We both cried a blessed curse then stilled to allow our bodies time to adjust. For me, adjusting meant spending the moment pleading with my balls not to fire off inside her.

"Are you okay?" I panted.

"I'm going to come as soon as you move. Fair warning."

I chuckled then stared at my cock slowly sliding out before filling her again.

"Ahhhh!" she cried out in ecstasy. "Stop watching and kiss me."

I wouldn't deny her that. I was desperate for her mouth again anyway. Dropping to my elbows, I less-than-gently covered her mouth.

Mmmm…mangos.

Levee clung to my back as her muscles tensed around my cock with every swipe of my tongue in her mouth. I didn't even need to move, but as her hips began to rock against me, it became obvious she did.

Looping an arm under her leg, I pressed it up to her shoulder, opening her even wider for me. With her nails raking up my back, I pumped into her. She wasn't exaggerating. Approximately four thrusts later, she came while crying my name. With her tight pussy milking me as she lost herself beneath me, I didn't make it much longer before I joined her.

I came on promises of giving her more.

What worried me was I didn't even know what kind of *more* I was offering.

The words didn't feel sexual even as I emptied inside her.

I just knew I wanted to give it to her.

So. Much. *More.*

chapter
ten

Levee

Fresh from a shower where Sam had used his fingers to give me earth-shaking orgasm number two, I watched him, wrapped in only a towel, smoking on my balcony. He was so obviously freezing his ass off, but it was a glorious sight. I hated that he was a smoker—but, God, he looked sexy as he did it.

It was after three a.m. when my phone started ringing on my nightstand. It was Henry, and while it wasn't out of the ordinary for him to drunk dial, it still worried me that he'd call so late.

I snatched it up immediately. "Hello?"

"Tell me he's lying?"

"What?"

"Please God, Levee. Tell me he's full of shit and you aren't seriously trying to kill yourself."

I froze. "What are you talking about? Who?"

"Whoever that guy is you're sleeping with!" he yelled before getting himself back in check. "He told Devon you go up to that bridge every night to jump. Damn it, Levee, what the hell are you thinking?"

My heart began to race as the blood drained from my face. "It's not. I mean… I'm… I don't…." I stumbled over my words as my eyes lifted to Sam on the other side of the glass.

"Stewart is losing his fucking mind right now that Devon was just this guy's first stop before heading to the press."

Oh God.

"Just tell me this is some kind of rumor."

As if he could sense my distress, Sam turned to face me. His golden eyes locked with mine, immediate concern painted his face.

"What?" he mouthed.

I couldn't reply.

Not to Sam.

Not to Henry.

Not even to myself.

It wasn't true.

It also wasn't a lie.

"Oh God," Henry gasped when my silence told him more than my words ever could.

Sam regarded me warily for several seconds before he dropped his cigarette and headed my way.

My world began to move in slow motion even as my mind frantically swirled.

He told Devon.

Betrayal chilled my veins, sending a shiver down my back.

"Levee?" Henry said, reminding me that I still had the phone to my ear.

"Yeah," I whispered absently, my eyes glued to Sam as he slid the balcony door open. A gust of wind blew the curtains in the air as he entered.

"I'm on my way. I'll be there in a half hour, okay? Stay put. We'll figure this out."

"I'm…really… I'm….umm…." My chin quivered as Sam stopped in front of me and tilted his head in a silent question. "I'm *fine*," I finished. A tear escaped my eye as Sam physically flinched from the word, immediately folding me into his arms.

"What's going on?" he questioned softly.

Why would he do this to me?

"I'll be there in a half hour," Henry repeated. "Devon's on his way now. Hang tight."

But I couldn't do that at all. The man who had been the only thing grounding me for the last week had just sold me out. The terrifying free fall rushed up at me from the ground, all but swallowing me even as I stood wrapped in his safe arms.

He wouldn't really tell anyone else… Would he?

If word got out that I was some sort of suicidal basket case, there was no way they'd let me help out at the hospitals anymore.

My pulse raced, and my hands got clammy.

I wouldn't let him take that from me—from them.

My ears pounded, leaving me unable to make out the words Sam was repeating into my hair. I wasn't sure if they were questions or soothing sentiments; it just broke my heart that *he* was uttering them.

He was the bandage—and, now, the wound.

Dropping my phone, I stepped out of his reach. After plucking his jeans off the floor, I threw them at him. "Get out."

His head snapped back. "What?"

"Get the fuck out of my house."

He put his hands on his hips, notably confused. "Excuse me?"

"Get out!" I screamed so loud that it echoed off the glass.

He didn't budge. Instead, he pulled his jeans on and then chewed on his bottom lip as his eyes flashed between mine, searching for some sort of answer. "Who was on the phone, Levee?"

I couldn't help but laugh. *Is he jealous?*

I was about to become front-page news and he was jealous?

This is not happening.

It really fucking was.

And, for that alone, I got pissed.

Really pissed.

"I won't let you do this to me. Your word means nothing against mine. You have no proof." I snatched the robe off the back of my door and wrapped it tight as if it could magically keep me from falling apart.

"What the hell are you talking about?" He tugged his shirt on.

"I will not let you ruin me because of some misplaced savior complex. I don't need you, Sam. So do me a fucking favor and keep your mouth shut about shit you don't know anything about."

"I'm so lost right now." He threw his arms out to his sides.

"You told Devon I was planning to jump off the bridge!"

His shoulders sagged in visible relief. "Well…yeah. Someone needed to know. I'm not going to just stand by while you kill yourself," he scoffed as if I were insane.

"I'm not going to kill myself!" I shrieked then began to pace around the room.

It was almost comical.

I was hurt

And pissed.

And floundering even more than ever before.

But Sam looked like he had just saved a litter of puppies from a burning building.

"Well, no. Not anymore you're not." He smiled proudly.

"Oh my God!" I threw my hands up in frustration. "You have mental issues." I should have looked up. I didn't. I kept pacing. "You seem to be so fucking hell-bent on saving me, but what about you?" I should have shut up. I didn't. I kept ranting. "You were planning to jump off that bridge too, Sam. Maybe I should run to your employees and share *that* little secret. But no, I wouldn't do that. Why? Because I'm a decent human being who respects your privacy. Congratulations, Sam. I didn't jump, but when this little secret trickles down shit creek, I'll wish I had."

When I finally—fucking finally—looked up, Sam was gone. He was still standing in the room, but he'd left me all the same. His face was pale, and his fists were clenched at his sides.

"Listen up, *princess*," he snarled. It wasn't a term of endearment that time. It was an insult that hurt far worse than any other name he possibly could have called me.

I didn't even have enough time to flinch from his verbal blow before he continued.

"Before you go around slinging insults from inside your glass mansion, you might want all the facts. Four months ago, my mentally ill sister went out for a stroll on the bridge. Two days later, they recovered her body from the bay."

My hand flew up, covering my mouth as acrid guilt settled in my stomach.

"The last conversation I ever had with her was that morning when she adamantly told me she was *fine*." He spat the word then cracked his neck. "She wasn't. And neither are you. Levee, I never wanted to die. I go up to that bridge because I want Anne to come *back*."

My vision swam. "Oh God."

"Maybe you were never going to jump, but you were up on that bridge for a reason. Don't worry. Your secret *is* safe with me. But I won't apologize for telling Devon. I'll gladly leave now, but one day, when I see your face again, it's not going to be on the news because they found your body washed up on the shores of the bay. You're fucking welcome." After snatching his shoes off the ground, he stormed out of my room.

"Sam, wait!" I followed after him, catching up just as he got to the front door—a cigarette already dangling from his lips.

"Don't," he snapped. "I can't deal with this. You're not at all who I thought you were."

"Sam, I'm sorry. I didn't know. I—"

"Or maybe you're exactly who I thought you'd be." He lifted his hands, motioning around my lush foyer.

That hurt. *A lot.*

But not as much as the idea of losing him.

"I'm sorry, please—"

The door slammed before I could even finish the apology.

"Wait!" I yanked the door open, but a sleepy Devon stood on the other side. "Move!" I tried to shove him out of the way.

But he only shook his head and backed me into the house. "Levee, stop. I had Carter take him home."

"You did what?" I screeched, rushing back to the door just in time to see the taillights disappearing.

"You have bigger shit to deal with than that jackass."

Gritting my teeth, I stalked in his direction. "You're fired."

"Oh please. I have a good mind to quit after the shit I found out you've been hiding from me," he bit right back.

"I wasn't going to jump!" I yelled for what felt like the millionth time, but when it cleared my lips, I realized it was the best lie I'd ever told.

Even I believed it.

Sam hadn't though.

Deep down, I'd seriously considered it. More times than I should have.

Daily.

My legs began to tremble, but they never even had a chance to give out before I was caught by Devon's embrace.

"Shh. I gotcha," he whispered into my hair. "Always, Levee."

"I, um… I think… I need"—*Sam*—"help."

"Then we'll get it."

Shit.

chapter eleven

Sam

It'd been another sleepless night for me. After some huge guy I assumed was another bodyguard drove me home, I'd sat on my porch with Sampson at my side and watched the sun rise. I was starting to feel like I'd never get a full night of sleep again. It didn't take long for me to regret having stormed out on Levee. She had problems, and I had done the one thing I'd sworn I'd never do again after Anne died—I'd walked away. But fuck, her explosive rant had cut me deep.

That's not completely true though.

Anne had cut me deep.

Levee had unwittingly rubbed salt in the already-gaping wound.

I needed to apologize. She didn't deserve that shit. If I went back over there, I could probably make her understand my over-the-top re-action.

But that was the last thing I really needed.

I had absolutely no business trying to pursue something with her. We came from different worlds—and only part of that had anything to do with her being famous. Hell, that was the easy part. We were both so filled with pain. Only she was determined to escape it, while I physically ached to stop her. We'd be a fucking train wreck together.

But that woman…

It'd only been a week and we'd only spent one night together, but, God, she'd felt like the *great* I'd always been searching for. Who cared if she had issues I would probably always stress about?

Oh, right. Me.

But, when we were together, it was easy to forget how we'd met. It was easy to get lost in her whiskey eyes and her contagious smile.

Her lithe body and her smooth, white skin.

Her soft breasts and her tight…

Damn it.

I desperately needed someone to talk to about her. But since Levee was such a public figure it made it tricky. I couldn't air her bullshit like she so obviously already thought I was going to do. My mom was still struggling with Anne's death. I couldn't bring this kind of drama up without upsetting her. She was just starting to get it back together.

I had one choice…

So, at nine a.m., I grabbed my wallet and headed out the door.

"Dude, what the hell are you doing up here?" Ryan asked when I walked into his office, closing the door behind me.

"I just hired you. I fucked up last night and I need to talk, but you can't say a word to anyone."

"What. Did. You. Do?" he said very slowly, pushing away from his desk and rising to his feet.

"By the way, I really wish I'd known you charged four hundred dollars an hour before I paid Jen for your time. Fucking hell, man."

He cocked an angry eyebrow. "One, stay the fuck away from Jen. Two, we're best friends! You didn't have to pay for my time, asshole."

"Yeah, I know, but I needed attorney-client privilege for what I'm about to tell you."

"Fuck, Sam. This does not sound good." He pinched the bridge of his nose as he perched on the edge of his desk, and then motioned for me to spill it.

"I've been kinda seeing Levee Williams, and last night, I slept with her," I rushed out.

His head snapped up. "Levee Williams, the singer?"

I quickly nodded.

"No shit?" he breathed. A grin spread across his face, but just as quickly, his eyes grew wide. "Oh, Jesus, did you hurt her? Is she trying to claim you forced yourself on her?"

"What? No!" I shouted, jumping to my feet.

"Then what the fuck did you do that you suddenly need a criminal defense attorney?"

"Nothing! I just wanted to talk to you without worrying that you're gonna run your big-ass mouth. For fuck's sake, Ryan! The first thing you assume is that I assaulted her?"

"I didn't think you necessarily *assaulted* her," he scoffed, crossing his arms over his chest and shrugging. "Maybe she didn't like the bionic cock? You never know."

I laughed without humor. "Don't be ridiculous. Everyone likes that."

"Including Levee Williams?" He smirked.

"Come on, jerkoff. Act like a professional."

"Fine. I'll ask that when we aren't on your dime." He walked back around his desk and, very businesslike, sat in his chair. "Now, Mr. Rivers. What can I do for you today?"

I sucked in a deep breath and settled back in my chair. "I met her on the bridge about a week ago."

He lowered his voice and mumbled a curse. "You have to stop going up there and torturing yourself."

I waved him off. I didn't need a lecture. I needed someone to tell me that I was insane for wanting to be with Levee. Then I needed someone to convince my body that it was insane, too, because all I really wanted to do was run back up that hill and lose myself inside her again.

"I didn't know who she was at first. She was always wearing shades and a wig, but I could see her intentions like a beacon of light." I cleared my throat. "She was going to jump. I know she was. She kept sticking her legs through the railing like she was testing out the wind on her skin. I couldn't stop worrying about her, so, on the third night, I struck up a conversation with her. I've been meeting her up on the bridge every night since, and last night, she finally told me her name, and after dinner, we...uh...went back to her place." I smiled and shook my head at how perfect the first half of the evening had gone. Then I groaned at the memories of how it had ended. "Anyway, I told her bodyguard that she was planning to jump, and when she found out, she exploded and kicked me out of her house. I have no fucking idea what to do, Ryan. I really want to go back over there and apologize tonight, but a woman like that is going to shred me. You remember how I was with Anne. I'd just be a sitting duck waiting for an instant replay. But I...um...*like* her."

He sighed. "You can't be with someone like that. Your personality cannot handle the crazy."

"Come on, dude. Don't call her crazy."

"I just mean you need someone a little safer and more on an even keel. You know I've always considered you a brother. But the fact that you made me lunch and folded my clothes every day in college definitely made it easy to keep you around."

I glared up at him, unimpressed.

"You're a caretaker, Sam. It's what you do. You did it for your mom when your dad died. You did it for me when..." He paused and swayed his head in consideration, "Well, you still do it for me. You did it for Anne. You do it for Morgan. And now, you're gonna try to do it for *Levee freaking Williams*. You did the right thing by letting someone know what was up, but I really think she'll be okay without you. If you want to have under-the-covers fun with her for a while, by all means, go for it. But, since I know your vagina doesn't work like that, you need to stop this now. What you really need is for someone to take care of you—not the other way around."

He was right.

I'd spent years of my life taking care of my father. Then even more years repairing the damage he'd caused our family when he'd ultimately hung himself in his workshop. Most recently, I'd spent my life trying to prevent Anne from sharing his same fate—a task I'd monumentally failed at.

Yeah. I couldn't do that with Levee.

Not again.

Clearing my throat, I pushed to my feet. "You're right."

He was so fucking wrong, and I knew it even as the agreement tumbled from my lips.

She was right.

We were right.

I was just too afraid to start the cycle of pain all over again.

So, like a coward, I repeated a lie. "You are absolutely right."

"Good." He stood up too and buttoned his suit coat in a very professional manner. "Are we done here?"

I sighed and nodded, preparing to leave, but Ryan stopped me first.

"You want to grab some coffee? Off the clock, of course." He winked and shoved his hands in his pockets.

"Yeah. I could seriously go for a smoke and some caffeine," I replied, deflated.

"Awesome. Now, spill it. Was she a freak in the sack? I can see her being kinky. And don't even try to avoid answering. You can't fuck the world's biggest pop star and keep this shit from your best friend."

I cleared my throat. "My best friend doesn't know I had sex with Levee. Just my attorney. And since you're off the clock…" I trailed off, tossing him a shrug.

"You are worthless." He pouted, and I made a mental note not to let Ryan ply me with alcohol any time soon.

"That's not what Jen said," I joked, dodging the punch that I knew would be heading toward my shoulder.

Ryan talked the whole way to the coffee shop, but I didn't have anything left to say. How was I supposed to just forget about her? Or stop worrying about her? Or stop myself from getting in my car and heading up to her house? God, I hoped Devon was going to truly get her the help she needed and stop taking her to that fucking bridge every night.

There was only one way to be certain about that though.

For seven days, I fought the urge and somehow managed to stay away from her. Her house was only fifteen minutes from mine, and my palms itched to touch her again.

For as much as I wanted to see her, it wasn't like Levee was reaching out to me, either. She had my cell number from the night I'd given it to her at the bridge, but I didn't know if she'd kept it. She knew where I worked though. I'd given the receptionist at rePURPOSEd full permission to give my cell number to anyone who called asking for it.

A million clients called; Levee didn't.

Anxiety wouldn't allow me to just write her off though. Every night, I marched up that bridge hoping to find a pair of designer shoes lurking in the shadows.

They never were.

For as much relief as it gave me each night when she wasn't there, an ache grew in my chest.

I miss her.

It wasn't long until I'd lived up to the nickname she'd given me and became a legit Internet stalker. During one of my many Google searches on her, I found that she'd canceled several of her upcoming performances. Tabloid speculation was that she was pregnant with Henry Alexander's love child. They'd even posted obviously edited pictures of her alleged baby bump. More reliable sources reported that she was headed to rehab. I couldn't imagine Levee being hooked on drugs, but how well did I really know her? And the pendulum of my anxiety swung, leaving me worried all over again.

Originally, I'd been grateful for the distraction Levee had provided me. If only I could have figured out how to distract myself from *her*. It wasn't like we had some torrid love affair I'd never be able to recover from. It was simply a flash-in-the-pan romance that never should have happened in the first place.

I needed to let her go and move on.

I just couldn't actually do it.

At all.

chapter twelve

Levee

"**I** really wish you would stay home," Henry said, sprawled across my bed.

When he'd arrived at my house the night Sam had walked away, he had done it with a huge suitcase wheeling behind him. I hadn't initially questioned it, but by day three, when a moving truck had shown up in my driveway, it had become abundantly clear that he was moving in. He hadn't necessarily asked if I was okay with living together again, but I hadn't exactly argued as a herd of movers had transformed two—yes, two—of my guest rooms into Henry's personal sanctuary.

"I have to get out of this house. I'm dying of boredom," I replied, stepping into a pair of washed-out skinny jeans. "Why don't you go out and do something tonight?"

After riffling through my drawers, I pulled on a New York T-shirt that hung off one of my shoulders. Simple, comfortable, and exactly what I needed.

"Hideous," Henry vetoed from the bed. "And no, thanks. I need some downtime."

I huffed then yanked the shirt back over my head and stomped into my closet. "When did you become such a homebody?" I called as I began searching through the rows of shirts.

"When the cockless love of my life decided she was going to jump off a bridge," he said, appearing in the doorway.

I closed my eyes and dropped my chin to my chest. "I'm sorry."

"Meh. I'll get over it. You just scared the piss out of me. I'm not much in the mood for going out without you these days." He smiled absently as he became enthralled with his reflection in the full-length mirror.

While I wasn't exactly in the know about Henry's schedule, I knew that it wasn't open. He was a busy guy. Yet, somehow, he'd managed to spend every waking minute of the last week at my side. Which meant he'd witnessed me obsessing and worrying about Sam firsthand.

Which also meant he already knew the answer when he asked, "Still nothing from Sam?"

Over the previous week, I'd slowly begun the process of getting my life in order while preparing for a month-long stint at a luxury resort. (Read: crazy camp/rehab.) I wasn't addicted to drugs, but according to the doctor Henry had forced me to see the morning after Sam's little revelation, depression, anxiety, and exhaustion were my poison. I couldn't say that I disagreed. I also couldn't say that I liked it. The press was going to have a field day, but Stewart assured me that we could keep it quiet. I laughed. Nothing was ever quiet in the music industry. The rumors were already circulating.

During all of it, I had mostly been concerned with what Sam would think when he heard the news. Would he be happy? Relieved? Still angry? Would he allow me a chance to at least apologize? I felt like an ass, but I missed his wicked grin and his golden eyes.

I missed the way his hands warmed me. And especially the way they sent chills down my spine.

Honestly, I missed the calm I felt with him just standing next to me smoking a cigarette.

"Nope," I replied curtly, taking the emerald-green tunic top he'd picked out from his hands.

"Then stop moping and call him, Levee. Put your damn pride aside and just call the man."

"And say what? 'Sorry I'm a basket case workaholic who can't even remember to eat on my own'? 'Sorry I kicked you out of my house for trying to help me'? 'Sorry I met you on the top of a bridge while contemplating suicide The exact same bridge that your sister jumped off. You want to go on another date with me?' Yeah. No, thanks." I laughed even as tears built in my eyes. "Let's not forget that, even if I could magically find the words to say, I have no one to tell them to. He hasn't exactly been beating down my door."

Just because I hadn't seen Sam since he'd stormed out of my house didn't mean I hadn't thought about him. I'd flipped my house on end but never could find that scrap of paper he'd given me with his cell number. I'd finally given up. I'd called rePURPOSEd more times than I'd ever admit, hanging up before anyone had the chance to answer, sometimes even before the first ring.

For a person who could tell an entire story within the lyrics of a three-minute song, I couldn't find the words to fix things with Sam. I was mortified about the way I'd acted the last time I'd seen him. Here was a guy I genuinely liked, who'd gotten a front-row seat to one of the biggest meltdowns of my life. Embarrassment couldn't even begin to cover it.

"Okay," he sighed. "Maybe you should lead with sex. 'Hey, I'm sorry, but can you at least stop by for another romp in the sack, and this time, let my pal Henry touch your cock?'"

My mouth fell open in a mixture of anger and disgust, but Henry threw his hands up to stop me before I had the chance to unleash it on him.

"I'm kidding!" He lowered his voice and mumbled, "Kinda."

I hurled a coat hanger at his head.

He dodged it.

It was very anticlimactic.

"You're lucky I love you," I warned, stepping into a pair of black pumps.

Henry cleared his throat. "Wedges."

I glared at him for several seconds but eventually stepped to the side and slid the nude wedges on instead.

"In all seriousness, Levee. I'm not sure a new boyfriend is what you need right now. But I certainly am not going to stop you. Reach out to him. Give him the chance to tell you to fuck off."

I flinched. That's exactly what I was afraid of.

"Orrrr...more than likely so he can apologize too. Have you stopped to think he might be feeling just as weird about the way things went down as you are? So what if he hasn't popped up on your doorstep like some lost puppy. That doesn't mean he isn't wishing you'd show up on his."

God, I hated when Henry made sense.

But what I really hated was knowing he made sense and being too afraid to listen to his advice.

"I have to go. I'm going to be late." I scrunched my hair one last time in the mirror before heading to the door.

"You're being ridiculous!" he called after me.

"See you in two hours. I'll bring back dinner," I replied as if he hadn't spoken.

"No sushi!"

"Then no dinner!"

I smiled when I heard him curse.

When I got to the bottom of the stairs, I found Devon waiting for me with a wide smile.

"You look beautiful," he said warmly.

"Thanks."

"You know he's just going to ask me to get him something besides sushi, right?" Devon said, fishing his phone from his pocket. He turned it to face me and lifted his fingers in the air to count down from three. No sooner had he tucked the last digit away than a text appeared on his phone.

Henry: Can you bring me back something to eat that doesn't taste like it washed up on a radioactive beach?

I burst out laughing. "What does that even mean?" I asked as he shoved the phone back in his pocket, ignoring the text completely.

"I've learned not to ask with Henry," he replied, using a hand at the small of my back to usher me out the door.

"Levee!" Morgan squealed when I walked into her hospital room.

"Hey there, pretty girl. How have you been?" I replied as my heart wrenched in my chest.

Little wires still dangled off her body, but her nasal cannula was gone and her color seemed somewhat better.

Her mother stood from a chair tucked away in the corner and extended her hand for a shake. I hugged her instead.

"What are you doing here?" she asked.

"I was thinking about Miss Morgan tonight." I squeezed her blanket-covered foot. "So I decided to come up here and see how things were going before I head out of town for a while."

"Wow. That's so sweet of you. We weren't expecting to see you again. I'm glad you came though. Morgan's been wanting to say thank you for all of the Henry Alexander stuff you left at the nurses' station."

"Aww. That was no problem. Henry was happy to do it. I promise I'll drag him up here one day. He's not big on hospitals, something about the nurses not letting him eat all the red Jell-O," I teased.

Morgan rewarded me with a giggle. "I made Henry a thank-you card. Could you…maybe…give it to him for me?" she asked nervously.

"Of course! He'll love it."

I laughed as she all but clapped in celebration.

"Mom! Get the card!"

"On it!" Her mom, whose name my frazzled brain couldn't remember, smiled as she moved to the other side of the bed. "Where'd you put it, sweetheart?"

"I put it between two books on my shelf to keep the glitter from falling out."

"Ohhhhh, Henry loves glitter," I exaggerated with wide eyes.

That time, she actually did clap.

Her mother laughed as she walked to the other side of the room. My eyes found her destination even before she did.

A familiar hollowed-out guitar filled with books leaned against the wall.

"Where… How…" I gasped as my heart pounded in my chest. "Is that a guitar bookshelf?" I asked as if it were an oasis in the desert that only I could see.

"Yep," Morgan chirped from her bed behind me.

I stood frozen in the middle of the room, but for the way my chest ached, I might as well have been transported back to the top of the bridge.

"*Oh God*," I breathed.

"Pretty cool, huh. My uncle Sam made it for me," Morgan prattled on, oblivious to my impending emotional breakdown.

"Levee," her mother called, forcing me to drag my attention away from the guitar. "Everything okay?"

"Did…um…Sam Rivers happen to make that?"

"Yeah. Jeez. That little punk must be doing better than I thought for you to recognize one of his pieces."

"Actually…I know him. He showed me a picture of that bookcase on his phone once." I cleared my throat to keep the quiver out of my voice.

"You know Uncle Sam?"

"Seriously?"

They gasped in unison.

I laughed to tamp down the tears I feared I wouldn't be able to hold back any longer. Turning back to face Morgan, I pasted on a smile. "We're... We used to be friends."

"Cool!" Morgan exclaimed.

When my gaze shifted to her mother, her face was soft in understanding. "So..." I paused sheepishly. "I'm sorry. I'm about to sound really rude, but I don't remember your name."

"Oh, that's okay. It's Meg."

"Sorry. I'm really forgetful sometimes."

"No need to apologize." She leaned in and whispered, "I'd way rather you remember Morgan's anyway."

"So, *Meg*, is Sam your brother?"

"Oh, God, no. He's my little brother Ryan's best friend. I guess we kinda grew up together. I've known that kid since he was a pimple-faced geek."

I couldn't imagine Sam ever looking anything but gorgeous, and disbelief must have read on my face.

"I'm serious," she insisted. "Before all of that ink, he was a dork. He sure grew up well though." She waggled her eyebrows.

I laughed again, and my cheeks blushed. "Yeah, he definitely did."

"He's always been a good guy though."

He really is.

I swallowed hard and glanced down at my heels.

"Small world. You'll have to tell him I said hi."

And that I miss him.

And want to see him.

And hold him.

And be with him.

"Sure," she drawled suspiciously.

I had to stop obsessing about him. *Time to move on.*

Squaring my shoulders, I walked back over and sat in the chair next to the bed. "So, Morgan, show me this card for Henry."

For twenty minutes, Morgan talked my ear off. She definitely wasn't shy anymore. I wasn't even sure she took a breath. I only had an hour before Devon was going to drag me out of there—doctor's orders. I kept waiting for Meg to chime in and give me an opportunity to move on to some of the other patients, but she just smiled and snapped pictures.

"Maybe, when my hair grows back, it will be curly and we can be like twins!"

"Maybe it will. But straight hair is pretty too. How about this? Send me a picture whenever it grows back, and I'll send you a curling iron if need be. We can still be twins."

"Okay!" Morgan excitedly agreed as someone knocked on the door.

"Come in!" Meg shouted.

"Well, I better get going. That's probably the nurse here to kick me out." I leaned down to hug Morgan when a deep, panty-drenching voice filled the air.

"Who's stalking who now, Designer Shoes?"

I closed my eyes, praying that he wasn't there and equally hoping that my ears weren't deceiving me. When I spun to the door, my chest seized as I found Sam standing with his hands in his pockets and a one-sided grin pulling at his sexy lips.

Sam

I couldn't help myself. The moment a text from Meg popped up on my phone with a picture of Levee and Morgan, my feet rushed from my house before my mind even had a chance to catch up. Her message scrolled through my head during my entire drive to the hospital.

Meg: Dumbass, I'm not sure how you know Levee Williams, but get your ass up here. She almost burst into tears when she saw the guitar.

By the time I came to my senses, remembering why I had stayed away in the first place, I was staring into her devastating, brown eyes from across the hospital room.

Fuck my senses.

Going to her was the right move—a fact I knew so deeply that I couldn't believe I'd managed to stay away as long as I had. The hospital was neutral territory. It didn't feel like I was forcing myself on her by showing up at her security gate, pleading for a piece of the celebrity. I just needed to apologize and see how she was doing. I'd be okay if nothing ever happened between us again, but I'd regret it if I never got a chance to apologize.

Then I'll let her go.

I had to. Self-preservation was a real bitch like that.

Our gazes locked as we both silently apologized. Words weren't even necessary. I could see it in her eyes, and I prayed that she could see it in mine.

I tried to remind myself that I was only torturing myself, that I'd never be able to fully relax with a woman like her. And, God, did I need a chance to relax after the last few years.

But, then again, she wasn't Anne.

She was Levee.

More than that, I wanted her to be *mine.*

As if she could read my thoughts, her chin quivered and tears sprang to her eyes. I tossed her a tight grin that said nothing but somehow also said it all.

Her red lips split in a breathtaking smile that instantly quelled the anxiety I'd been living with for the last week.

Jesus Christ. What is wrong with me?

She was standing right in front of me, and my body ached to hold her.

To feel her.

To help her.

To allow her to heal…*me.*

Fuck it. I couldn't let that go.

Not because of a garbage truck full of what-ifs. I'd told Levee once that I wasn't perfect and I didn't want her to be, either, but then, at the first sign of trouble, I'd hit the road to spare myself. I'd known from the first moment I laid eyes on her what I was getting into. I might not have known she was some super celebrity, but I'd known she was damaged. We'd met on the top of a bridge for God's sake, yet there I stood as if I were surprised she had issues. I'd known it then, and I'd known it when I'd decided to take her to bed. But, worst of all, I'd known it when feelings above lust or worry had begun to spiral out of control. I hadn't been sure what those feelings were, but I had known they were there.

And I knew I wanted them to stay.

I was a man, and it was time to start acting like it. I could survive the tumultuous wake Levee Williams would surely leave behind. But what I couldn't survive was letting her walk away without even trying. In the span of five seconds, I'd thrown all of my apprehensions out the window and come to the decision that I desperately wanted something with her. I just needed to figure out a way to make her come to that decision too.

"C'mere," I whispered, hoping she'd at least give me that.

A sob bubbled in her throat, but she rushed in my direction, not stopping until she collided into me.

"I've missed you so much," she told my chest, and relief flooded my veins.

Well, that was easier than I expected.

I chuckled, wrapping my arms around her waist, kissing the top of her head.

"Don't laugh at me," she sniffled, squeezing me tighter.

Of course, that only made me laugh harder. Her head tipped back, and a scowl covered her gorgeous, tear-stained face.

Tucking stray curls behind her ears, I smiled down at her. "I've missed the view."

Her gaze jumped away. "I'm not allowed to go to the bridge anymore."

Using her chin, I tipped her head back. "Good," I breathed, kissing her forehead.

"You haven't been going up there either?"

"I've been there every night, but that's not the view I've been missing."

Her cheeks pinked, and her eyes smiled.

Her mouth didn't.

Because it was suddenly on mine.

Her tongue invaded my mouth as mango overwhelmed my senses. *Levee.* My whole body slacked as I slid a hand down to her ass.

"Uhhh…" Meg's voice stole my attention and reminded me that we weren't alone the way I so fiercely wanted to be.

Levee giggled and tucked her face into my neck.

"Hey!" I greeted Meg awkwardly.

"Nice to see you too, Sam." She rolled her eyes then flashed them to Levee's back in a silent question.

I shrugged. "Well, it's good to know your loud-mouth brother at least takes attorney-client privilege seriously."

"Shut. Up," she whispered. "Ryan knew about this and didn't tell me!" Her face morphed from humor to anger.

"Yep." I rubbed it in just to be sure Ryan thoroughly got his ass handed to him later.

"Mom," Morgan choked.

We all looked down at her, including Levee, who spun in my arms. Morgan's face was pale as tears welled in her bright-blue eyes.

"What's wrong?" Meg asked, settling on the bed next to her.

"Does this mean that Levee is going to be my aunt?" A trail of tears streamed down her cheeks.

"Well…" Meg stalled then leveled me with an annoyed frown. "Sam? Levee? You got an answer here?"

Levee blew out a sigh of relief. "Maybe."

Panic followed by a tinge of elation filled my chest as I swung an incredulous glare in her direction.

She shrugged then went back to talking to Morgan. "But maybe not. You mind if I step outside with Sam and talk about that?"

Morgan jumped to her knees and folded her hands in a prayer. "Oh, please say yes, Levee. Please. If you're my aunt, you get to come to dinner at Nana's every Sunday. And Christmas. Oh my God! Christmas is so fun. Sam always shows up smelling like smoke, but I promise I'll put a toothbrush in his stocking in case you want to kiss him some more."

Levee bit her lips to stifle a laugh.

"Uncle Sam, did you bring a ring? You need a ring if you're going to marry her."

I threw my hands up in defense and slowly backed toward the door. "I have no idea what you are talking about right now."

Meg doubled over in laughter as Morgan's expression turned murderous. "Girls need a ring! Come on, Sam. My friends would die if Levee was my aunt. Don't mess this up for me."

Levee barked a laugh. "Yeah, Sam. Don't mess this up for her." She flipped her hand up for a high five, which Morgan enthusiastically returned.

"Don't encourage her," I whisper-yelled at Levee, but the huge grin I was hopeless to hide gave me away.

After offering Morgan a quick hug, Levee headed toward the door, bumping my shoulder as she passed. "Come on, Sam. We need to talk about this ring." Just as she got to the door, she shouted, "See ya later, Morgan!"

"See you at dinner on Sunday!" Morgan casually called after her.

I couldn't help but laugh at the exchange, and as the door clicked behind her, I heard Levee laugh as well.

I quickly kissed Morgan on the top of her head then pulled Meg into a hug. "Thanks for the text."

"You have so much explaining to do," she bit out but immediately started shooing me out of the room.

I wandered into the hallway, where I found Levee whispering with Devon.

"Sup, big man." I clapped his meaty shoulder, looping the other arm around Levee's waist.

He glowered at me, but his words were for Levee. "We need to go. Time's up."

She shyly peeked up at me. "You want to maybe…come back to my place for a little bit so we can…talk."

"Yeah. Sounds good." I dug my car keys out of my pocket, and Levee's whole face lit up.

"I'm riding back with Sam!" she announced, bouncing on her toes.

"No," Devon snapped.

"Yes."

"No," he replied firmly.

"Yes," she repeated with a smile.

"I'll take you both back, but no way in hell am I letting you go with this guy alone."

Offended, I jumped in. "Hey! What the hell's that supposed to mean?"

Neither of them acknowledged me.

"Too bad you don't get a say in that." Levee grabbed my arm and dragged me away, leaving Devon cursing behind us.

As we marched down the hall, I leaned down and whispered in her ear, "I'm parked in the back lot."

She slammed on the brakes and groaned in frustrated. With a quick U-turn, we headed back toward a hopeful Devon.

He opened his mouth as we got close, but Levee interrupted him as we breezed past.

"Nope. Still riding with Sam. Don't forget Henry's dinner."

"Goddammit," he seethed through gritted teeth, but Levee seemed unfazed.

Well, okay, then. I guessed she was riding with me.

chapter thirteen

Levee

"**F**uck. Me," Sam moaned when I mounted him just as he slid behind the wheel of his Jeep.

"If you insist," I mumbled, crushing my mouth over his; smoke still lingered on his lips.

"Levee," he warned as I dropped a hand to his zipper. Grabbing my wrist, he attempted to stop me, but I retaliated by gliding my hips over his stiffening dick. "Shiiiiit." He gave the fight up and kissed me, thrusting a hand into my hair to use it for leverage.

With a gentle tug, he turned my head and latched onto my neck—nipping and sucking his way up to my ear. The bite of his hand in my hair sent blood rushing to my clit while his breath against my ear forced chills down my spine.

"Come back to my place. It's closer than yours."

"Okay," I answered without a single second of hesitation. I'd go wherever he wanted just as long as he was going too.

Shocked, he held my gaze. "Are you *allowed* to do that?"

"I'm a big girl, Sam. I'm *allowed* to do whatever—or whoever—I want." I went back in for another kiss, but Sam lifted me off his lap and deposited me onto the passenger's seat.

"Put your seat belt on," he growled, adjusting his pants.

Sam's Jeep was exactly what I would have expected from him. It was older but in perfect condition. There were no windows or doors to shield us from the sure-to-be freezing wind, but the idea of freedom was more than worth the price. A loud beat from his speakers filled the air the second he started the engine.

"Sorry." He turned it down as he slammed the five-speed into reverse. Tossing his arm around the back of my seat, he zipped us out of the parking spot and onto the streets of San Francisco.

With my hand on his thigh and the wind whipping through my hair, Sam navigated us back to his place. I was going to look like a shivering, matted poodle by the time we got there, but I couldn't have cared less. Sucking in a deep breath, I closed my eyes and smiled to myself. I didn't ever want to leave that moment. And that was the first time in as long as I could remember when I could honestly say that.

Something happened when I was with Sam.

I didn't know what that something was, but it happened all the same.

He wasn't a magical fix. I knew that the free fall was still waiting for me at the end of the night. But I didn't feel like I was plummeting when I was with him.

"What are you smiling about?" Sam asked when we pulled up to a red stoplight. His hand sifted through my hair then gently wrapped around the back of my neck.

Like a kitten, I purred, leaning into his touch. "Mmm, the way I feel right now." I opened my eyes to find him watching me with a content grin.

"You're beautiful," was all he said before the light turned green and we were off again.

Being told I was beautiful wasn't an anomaly.

It was Sam though.

That was *everything*.

Less than a minute later, Sam pulled up to a gorgeous two-story brick house complete with a wraparound porch that almost made me moan. It was so quaint and homey that I instantly felt drawn inside.

"Put your gooey eyes away. This is my mom's place. I live in the basement."

"Oh. You live with your…mom?" I'd done my best not to sound disappointed, but judging by the sound of his laugh, I'd failed miserably.

He arched an eyebrow. "Is that a problem?"

"No. I mean… I just." I stumbled over my words. It wasn't a problem. Well, not totally. It just wasn't what I expected. And suddenly, in that moment, I realized exactly how much I didn't know about Sam. "I thought…"

I continued to ramble until he leaned over and pressed his lips to mine. He didn't take it any deeper, and I was very aware of his shoulders shaking in amusement.

"Chill, Levee. I'm just giving you shit. It's my house. I bought it two years ago and have been fixing it up ever since. Rest assured, my mom has her own place across town."

I breathed an audible sigh of relief then squeaked, "It's a pretty house."

"It is. But it's still a work in progress, and I can't promise how safe my handiwork is, so don't step on the cracks or the whole floor might cave in." He unbuckled himself and climbed out.

"Uhhh," I stammered as I got out, meeting him at the hood. "Seriously?"

He shook his head and looped an arm around my waist. "Why are you nervous?"

"What? I'm not." I swayed in his arms with a herd of butterflies stampeding in my stomach.

"You haven't called me on my shit once since you got in my car. You're nervous. Now tell me why."

"I'm not—" I started, but he twisted his lips, unconvinced.

"You want me to take you home?"

"No!"

He dropped his hand to my ass. "Then tell me what's got you so distracted."

I chewed the inside of my cheek. How the hell did I answer that?

You, Sam! You have me distracted. I'm nervous because I can't say the wrong thing again. Not if I want you back. And, God, do I want you back.

I kept that to myself.

After backing me up, he pinned me against the hood with his body. "Levee," he prompted.

"I have crabs!" I blurted out when the truth got lodged in my throat. "I didn't want to tell you, but since we had sex, it's only a matter of time before those critters get you too."

I didn't expect him to believe my joke, but I figured he'd at least laugh. Instead, he groaned, sliding a hand under my shirt and over my breasts—his rough fingers dipping inside my bra to tease my nipples.

"Fuck, I've missed you."

"Mmm," I moaned. Closing my eyes, I slipped a hand down the back of his jeans—strictly for balance, of course.

I whined in complaint when he suddenly stepped away.

"Get your ass inside. I need to smoke."

"Are you crazy? I'm not going inside my stalker's house alone."

He cocked his head to the side. "Should you ever really go in your stalker's house at all?"

"Excellent point. We should definitely do it in the driveway." I reached for the button on his jeans, but he backed out of my reach.

"Jesus, Levee." He pulled a pack of cigarettes from his pocket. "Aren't we supposed to be talking?"

I nervously began chewing on the inside of my mouth again.

Talking was going to suck. Sex definitely wasn't.

But sex didn't mean I got to keep him. Talking hopefully would.

My eyes flashed to the ground. "Yeah. You're right."

I heard his lighter spark to life. Then his shoes entered my field vision. Threading our fingers together, he lifted the back of my hand to graze over his dick bulging behind his denim.

I sucked in sharply as his warm breath whispered over my neck.

"I've never in my life wanted to lose myself inside a woman more than I do with you. In my driveway. In my bed. In my car in the middle of a hospital parking lot. *Anywhere, Levee.*" He draped my arm around his neck then dropped his forehead to mine. "I've also never wanted to make something work with a woman more than I do with you. So, if talking is what I have to do, then let's do it. But, after all of that's settled—and I swear to God it *will* be settled—we'll get back"—he roughly tugged me against him, pointedly rolling his hips—"to this."

I'd been wrong.

That was everything.

I immediately looked away, and I did it smiling.

Huge.

Taking my hand, Sam smoked as we walked up the short sidewalk to his front door. While he fumbled with his keys, my eyes were drawn to two antique white doors that had been transformed into a porch swing.

I lifted our joined hands to point. "Did you make that?"

He tossed me a proud, lopsided grin. "If it's in this house, I made it."

"That's amazing. I can't imagine being that talented."

He barked a laugh as he pushed his door open. "Says the woman with a mantel full of Grammys."

"Oh, shut up. I meant talented with my hands, smartass." I pinched his nipple.

"Ow! Shit!" he complained before reaching out to pinch mine in retaliation. His was definitely gentler, and I might have secretly wished that he had done it again. *Repeatedly.*

He didn't though. He dropped his hand and flipped the lights on.

The outside of his house was amazing, but it didn't do justice to the inside in the least. Dark hardwood floors covered the expanse of the den, and a rugged, brown leather sectional butted up against the wall, facing a flat-screen mounted above a stone fireplace. The whole area was open, and his galley kitchen sat in the back with only a granite-top bar dividing the rooms. The house appeared to be older from the curb, but inside, it was as modern as it could get.

Sam's house definitely wasn't the bachelor pad I'd expected. It was unnaturally clean. I had a full-time maid and his place made mine look like a stable.

What single guy keeps a house this neat?

I gasped. "Oh my God, you're married!"

"Shh! You'll wake up my wife," he replied, touching his lips to my temple. "Don't worry. She's okay with you being here. You were on the top of my celebrity sexception list."

A laugh escaped my throat. He waggled his eyebrows as he moved to the small table next to the door. After flipping through the mail, he extended an envelope in my direction.

"Text my address to Devon. I don't need the SWAT team breaking down my door when he realizes I didn't take you back to your place."

He had a point. And, given my situation, Henry would probably stroke out too.

Upon retrieving my phone from my back pocket, I sent a message to Henry and asked him to pass the word along to Devon as well. His reply pinged in my hand, but I didn't bother reading it before powering my phone down.

"You want a beer?" Sam asked, bypassing the fridge and heading to a sliding glass door off the back of his kitchen.

"Sure."

"Okay. Be right back." He disappeared out the door.

Less than a moment later, a black lab came barreling in.

"Sampson!" Sam yelled behind him.

I immediately backed away. He didn't exactly look ferocious, but I'd become too fond of my legs to chance having them gnawed off.

"Sit," Sam ordered, appearing in doorway with four beers cradled against his chest.

The dog skidded to a halt then dropped to his hind end less than an inch away from me. His tail thumped against the hardwood as he eagerly stared up at me.

"You have a dog?"

"Very astute observation. Levee, meet Sampson," he laughed, twisting the tops off two domestic beers.

"Your dog's name is Sampson?"

"Yep," he said before tipping the beer to his lips and offering one in my direction.

"Your name is Sam and you named your dog Sampson. That's a bit egotistical, don't ya think?"

"Well, the guy who does my ink wouldn't give us matching tattoos. I was really limited in my narcissistic options."

"Right." I reached down to scratch behind Sampson's ears.

"I got him at the pound a few years back. I saw the name tag on his kennel and took it as a sign." He whistled and Sampson rushed to his side. Tilting his beer toward the couch to signal for me to sit down, he asked, "You a dog person?"

Following his unspoken order, I settled on the end of the couch, slipping my heels off so I could tuck a leg underneath me. "Yeah. I've always wanted a dog, but by the time I could afford to take care of one, my life was chaos. I travel way too much."

"Gotcha," he said, sitting beside me on the couch.

With a snap and a point from Sam, Sampson lumbered over to a dog bed in the corner, grunting before flopping down.

We both stayed silent, awkwardly drinking our beers. Small talk was officially over, but it seemed Sam wasn't any more excited to start the heavy conversation than I was.

"You hungry?" he asked as I nervously polished my beer off.

"I'm good, thanks."

He nodded and went back to staring into space. "Sooo..." he drawled but didn't say anything else.

Without looking at him, I broke the silence. "Are you positive that we can't just start with sex?"

Chuckling, he dropped his head back against the couch and turned to look at me. I met his gaze with a grin, hoping he was about to give in. Instead, his smile fell and his eyes softened.

"I'm sorry I stormed out the way I did, but I really can't apologize for telling Devon. Levee, I have a really fucked-up past, and it terrifies me to start something with someone like you."

Someone like you.

I swallowed hard, trying not to flinch from the sting of his words. "Oh." I scooted to the edge of couch and slid my shoes back on.

He caught my elbow before I had the chance to push to my feet. "Hear me out. Please."

"Yeah, of course. I was just gonna grab another beer." I smiled tightly, but he didn't release my arm.

With one hand, he grabbed the neck of my empty beer between two fingers and replaced it with his half-full one. "Stop and listen. That's all I'm asking."

A nod was my only response.

"My fondest memories from when I was a kid are when I was with my dad. I remember him spending hours running around with Anne and me in the backyard. He was so fucking funny and energetic. I swear we were always laughing with him. The problem was that my mom would sit at the kitchen window crying because she knew what would follow. My dad had been diagnosed as bipolar long before he met my mom. But he had meds, and even though they weren't a fix-all, they helped. Just like basically everyone else who struggles with the disorder, he had a hard time sticking to the medication regimen." He scrubbed his palms over the thighs of his jeans then dragged his cigarettes from his pocket. He glanced over at me then sighed, tossing them on the wagon-wheel coffee table—his creation, no doubt.

All of my hurt disappeared as I watched something far worse appear on Sam's face. I didn't necessarily want to encourage his habit, but I'd have done anything to erase that pained expression.

"You want to take this to the porch swing so you can smoke?" I asked, folding my hand over his.

"Yes. But I need to stop compromising your breakup with lung cancer. So no." His lips twitched as he intertwined our fingers. Groaning, he continued. "There were times when my dad would disappear to his workshop in our backyard for a week or more. It was a way of life, and Anne and I learned to stop asking questions. Despite all of his shit, he was a great dad." He squeezed my hand and pointedly held my gaze as he said, "I miss him a lot."

That does not sound good.

I'd figured the whole walk down memory lane was to set up Anne's story. But I was quickly realizing that, unfortunately, she might not be the only stop on the ride through Sam's self-proclaimed fucked-up past.

He ran a hand through his hair. "When I was fifteen, Dad lost his job and went into one of his typical lows. No one really paid it any attention. We were overly used to it by then. Mom used to have us deliver his dinner out to the shop. He wasn't always as patient with her as he was with Anne and me. When he was up, Mom was the center of his universe. When he was down…he was a fucking dick."

He lifted my hand to his mouth as I waited on pins and needles for what I prayed wouldn't be the ending I feared he was about to give me.

"Anne was twelve and thankfully spending the night at the neighbor's house the night I found him hanging from the rafters. I knew he was dead as soon as I opened that door. But I still frantically tried to save him." He sucked in a deep, agonizing breath then dragged me onto his lap. Holding me as if I were the only thing anchoring him to the present. "Levee, that's why I told Devon. I'll never forget those seconds when I was the only one in that room, begging the universe for help to save him—help that was never going to arrive. I just couldn't risk that I'd be alone in that room with you too. Someone else needed to know. I couldn't be solely responsible for losing someone else. Not like that."

Ice chilled my veins as a reality sliced through me.

Oh God.

I couldn't let that happen either.

Sam really can't be with someone like me.

chapter fourteen

Sam

"I have to go," Levee said, scrambling off my lap.

I had just dredged up memories I'd spent my entire life trying to forget in order to explain my past. I had close friends who didn't know about the skeletons I'd pulled from the closet and all but put on display for her. And now she was darting?

"Where the hell are you going?" I bit out entirely too roughly while pushing to my feet after her.

She began messing with her phone until it powered on with a chime. "I have a busy day tomorrow. They rescheduled my concert in LA for tomorrow night. I should probably head home. I'm taking off on vacation for a few weeks. You know, rest and relaxation and all that jazz. I'll just call Devon for a ride." She lifted the phone to her ear.

Fuck.

That.

"Put the phone down, Levee," I growled.

She squeezed the phone between her shoulder and ear and lifted the empty beer bottles off the table. "I'll just put these in the trash." Then she flittered to the kitchen, grabbing a rag off the side of the sink and wiping away imaginary dirt from my spotless counters.

What hell is she doing?

"Levee?" I called, but apparently, Devon had just picked up.

"Hey. Can you come get me?" she asked quietly, but not quietly enough, because I'd heard the quiver in her voice loud and clear.

And that was all it took to get my legs moving in her direction.

Her back was to me, but I reached over her shoulder and snatched the phone away from her ear.

"Hey!" she shouted, spinning to face me.

My nerves were still raw and exposed from the little journey back in time, but I was mainly frustrated beyond belief.

With my gaze locked on hers, I lifted the phone to my ear. "Hey, Devon. I'll bring her home in a little while."

"No, the fuck you won't," he barked, but I pressed the end button.

She swallowed hard and pasted on a sweet smile that definitely belonged to *the* Levee Williams.

It just didn't belong to *my* Designer Shoes.

Not at all.

"Sam, you don't have to take me back. Give me the phone. Devon can be here in a few minutes."

Tossing her phone onto the counter, I took a menacing step forward.

Her eyes grew wide as she backed away. "Sam, I have to go."

I sucked in a calming breath that did nothing to quell the frustration brewing inside me. "No, you don't. You're freaking out about something, so open your mouth and tell me what that is." I continued to advance. "I spill my darkest secrets and suddenly you have shit to do tomorrow? Well, guess what, Levee? I have shit to do tonight. And it starts and ends with you."

Finally, she'd exhausted the space in my kitchen, and her back hit my sliding glass door. "I don't know what to say. I just need to go," she said so matter-of-factly that, if it hadn't been for the tear that rolled down her cheek, I might have believed her.

I caught the tear with the pad of my thumb and slowly lifted the moisture into her line of sight. "Liar."

"Sam—"

"Whether it was on the bridge or in a hospital room not even two hours ago, your tears have always told me the truth." I dropped my damp thumb to her lips. "These are not as honest. Don't tell me you're fine. Don't tell me you have to go. Don't tell me that everything is okay. Just tell me the truth your eyes are so desperate for me to hear."

She held my gaze for only a beat longer before she broke.

Completely.

As she threw her arms around my neck, the waterworks came full force. Scooping her off her feet, I carried her to the couch, settling with her on my lap.

Her face was buried in the crook of my neck as she rambled a million miles a minute. "I have no idea what to do here. I like you, but you're right. You can't be with someone like me. And, more than that, you shouldn't have to. Over the last week, I've been doing a lot better and finally feeling better than I have in years. But I don't know if it will stay that way. What if I find my feet on that bridge again? " She suddenly sat up. "I can't put you in that position. Not after everything you've been through." She rested her head back on my shoulder. "You're amazing, Sam. I'm so fucking sorry that you had to deal with all of that in your past, but I can't ask you to potentially deal with my issues in the future. And it hurts because I lied. I more than like you. I hardly know you, but I want to keep you. Just the way you are. Maybe forever."

A lump formed in my throat, and an unlikely smile tilted my lips. I'd learned early on that, no matter how I tried, I couldn't fix everything for everyone. I couldn't make my Dad better any more than I could Anne.

But I could fix *this*.

With a sigh, I whispered into the top of her hair, "Then do it."

Her head popped up, confusion painting her tear-stained face.

"Levee, I'm not the one trying to leave. You're right. This is going to be a struggle for me, but while I have no idea what issues you do have, I do know you're not my dad or Anne."

Framing her face with my hands, I pulled her in for a kiss. She was still visibly upset, but I couldn't deny that the brief contact was more for me than it was for her.

"Levee, when Anne was a teen, she started exhibiting a lot of my father's typical behaviors. My mom immediately hauled her into the doctor, begging for them to do something...and they did. She battled with what we thought was bipolar disorder for years, but when she was twenty, everything went downhill fast. She started hallucinating and flipping out over nothing. My mom and I did the best we could, but nothing seemed to help. At twenty-one, Anne was officially diagnosed with schizophrenia. I have no idea if that's what my dad had too. After seeing Anne, it's not exactly a stretch that he could have been misdiagnosed also." My pulse slowed, and the truth I was prepared to admit ebbed any residual fear from my body. "But I do know that it's not what *you* struggle with."

Her eyes filled with tears all over again. "No. I don't think it is, either. But that doesn't change the fact that you deserve someone different than me. Someone better." She climbed off my lap, but I no longer worried that she was going to bolt.

If she wanted space to think, I'd give her that.

Gnawing on her thumbnail, she began to pace. Then she stopped and turned to face me, her shoulders rolled forward in defeat. "You need someone you didn't meet on the top of a bridge."

But I didn't give a single fuck what Levee thought I needed.

I'd made my decision.

With all of my unease about pursuing something with her organized inside my mind, a familiar levity washed over me. Reclining back against the couch, I folded my hands behind my head and propped my feet on the table.

"You're right," I replied curtly, and her whole body sagged as she looked away. I smirked to myself. "The only problem, Levee, is I just want *you*."

Her gaze snapped to mine, and her eyes were filled with a mixture of surprise and hope. As her chin fought to suppress a smile, it gave me hope as well.

I walked over and wrapped her in my arms. Then I repeated familiar words that were suddenly more fitting than ever. "I'm not perfect, and I'd like to pretend you aren't, either."

She dropped her head to my shoulder as her arms dangled at her sides.

I kissed her hair and whispered, "There isn't a woman in the world who doesn't have demons of some sort. No matter who I end up with, it's always going to be a struggle." I kissed her hair again, letting it linger as if my lips were able to transfer the truth of my words. "Levee, I'd like to struggle with you."

That should have been my big finish, but she didn't even acknowledge that she'd heard me. She stood impossibly still in my grasp. She wasn't moving away, but she wasn't returning my embrace either. I couldn't see her face to get a read on her reaction, and after a few moments of silence, it began to unnerve me.

"I meant that in a good way," I whispered, squeezing her tight.

She tipped her head back to look into my eyes and mumbled, "I'm going to need you to sign a release."

"Huh?"

"I need you to sign a copyright release, because I'm using every single bit of that speech in a song. Jesus, Sam. 'I'd like to struggle with you.' I'm so freaking jealous that I didn't write that."

I smiled as she finally circled her arms around my neck. "You can have it. It's not like I can use it again at this point."

"I don't know. You did a pretty nice job at recycling the 'perfect' thing."

"I didn't recycle—I *repurposed*," I exaggerated with a wink.

She laughed then leaned her head back to my shoulder. "Sam, you have no idea what you're getting into."

"No one ever does. It's the beauty of taking risks."

"Oh my God," she breathed. "I'll need a release on that too."

I chuckled, dropping my hands down to her ass. "Look at me," I urged with a squeeze.

Reluctantly, her red-rimmed eyes met mine.

"I shouldn't have stormed out on you the other night, but I swear it won't ever happen again. You need to talk about...*anything*. Hell, even if you get sick of me and ditch me for some big-time bazillionaire actor tomorrow, I'm still here."

She narrowed her eyes.

"I'm just saying, I'm here no matter when, where, or why. I don't want you holding back because of my history. Okay?" I didn't care if she answered or if she thought it was okay. It made me feel infinitely better to know I'd put it out there.

"Ugh." She lolled her head back down. "You're such a good guy."

"Not always. I'm a real dick if you try to use my toothbrush in the morning."

Her shoulders shook as she laughed. They stilled when her lips brushed against my neck. "I'll keep that in mind."

"Good." I squeezed her ass again.

"This is going to be a train wreck for you, Sam. But I really want to see if we can make something work. I believe I can get better and get my life in order, but struggling *with* me is exactly what you'll be doing while I try to find some sort of balance. Besides all my *issues*, my life is crazy town." She never looked up as she continued. "There's no such thing as dinner and movie dates with me. I can't even leave the house without security. I work nonstop and get recognized virtually everywhere I go. I travel for six months out of every year, and my free time is usually spent at children's hospitals." She sighed. "I don't know how to date anyone anymore, especially someone who isn't in the industry. The press is going to eat you alive, so we'd have to keep this quiet."

I could feel her heart pounding against my chest, and her breathing was labored as if she'd just finished a marathon.

"Nobody can know." Sure, she was talking to me, but she wasn't telling me anything new. All she'd managed to do was work herself up into a frenzy.

"Calm down." I hugged her tight. "We don't have to figure out all of this tonight. Hell, we don't actually have to figure it out at all. The rest will work itself out. We'll keep things chill for a while. I'm okay with date nights at casa de Rivers. It has a convenient private bedroom at our disposal." I glided a hand down her back, but she didn't laugh.

She continued to freak out. "You don't understand how much this is going to change your life," she whispered.

She was absolutely right. My life would never be the same again.

And it was *invigorating*.

I understood that dating a woman like Levee was going to be difficult, but if she was the *great* at the end of the day, I was more than up for the challenge.

"I'll be okay. I promise."

"You say that now…but—"

"Levee, stop. Take a deep breath and relax. No matter what you say, you're not talking me out of this. I want to make something work with you, and you've made it clear that you want something with me. So let's do it. End of story."

"Sam," she objected, clearly not done talking.

But I was.

"What's your schedule look like tomorrow? I want you to spend the night."

"I have to leave in the morning for LA. I have a concert tomorrow night. Then I'm scheduled for a month of"—she lifted her hands in a pair of air quotes—"'vacation.'"

"Are there going to be doctors on this vacation?"

She nodded.

"Good."

"Yeah, fantastic," she deadpanned.

"Oh, hush. It will be fantastic. Now, spend the night and tell me who I need to sleep with to get tickets to your show tomorrow night? I have two days until you're gone. I'm maximizing my time whether you want it or not."

"Are you sure?"

I reached up and pinched her lips between two fingers. "Zip it. I'm positive."

She sighed, and her whole body relaxed.

As anxiety drained from her face, my Designer Shoes appeared before my eyes with an enticing smirk. Pushing my hand away, she pressed a kiss to my mouth. "I might know someone who can get you tickets, but I hear she's pretty needy in bed."

"She can't be any needier than you." I kissed her again, greedily opening my mouth for a taste I had been longing for.

She was leaving in two days, but for the first time since I'd met Levee, I knew for certain she'd be coming back.

To me.

chapter fifteen

Levee

If Sam could pretend that sheer force of will was enough to overcome our issues and attempt a relationship that was obviously destined to fail, so could I.

Hell, I could probably pretend for the rest of my life if he continued to hold me the way he did.

Kiss me the way he did.

Touch me the way he did.

Save me the way he did.

With a firm squeeze around my waist, he lifted me off the ground. Never breaking the kiss, he carried me, dangling in his arms, to the couch.

He sat on the cushion and attempted to pull me on top of him, but I sank to my knees instead.

"No," he objected as I went to work on the button of his jeans.

"Yes."

"Levee, no." He shoved his hands under my arms and lay down, dragging me with him.

"Stop!" I laughed as I fought against him, but somehow, he'd managed to wedge me between the back of the couch and his body.

Pinning both my hands above my head with only one of his own, he rolled on top of me. "I'll stop when I'm done eating your pussy." He slid a hand between my legs and used the seam of my jeans to rub glorious circles. "But, when I'm done, I promise I'll give you my cock anywhere you want. Mouth." He popped the button on my jeans open with one hand. "Pussy." Releasing my hands, he tugged my pants over my hips as I kicked my shoes off. Pausing, he arched an eyebrow. "Ass."

I scowled, which caused him to chuckle as he pulled my panties off as well.

"Okay. Okay. So maybe no ass."

"Good call," I said, sitting up to remove my shirt. It was still in my hand when his mouth crushed over mine and his hand dove between my legs. "Sam," I gasped as two fingers suddenly filled me.

"Sit up," he ordered, kneeling on the couch while continuing to piston his fingers in and out.

I wasn't going to argue. I was, however, going to take it further.

While Sam used one skilled hand to unsnap my bra, I flipped the button on his jeans and snuck my hand inside.

"Fuck," he cursed.

A moan escaped my own throat as I closed my hand around his length.

Sam's dick was incredible—the perfect combination of long and thick women dreamed about. However, it was the memories of the barbell that graced the head that had caused me to kill more than one set of batteries over the last week. I'd never been with anyone who'd been pierced before, but after having felt the metal glide over what I assumed was the elusive G-spot, I knew it was about to become a requirement for all future boyfriends.

Or maybe, somehow, someway, I'd be lucky and get to keep Sam.

Leaning down, he took my mouth in another hasty kiss. I matched the rhythm of his hand until he suddenly stepped out of my reach. He removed his fingers and peeled his shirt over his head. I would have complained about the loss, but his fingers quickly returned, and within seconds, his mouth followed, sealing over my clit.

"Oh God." I arched off the couch as Sam attempted to settle between my knees. His tall body wouldn't fit on the couch, so he hooked my legs over his shoulders and turned us so he could kneel on the ground in front of me.

My fingers tangled in his hair as he trailed a hand up to my breast, deliciously rolling my nipple while his mouth worked me from all angles. It wasn't enough though. He was devouring me, and I could have easily come within minutes, but I wanted more. We were wrong on so many levels, but the way he made me forget about the free fall while he was inside me made it absolutely right.

At least, for me.

After the night we'd had, I didn't want to come against his mouth. I wanted his weight on top of me, grounding me while reminding me of what we now had. And, better than that, what we could possibly have in the future.

Giving his hair a rough tug, I said, "I want you inside me."

His tongue continued to flick against my swollen clit, but his eyes lifted to mine.

"You're driving me mad, but I need you inside me. I need to know I'm driving you mad too."

"No," he murmured. Then his tongue darted out.

"Sam, please," I cried, pulling on his hair.

His hand left my breast and disappeared out of my view. His shoulder moved against my leg as he stroked his dick while he watched his fingers moving inside me. "Rest assured that you're driving me in-fuck-ing-sane. But I get one night with you. Then all I'll have for the next month are those memories. Stop fighting it, and give me one of this sweet cunt coming on my mouth."

Jesus.

Like I was going to say no to that.

Who was I to deny the man a memory?

I was going to need the memories too.

"Okay. Umm…I guess you should stop talking and get back to work, then."

A devilish grin grew on his lips.

Then he did just that. Sam licked and teased with a fierce determination. His tongue swirled and his fingertips circled, working me harder and pushing me higher than ever before. I still wanted to feel him inside me, but once I let myself go, I was no longer willing to lose his mouth.

As my muscled tensed, attempting to fight the impending climax, Sam's hands disappeared. His tongue stayed the course, and even with as lost as I was, I became vaguely aware of his shoulders shifting and the familiar crinkle of a condom wrapper. I lifted my hips, silently asking for more, and Sam more than answered. Two fingers thrust inside me, curling as he sucked hard on my clit. I couldn't even fight.

I sat up straight and ground against his face as the orgasm tore through me.

I was still pulsing and riding the high when Sam was suddenly gone.

Less than a second later, he was *everywhere.*

His body covered mine, forcing me down to the couch just as he slammed to the hilt inside me. He cursed loudly, but all coherent thoughts had escaped me. A new orgasm sparked within even before the first had left. My legs shook as he wrapped them around his hips. His hand snaked into my hair, and he roughly drove into me, each thrust deeper than the last.

Sam's golden eyes filled with feral possession as they rose to meet mine.

In that moment, the perpetual free fall was no match for the way he made me feel.

I was still falling at unstoppable speeds—only, in his arms, as his body claimed me without a single word spoken, I was suddenly falling…up.

A tear slipped from my eye and a smile tilted my lips as I clung to his back while another orgasm washed over me.

Sam continued to chase his own release until finally he came whispering my name. It was more musical to my ears than any note I had ever sung, written, or played.

"Hey." His gravelly voice caught my attention as he pushed up to catch my gaze. "Good or bad?" he asked, using the pad of his thumb to wipe away the wet trail then pressing it against my lips.

"Good," I mumbled around it. "Really, *really* good."

"Good," he whispered, replacing his thumb with his lips. He breathed deeply, but kept it chaste. "Let me get rid of the condom. I need a smoke. Then we can take a shower." He winked, climbing off me and sauntering away.

Sitting upright, I collected my clothes off the floor with a silly smile.
Yeah. We can do this.

"You want something to sleep in?" Sam asked, emerging from the hallway in a new pair of jeans riding low on his hips with a shirt slung over his shoulder, an unlit cigarette already dangling from his lips.

He looked downright edible. My eyes raked over the tattoos covering his chest and down his arms and his sides.

Under my scrutiny, he stood proudly, flexing to define his six-pack. "Fuck, I love when you look at me like that."

"Perfect, because I love looking at you like *that*." I motioned my finger up and down his body.

"It's official. I'm burning all of my shirts. You want to rescue this one from the fiery pits and sleep in it tonight?" He offered me the one off his shoulder.

"Please." I laughed as he threw the cotton top in my direction.

As I tugged the oversized rePURPOSEd T-shirt over my naked

body and stepped into my panties, he slowly made his way over to me.

Cupping my jaw, he rubbed his thumb back and forth over my cheek. "I'm really fucking happy you're here."

"Me too." I smiled.

He removed the cigarette from between his lips and was bending over to touch his mouth to mine when a sudden pounding on the door stopped him. Sampson went nuts barking, and Sam's eyes narrowed with suspicion.

"What the fuck?"

Devon's angry snarl permeated through the wood. "Open the fucking door."

Henry's voice quickly followed. "Would you calm down? She's probably getting the dick right now."

"Oh God," I groaned.

This is not happening.

Devon replied, "Or she's dead on that dick's floor."

"She's fine."

"You don't fucking know that. You should have heard her on the phone."

The loud pounding returned, and Sam stared at the door as he said, "I think that's for you."

"She is going to kick your ass," Henry scoffed.

"I'll survive. Besides, you were the one who gave me the address. She'll probably kill you first," Devon continued to argue as I stomped to the door and snatched it open.

"What the hell are you doing here?" I seethed at them.

Their eyes raked over my outfit—or lack thereof—and Henry's smile spread as he elbowed Devon in the side.

"See? Told you. She was getting the dick."

"Let's go," Devon barked at me.

"Yes, please *go*," I snarked, slamming the door in their faces, but Devon snuck a foot inside preventing it from closing completely.

"You called for a ride home. I'm here. Get in the car," he replied, pushing the door wide and stepping inside.

Sam's arms suddenly folded around my hips from behind. "Go get dressed. We can have this conversation when you aren't half naked with my front door wide-ass open."

I knew the moment Henry saw Sam. His jaw slacked open and cartoon hearts might as well have floated from his eyes. Sam and Devon recognized the moment too, because Devon's eyes flared wide and Sam instinctively took a step away with me securely tucked into his side.

Henry prowled forward as Sam's gaze bounced down to me in bewilderment.

"You probably should have been the one to get dressed first," I told Sam as Henry continued his nonconsensual eye-fucking of my boyfriend.

Boyfriend?

Maybe that's a bit much.

Is it?

Sam's hand flexed at my hip, and I couldn't help but smile at the idea. I hadn't been so excited about the idea of calling someone my boyfriend since fifth grade, when Jay Rogers passed me a note asking me to check yes or no.

I was still lost in schoolgirl musings when Sam interrupted my thoughts.

"Hey, so, I'm Sam. You must be Henry." He extended a hand forward.

I laughed when Henry looked down at his hand then bent to the side, licking his lips as he openly checked out Sam's package. Then I laughed even louder as Sam shifted me in front of him to block Henry's assessment.

I should have said something to defuse the insanely awkward situation, but where was the fun in that? I looked up at Sam and very matter-of-factly said, "I told you he was going to try to woo you."

"This is wooing?"

"You would be surprised how many men have fallen victim to him with far less."

Devon shook his head as Henry continued to stare in awe, pacing a tight circle around us.

"Is he going to say something?" Sam whispered.

"Unfortunately, yes. And when he does, you'll wish for the weird silence again."

Suddenly, Henry stilled and peeled his shirt over his head, announcing, "Threesome."

"Excuse me?" Sam questioned as Henry advanced.

"Fine, twosome, but Levee gets to watch. She is my best friend, after all."

I giggled as I pressed a hand into Henry's bare chest. "Put your damn shirt back on and leave him alone."

He groaned, finally dragging his eyes off Sam. "This is so not fair. Why would you flaunt this fine specimen of a straight man in front of me and not even let me nibble. Do you not love me at all?" He pouted.

"No one is nibbling anything," Sam quickly added.

Henry winked. "Yet."

Sam stepped away and dug into his pocket. "Jesus, I need a cigarette."

"Oh, me too. Let's go outside," Henry agreed, starting to follow after him.

I caught his arm. "Don't you dare! First of all, you don't smoke. Second of all, Sam is completely off-limits to you. Let it go."

His shoulders sagged in defeat. "You're so selfish," he whined, pulling his shirt back on.

"Maybe, but if you quit your bitching, we could watch him walk away together. His ass is insane."

"Seriously?" Sam asked cynically.

"Well, now, you're just being mean. But I accept." Henry tossed his arm around my shoulders.

We both turned to Sam, who was squinting his eyes in disbelief at our objectifying exchange.

Henry made the shooing motion toward him. "Go ahead, hot man. Smoke your cigarette. And, before you ask, yes, I'm perfectly okay with you envisioning it's me you're putting in your mouth."

"Henry!" I scolded then burst into laughter.

"What?" He feigned innocence.

Sam curled his lip in disgust then barked a laugh while scratching the back of his head in what could only be described as astonishment. "Yeah. I…uh… Come on, Sampson."

The dog trotted after him.

I slapped Henry on the chest. "You dumbass. Don't screw this up for me. You know I like him."

"Yes, I do. And I completely know why now. Fuck, that man is sexy."

"He really is. And he's such a nice guy." I sighed. "He deserves so much better than me."

Henry rubbed my arm. "Nonsense. If he's smart, he's probably on his knees out there, thanking God that he gets to be with you." He swayed his head from side to side. "And, since he's already on his knees, maybe I should go check on him."

I slapped his chest again. "Shut up! Leave him alone."

Henry chuckled, throwing his hands up in defense. "Okay, okay."

Devon spoke up, interrupting our conversation. "Show's over. I'm bored. Levee, get your clothes and let's go."

"I'm not going anywhere. Come get us in the morning."

Devon's eyes flared wide. "Us?"

"Sam's going with me to LA. He can ride back with you after the show."

"Awesome," Devon mumbled.

I wasn't sure what Devon's problem with Sam was, but he'd made it blatantly obvious he had one. He'd always been protective of me. It was his job, after all. Literally. But our relationship was more than just employee-employer. Over the last few years together, Devon and I had forged a friendship that had eventually evolved into more of a brother-sister bond. I loved and hated it all at the same time.

It would have been nice to have an employee who just did what I said. But I loved knowing that Devon was always there for me, no matter what the task.

"So, who wants a beer?" Sam asked as he came back inside wearing a wrinkled hoodie and holding a six-pack of brews.

"Where do you keep magically producing beer from?" I inquired.

"I have a stocked fridge in my shop out back."

"And the hoodie?"

His eyes flashed to Henry. "My Jeep. I didn't think it was safe to come back in without a shirt."

"Smart move," Henry said, walking over and pulling a beer from his hand. He winked as he twisted the top off and tipped it to his lips.

"Okay. As very entertaining as this has been, can you two please leave? It's late, and Sam and I were just about to take a shower."

Henry's mouth was full, and he lifted a finger as he swallowed.

"No, you can't join us!"

"Why are you so hateful?" Henry grumbled.

"Take him home. Please," I begged Devon, who was glowering at the whole situation—and especially at Sam.

"Levee, we need to talk. Stewart isn't going to be happy about you being here. We don't know this guy, and a lot of things are going down for you right now. We need to keep this among the family for a while."

I walked over and stopped in front of him, craning my head back to meet his eyes. "A lot of things *are* going down for me right now, but Sam has had a front-row seat to everything for a while. There's nothing he doesn't already know."

"Levee—"

"Devon, I'm good. I swear. I know you're worried, but there's no talking me out of this. Now, please, just take Henry and go. I'll see you in the morning."

He stared down at me blankly for several beats before rolling his eyes and calling out, "Henry, we're pulling out."

Henry set the beer down and headed toward the door, pausing to give me a hug. "I'll see you in the morning." Then he shouted over his shoulder, "Night, Sam! Call me if you change your mind."

I groaned.

Sam walked over, draping his arm around my waist, and called back, "Will do! Goodnight."

As soon as the door clicked behind them, my whole body sagged. "God, I'm sorry."

"Don't be. That was…interesting."

I laughed. *Interesting* didn't even come close to it. But as I nervously peeked up through my lashes to get a read on Sam, he was sporting a huge smile.

"It was fun, Levee. Don't look so worried. It's going to take more than Henry Alexander trying to get in my pants to run me off."

"I'll make him quit. I swear. I'm not sure I can promise the same about Devon though."

"Stop." He folded me into his chest and kissed the top of my head. "You're stuck with me."

I breathed in deeply, praying that that was true.

"Let's shower. You stink." I tugged at his hoodie.

"Yeah, this thing is filthy." He pushed me back a step and dragged it over his head. "Sorry, but there was no way I was coming back in half naked."

"I can't blame you there." I giggled into his chest.

He glided a hand over my ass. "Hey, next time people show up at my door, clothing is not optional for you."

"Oh, please. It's just Henry and Devon."

His other hand snaked into the front of my panties and through my wet folds. "Maybe. But this is mine now. No more peep shows."

A moan escaped my throat, and it was only partially because the tip of his finger had dipped inside me.

"This is mine now."

"Yes," I breathed before his mouth landed over mine.

chapter sixteen

Sam

Levee and I ended up taking a shower. Then she rode me until p.m. slipped to a.m. Neither of us was in any hurry to go to sleep, especially knowing that the next day was going to be our last for a while. But I reminded her as many times as possible that it was only temporary. She tried to argue that this kind of separation would be frequent in her line of work. I kissed her indecently every time she so much as started trying to talk me out of being with her.

There was nothing she could have said to change my mind.

Eventually, she gave up, and as the sun started to peek in my bedroom window, she nodded off in my arms.

Sleep never found me. Like a true stalker, I stayed awake watching her sleeping safely tucked into my side. Her legs were tangled with mine, and her arm was slung over my hips.

I hadn't felt that kind of peace in as long as I could remember.

And it was going to fucking suck to lose it.

But, when the alarm on her phone started going off, I released her, knowing she'd be back. I'd make sure of that.

With only a combined three hours of sleep between us, Levee and I slept wrapped in each other's arms the entire five-hour drive to LA. When we arrived at the arena, Levee had Devon drop me off first. She was adamant that we not be photographed together, and while it stung, I understood. With an all-too-quick kiss, I was dropped off by the tour buses parked out back, where I met Levee's band and backup dancers.

Simon, her guitarist, greeted me with open arms and stuck by my side. Apparently, Levee had called and put him in charge of babysitting me. He was a nice guy—they all were, actually. It wasn't at all the rock-star feel I'd expected. For hours, I chilled on a bus, bullshitting with the members of her band and a few of their wives, and I was surprised to discover that one even had his three-year-old daughter with them. They were curious as hell about me, and I couldn't even begin to count how many times I dodged the question of how Levee and I had met.

I'd checked my phone incessantly, waiting for a message from her, but nothing ever came. I assumed she was busy, but the fact that she was in the proximity made me edgy to be with her. I wasn't going to be *that guy* though. She'd left me out back for a reason. I'd give her whatever space she needed to prepare for her show.

Finally, four hours later, the door to the bus opened and Devon informed me that Levee was asking for me. He handed me a small amp to carry, dropped a staff lanyard around my neck, and then led me to a roped-off side door. Fans huddled around the area, only glancing up long enough to deem me as unimportant.

We made our way through a maze of backstage hallways before finally stopping at an unmarked door.

Devon knocked and then took the amp from my hands.

"Come in," Levee singsonged.

Disgruntled, he shoved the door open and silently motioned for me to enter.

My breath was stolen from my chest the moment our gazes locked. With her hair teased in the process of being done and heavy makeup covering her smooth skin, it was the first time I'd ever laid eyes on Levee Williams, the superstar. I recognized the brown eyes that stared back at me, but everything else was that of the woman who graced the pages of magazines.

This woman was undeniably beautiful, but I definitely preferred the one who'd spent the night naked in my bed.

"There you are," she said quietly as a woman continued to work on her hair.

"I was starting to think you forgot about me." I took a step forward with full intentions of kissing her painted-pink lips then stopped long enough to flip my gaze to the stylist in question.

"Oh! Sorry. Madison, this is Sam. Sam, this is Madison."

The woman looked up and smiled warmly. "Ohhhh, you are pretty."

"Thanks?" I replied, curiously flashing my eyes back to Levee.

"Henry called Madison this morning just to rave about you."

"Oh, Jesus," I groaned, making them both laugh.

"He likes you. But don't let Levee lie. She's been rambling about you since she sat down," Madison said.

Even under what looked like a suitcase full of makeup, I saw Levee's cheeks turn pink.

I fucking loved that I had that effect on her.

"Is that so?" I asked with a smirk.

Levee shook her head and knotted her hands in her lap. "I was just worried about you. You never know when Henry might attempt to abduct you and force you into sexual slavery."

I fisted my hands on my hips and said seriously, "The threat is real."

Madison chuckled, dropping a comb on the small rolling table. "I'm gonna grab a coffee." She arched an eyebrow at me. "We can fix the lipstick, but don't fuck with the hair. *Capisce*?"

I kept my eyes glued to Levee and nodded.

No sooner had the door shut behind her than Levee stood up and planted a kiss on my lips. Then, using the back of her hand, she wiped it away. "I missed you. Where have you been hiding?"

I circled my arms around her waist and pulled her flush against me. "I was chilling with the band. Same place you dropped me off."

She leaned away and eyed me suspiciously. "Devon said you weren't out there anymore. He's been looking for you for the last three hours."

"He must not have looked very hard, because I didn't go anywhere. Ask Simon." I touched my lips to her temple.

"Hmm." She twisted her lips in confusion. "Well, okay. You're here now, I guess."

"Yep. Now, if only I could find Designer Shoes. She seems to have gone missing. I'm terrified she's been buried alive by a makeup artist."

Levee giggled and squeezed me tight. "You should see the sand-blaster they use to scrub it off at the end of the night."

"Oh, they repurpose you!" I teased as she shifted impossibly closer.

"Basically," she mumbled. "I hate that you have to go home after the show. I feel like we haven't gotten to spend any time together today. You were either drooling on my shoulder or snoring on the way here. Now, I have to perform."

"Don't you even try to pretend that I was the one drooling. I woke up to find myself sitting in an honest-to-God wet spot. And not the good kind."

"Shut up, liar."

"No, you shut up, Drooly."

We both laughed, but she once again sighed in frustration. "I don't want you to leave tonight."

"Then I won't. You aren't leaving until the morning, right?"

"Right, but Devon has to drive you back tonight when he picks up the rest of my stuff and Henry. They're dropping me off tomorrow."

"I'm not ten, Levee. I don't need a ride home. If you want me to stay tonight, I'll catch a flight back in the morning."

Her eyes perked. "Really?"

"Yeah, really, crazy woman."

"I mean, I'll pay for it. Just tell me when you want to leave and I'll have someone book it right now."

I chuckled. "I'm also not a male prostitute. You aren't buying my ticket just so you can have your wicked way with me. But yes, I'll stay."

"You sure?" she asked hopefully.

"I'm positive. I'm not kinky enough to be a prostitute."

She pinched my nipple. "That's not what I meant. And now, I'm disappointed to find out you're not kinky."

I pinched her nipple back, letting my fingers linger as I grazed my teeth over her neck. "You didn't seem disappointed last night."

She gasped and swayed into my touch.

"And, before you smart off, I promise you won't be disappointed tonight, either. I'll buy my ticket. You entertain thousands. We sandblast you back to life. Then I'll fuck you whatever kinky way you want until you are physically unable to forget me for the next month."

"Yesss," she hissed, sliding her hands over my ass.

I nipped at her earlobe as my cock swelled between us. I'd have given anything to skip to the end of that scenario—even past the losing-myself-inside-her-later-that-night part. I wanted to be at the *very* end—when she came home.

Healthier.

Happier.

And all fucking mine.

I was about to take her mouth in a needy kiss when Madison knocked on the door.

"Everyone dressed?" she asked, cracking the door open but not coming in.

Levee groaned and leaned her forehead on my shoulder. "Unfortunately. But give us a minute."

"Sorry. I need to finish you up. They're calling for you back in wardrobe."

"Right," Levee said, stepping away. Glancing down to my cock bulging in my jeans, she whispered, "What a waste of a perfectly good hard-on."

I laughed, adjusting myself. "Later. I promise." I pressed a chaste kiss to her lips then closed my eyes and started alphabetically listing types of wood.

Watching Levee perform was one of the most exhilarating experiences of my life. Sure, she put on one hell of a show, complete with dancers, wardrobe changes, and pyrotechnics, but even without the fanfare, she was mesmerizing. The way she commanded that stage, owning every note that escaped her sexy mouth, was cock hardening. I couldn't have dragged my eyes away even if I hadn't been utterly falling for her.

I'd heard Levee's music on the radio. I recognized the beats and the melody. But, after having gotten to know the woman who'd written them, I realized that the words were the most beautiful of all. Through her songs, it was clear Levee had been struggling for a while, but the most staggering part was how much hope and fight were woven into her lyrics as well. And, because of that fight, I found hope as well.

She's going to be okay.

And so would we.

I still didn't know why Levee had been on that bridge night after night. I'd gathered that her life was stressful, but when I saw the way she came alive the moment she stepped on stage with a mic in her hand, I couldn't imagine her wanting to escape it all. I was well aware that life wasn't always what it seemed to an outsider. Something else had to be going on with her, and as her eyes continuously found mine in the front row, I had a sudden and burning desire to figure out exactly what that was.

As the concert drew to an end, Devon retrieved me from my seat and escorted me to Levee's dressing room. As usual, he was pissed the fuck off about something, but I was starting to believe that that was just his natural disposition rather than it having anything to do with me.

The sound of Levee's encore was blaring into the room as I relaxed on the small couch and propped my feet up. Closing my eyes, I breathed in deeply and began replaying the last twenty-four hours in my mind. Before I realized it, my cheeks were aching from the huge smile that covered my face.

I was so fucking happy.

And, if the twitch of my cock was any indication, I was horny too. The memories of Levee strutting across the stage had spurred that.

When the last beat of the drum finally fell silent, I began to stare holes in the door. The concert had been surreal, and I was desperate to get my hands on Levee and remind myself just how real we really were.

I jumped to my feet when the door swung open and people filled the room. Probably only five or six others came in, but the moment Levee entered the room, it felt like we were still in the middle of that sold-out arena.

We'd agreed to keep this thing with us on the down low for a while, so even though she was standing directly in front of me, she was completely unreachable in the room full of people.

Her face was slicked with sweat, and her makeup had begun to melt away. Tiny curls were frizzing from the top of her hair, boldly escaping what could only be described as hairspray's death grip. But, as she stood in front of me in a tiny, black dress with desire filling her eyes, she was more gorgeous than ever.

It took every ounce of self-restraint I had not to pull her into my arms, but since my eyes were glued to hers, I had no idea who else was in that room or if they knew about us.

I did know they needed to get the fuck out.

"You were incredible out there," I whispered, and a shy smile pulled at her lips. Dropping my voice so low that it was barely audible, I buried my hands in my pockets and bent toward her, saying, "Now, get rid of these people so I can strip you naked and show you what watching you on stage did to me."

I backed up just in time to see her eyes darken, and a silent breath breezed through her parted lips. That simple reaction sent blood rushing to my cock and an intoxicating feeling I wasn't ready to acknowledge yet spreading throughout my chest.

Levee held my heated gaze as she shouted, "Everyone out! I need a few minutes alone."

The crowd continued to talk amongst themselves, but without a single question, the room cleared.

If we wanted to keep up the façade, I probably should have followed them out then snuck back in, but I was more focused on the woman I was about to maul than devising an actual plan.

My heart raced.

Her nipples hardened.

My nostrils flared.

Her teeth grazed her bottom lip.

My fists clenched at my sides.

Her eyes flashed to my cock.

The door clicked.

Our bodies slammed together.

Her hands were in my hair as my mouth dominated hers. Moans and growls mixed in a symphony of desperation around us. I couldn't wait a second longer. Palming her ass, I lifted her off her feet and backed her against the wall. Her legs wrapped around my hips and her arms folded around my neck in a frantic need to be closer. There was only one way to possibly do that though, and it required me to let her go and roll a fucking condom on.

I'd have given anything to rip her panties down and bury myself inside her wet heat bare. To lose myself in the moment and show her exactly how ravenous I was for her. I wanted raw and rough to quell the visceral need she made me feel when we were together.

However, I wasn't putting her in that position yet. No matter what fucked-up pattern my chest was banging out for her, it was too soon to ask her to trust me that deeply.

Even if, in some ridiculous way, I already trusted her.

"Hold on," I ordered, releasing my grip on her ass.

She clung to me as I kept her propped against the wall with my thigh between her legs. Her mouth attacked my neck as I raced to get the condom from my wallet in place. It wasn't easy, but I was fucking her against the wall even if it killed me.

After barely getting my jeans down over my ass, I scooped her panties to the side. Finding them soaked, I bypassed all preparations and roughly drove inside her.

She cried out, but I gave her no time to adjust. I went wild.

I wasn't gentle as I took what was mine, but I knew that it was what we needed as I gave her what was hers.

And that wasn't just an orgasm.

It was me.

I never slowed in my hunt to possess her. Her nails dug into my shoulders as she rolled her hips against mine, forcing us both toward the edge of release.

No words were exchanged. Everything had been said as we both came on the gasp of the other's name.

I'd claimed her. And, in turn, she owned *me*.

It was almost as exhilarating as it was terrifying.

Almost.

chapter seventeen

Levee

I didn't want to leave Sam. After an unbelievable night together spent with our bodies joined in one of a myriad of ways, I feared that, if I left for a month, I might lose what we had started. But I needed to get my life together so we could restart our relationship in a healthy place for us both—instead of on the top of that bridge. And, unfortunately, no matter how much it sucked, I had to do that alone.

So, with that in mind, at nine the following morning, I blew Sam a kiss from the wrong side of the window as Devon pulled away. He stood, hot as ever, with his hands shoved in his pockets, rocking from his toes to his heels. It made me feel marginally better that he hated watching me leave every bit as much as I did going.

"He'll be here when you get back," Henry said, patting my leg when I began to tear up.

"I hope so." I swallowed hard and rested my head on his shoulder.

"You want me to keep an eye on him while you're gone?"

I chuckled. "You mean the kind of eye where he wakes up in your bed each morning?"

"I do believe that would be the most effective method for keeping tabs on him."

I shook my head. "Stay away from him. I don't need you spending the next month trying to get your claws in his pants while I'm not here to protect him."

"Oh, please. Even if I didn't have a dick, it would be a worthless attempt. He's been hit by the Levee Williams effect. Complete with googly eyes and breathy sighs."

My insides warmed, and my shoulders relaxed. "He looked at me like that even before he knew who I was. That's just Sam."

Henry tossed an arm around the back of my seat and squeezed me tight. "That's how you know he got the full effect."

I closed my eyes and sighed.

One month.

It had to be done. The high I felt with Sam was only a patch. He deserved a whole woman, and as we headed to the airport, I was determined to be that woman.

Two private jets and six hours later, I arrived at a rehabilitation center in Maine. It looked like a luxury hotel from the outside, but as soon as we walked into the back door there was no doubt it was a medical treatment facility.

I'd been worried for days that we would be greeted by the paparazzi, but luckily, we arrived under the radar.

Since we'd canceled most of my appearances, it had been speculated that I was going away for rehab. Everyone assumed drugs, but I'd taken to Twitter a few nights earlier, explaining that my body was worn out after my tour and I needed some time off to rest up. Fans seemed to be supportive and understanding, but it was the media who would ulti-mately cast the final judgment. Stewart was working his ass off, along-side my publicist, to give my "vacation" a positive spin.

"Miss Williams, it's so nice to meet you. I'm Doctor Terrance Post." The elderly man with thin-rimmed glasses extended his hand in my direction.

"Nice to meet you too. Stewart spoke highly of your facility."

"Well, that was kind of him." He smiled. "Come on. Let's get you checked in."

The doctor walked away, but my feet remained rooted. My stomach twisted with nerves. I didn't want to do this anymore. It wasn't neces-sary. Well, that was a lie. It was totally necessary, but it still scared the shit out of me. I was already feeling better, so maybe all of this was over-kill. Sure, something had to change, but like this?

Henry linked his arm with mine and tugged me forward. "Stop freaking out."

"I don't want to do this anymore. I want to go home."

"Well, I want you to get better. So suck it up."

"Henry, please."

He released my arm and stepped away. "No. You're not talking me out of this. Going home and falling back into your same routine isn't going to help anyone. Not you. Not me." Then he pulled out the big guns. "Not Sam." He arched a knowing eyebrow. "You're only freaking out because shit just got real. Well, guess what? Shit got real for the rest of us when we found out why you were really going up to that bridge every night."

I frowned, but we both knew he was right.

"Just let these people help you for thirty days. That's all I'm asking, Levee."

His little guilt trip didn't still the angry butterflies in my stomach, but it did get my feet moving.

"Thank you," he said softly.

"Shut up," was my only response.

chapter eighteen

Sam

Three days.

Three fucking days without a single peep from Levee. I was losing my fucking mind. I wasn't riddled with self-doubt or insecurity. Whether she knew it or not, she was mine on every possible level. I was, however, overwhelmed with worry. How was she doing? Had she made any breakthroughs? Why the fuck was she even there?

Oh yeah, I'd chickened out of that conversation big time the last night we were together. After we'd had sex in her dressing room, she'd seemed so happy. The last thing I'd wanted to do was fuck all of that up by easing my own curiosity. So, instead, I touched nearly every inch of her body. I had a feeling she'd enjoyed that more than talking about her past anyway.

I'd told myself that I was going to give it a few days to let her get settled in, but after that, I was going to head up to her house in search of

Henry. I was sure he wasn't in the dark about her, even if I was.

Thankfully, that was rendered unnecessary when my phone pinged in my pocket while I was working on an old piano I was transforming into a dining room table.

Levee: I just wrestled a bear for custody of my phone.

Me: A bear?! That sounds dangerous. But it explains all the "rawr" texts I've gotten over the last three days. I thought you were just being kinky.

Levee: Ha! We've already established you aren't kinky, but trust me, there is nothing even remotely sexy about this place.

Me: Well, obviously. I'm here.

Levee: Obviously. Anyway… Hi. How are you?

Me: My soul is trembling that I'll forget your touch.

Levee: Hey, plagiarist! I wrote that!

Me: Yeah, I know. I binged on your music last night. It's pretty good. I bet if you keep practicing you'll be able to make music a full-time career one day.

Levee: Hilarious.

Me: I do what I can. How's the vacation going?

Levee: Actually pretty good. The place is nice and I really like my doctor. My "helper" (aka: nurse) is a forty-year old man who's covered in hair and makes Devon look like a member of the Lollipop Guild.

Me: The bear I assume?

Levee: Yep. He's been holding my phone hostage since I got here.

Me: So does this mean you have it back for good now?
Levee: Double yep. Now, I have to go, but when I get back, I expect my phone to be filled with beer and chicken pictures. ;)
Me: Sweet! Do I get kitty-cat pics?
Levee: Be real, Sam. They don't allow pets here.
Me: Improvise.
Levee: I miss you.
Me: I miss you too.
Levee: I'll call you tonight.
Me: I'll probably answer.

I smiled to myself as I lifted my shirt and flexed my abs for a quick picture. I'd barely pressed send when I noticed my mom standing in the doorway of my shop.

"Did you just text someone a crotch shot?" she asked in her best "mom" tone.

"Oh, God, Ma. No." I walked over and pulled her into a hug. I couldn't wipe away the grin that was threatening to split my face in half after even such a brief conversation with Levee.

Mom hugged me back before stepping away. "You know, women share those pictures with all of their friends. Just last week, this guy sent me one of his bait and tackle and I showed it to—"

I curled my lip in disgust. "Jesus. Why was some asshole sending you dick pics? And better yet, what in the hell made you think I would want to know that?"

I was still riding my Levee high, but my mom's talking about anyone's "bait and tackle" was more than enough to ruin it.

"I just want you to be prepared. You show one woman, you might as well just send it out as a group message, because all of her friends are gonna see it eventually."

"Thanks for the heads-up, but I didn't send any 'crotch shots.'" *Yet.* "Thanks to you, my genitalia is safe for yet another day."

"Oh good. That will make it even more special when you finally lose your virginity on your wedding night." She gave me a look that dared me to argue otherwise.

Given the fact that she'd walked in on me having sex with Stacy Davis when I was seventeen, she knew better. However, I assumed she didn't want to know any more about my "bait and tackle" than I did about her looking at pictures of some random dude's.

Patting me on the chest, she headed over to the claw-foot loveseat in the corner, which was still waiting to be picked up. "This is gorgeous, baby."

"Thanks. I love the way it turned out. You should have seen it before I started. There were—"

"Yeah yeah yeah. Save your breath. You know I don't understand a lick of what you say when you get all technical about tools and stuff. Besides, we have stuff to talk about." She lifted my overflowing ashtray in my direction. "This is ridiculous, Sam. You have to quit. I will not bury anyone else. I can't…lose you too." She glared at me.

She and Anne had been on my ass to quit smoking for years. I couldn't count how many times I'd promised them I would. But, after Anne had passed away, I'd found myself with a cigarette in my hand more often than not. Guilt will do that to you. I needed to stop—I knew that much. But knowing and doing are a totally different story though.

"I'll stop," I said, sheepishly shoving my hands in my pockets.

"Swear to me," she pushed further.

"Come on, Ma. I said I'll stop."

She dropped the whole ashtray into the trash can and took a large step forward. She was all of five feet five and a hundred and twenty-five pounds, but she was my mom. That one step was scary as hell.

"Swear. To. Me."

"Fine. I swear," I huffed like a sullen teenage.

"Good," she exhaled in relief, and a loving smile warmed her face.

"Okay. Now that we've dealt with that." She took another step toward me and turned serious once again. "Meg tells me that you're dating Levee Williams."

"What? Since when do you talk to Meg?"

"Since my son doesn't feel the need to tell his mother anything anymore." She crossed her arms over her chest and leveled me with a glare of guilt only women are able to shoot from their eyes. "You're dating a celebrity, Sam. You didn't think, 'Hey, maybe I should call and tell my mom.'"

I twisted my lips and arched an eyebrow. "Mom, don't even pretend that you know who the hell Levee Williams is."

"No. But I'd like to know now that my son is sending her crotch shots!"

I barked a laugh and threw my hands out to my sides. "It was just my abs! And, for the love of God, stop saying crotch."

She narrowed her eyes then very slowly enunciated each letter as she said, "*Crotch.*"

Even as she continued to glare at me, I couldn't help but laugh, and because she was crazy in the best possible way, she did too.

When we both sobered, she went right back to the serious. "All right. Tell me about this Levee girl."

"I'm not supposed to talk about this, Mom. I need to call Meg and tell her to shut her mouth."

I was fucking smitten, and if I'd had my way, I would have told the world.

However, I was smitten with *Levee Williams*, so the world would have to wait until she was ready to tell them. It sucked, but whether people knew or not didn't change our relationship.

She was still mine.

I smiled to myself, and I knew that my mom saw it when she laughed.

"Don't think I'm letting this go. I Googled her. She's a kind of a big deal."

I'd told Levee that we'd keep things quiet for a while, but my mom was safe. *Right?*

"I guess. I mean, she's not *that* famous. She's never done a duet with Lionel Richie or anything," I teased, knowing the distracting effect it would have on my mom.

Her eyes grew wide at the mere mention of his name. "Do you think she *knows* Lionel?"

I slung an arm around her shoulders. "I doubt it, but if it will stop the inquisition, I'd be happy to ask for you."

"No, you are going to ask her because you know I'm obsessed with that man. The inquisition will most definitely continue. Tell me about her. Are you two serious?" She tugged on my arm until I followed her to our old dining room table, which I'd been using as my desk for the last few years. I'd never even taken the time to refurbish it. Or, more accurately, I didn't want to change it. Dad had built that table. Even repurposing it felt wrong.

I settled on the wooden stool next to her. "We haven't been dating long, but I think it might become serious."

I'm in love with her.

Fuck.

"Nice girl?"

"I really think you'd like her."

"Well, I can't like her any less than I did that last one. What was her name again?"

"Lexi."

"Yes." She lowered her voice and mumbled to herself, "I hated that bitch."

"Mom!" I scolded on a laugh.

"I'm sorry. She was"—she exaggerated a shiver—"toxic."

"She wasn't *that* bad... Well, not all the time. But yes, Levee is definitely better. She's so funny." I glanced away, smiling as I remembered her laugh. "And smart. She's not at all who you'd expect her to be. She's really down-to-earth and kind."

I scrubbed my hands over my jeans, wishing Levee weren't so far away. How the hell was I going to go a month without that woman? I looked back up to find my mom watching me with a gentle smile.

"She's amazing," I breathed.

Her smile grew. "I already like her, then." She patted my leg, squeezing it firmly before asking, "How'd you meet Miss Fancy Pants?"

I scratched the back of my neck. *Shit.* I'd known that this question would eventually come up, and while I hated to lie to my mom, there was no fucking way I was telling her the truth. She would have freaked if she knew how I'd really met Levee.

Evade.

"We...umm, frequent one of the same places. I saw her a couple times before I got the nerve to talk to her." After the partial truth, I decided to switch gears and distract her with humor. Waving my hands over my chest, I said, "I mean, no way she could resist all this." I threw in a bicep curl for good measure.

"Oh, please. Put those wet noodles away. I saw a picture online of her with her ex-boyfriend. All I'm going to say is you're lucky you got my sense of humor."

"Wait? Who's her ex-boyfriend?"

"I can't remember his name. One of those big football players." She waggled her eyebrows while fanning herself.

I wanted to gag—then Google this guy. "Gross!"

She laughed, pushing to her feet. "Okay, well, I have to get back to work. Bring Levee over for dinner sometime."

"Okay, Ma."

She gave me a quick hug then headed for the door. "I'll see you later. Don't forget what I said about those crotch shots."

That time, I really did gag.

I was sitting outside on my porch swing with a cigarette burning between my fingers and Sampson at my side when my phone finally rang.

"Hello," I answered, thrilled to hear Levee laughing on the other end.

"On the first ring? Really, Sam? You couldn't even make it look like you weren't holding your phone."

"Laugh it up, Designer Shoes. I was only holding my phone because I was reporting a video montage on YouTube of you tripping and falling."

She groaned. "Oh, God. Please tell me you're lying."

"Nope." I popped the P at the end. "User HenryisMine7765 set it to a lovely remix of Henry's song 'Goodbye, Lover.'"

"Great," she huffed. "So many of his fans think I'm their competition. You have no idea how many of those videos there are out there."

"Ohhhh, after the last few hours, I have a pretty good idea. Don't worry. I've got your back. I reported all of them," I stated proudly.

"You're too good to me," she whispered teasingly in a tone that made me miss her that much more.

"Nah. I'm not that great. I watched them all first." I put the cigarette out and headed back inside, ready to sink into my bed and keep Levee for whatever time she was willing to give me.

"Well, I forgive you."

"Good, because some of them, I watched twice," I admitted. Then I quickly amended, "But it was only because I liked the way your boobs bounced when you jumped back up."

She laughed, and it forced a smile to my face.

"I guess I can't be mad about that now, can I? So, how did you end up watching YouTube videos of me?"

"It started earlier when, against my better judgment, I looked up pictures of you with Thomas Reigns. I have to say I'm feeling a little inadequate now."

"Oh, whatever. Your cock is way bigger than his."

"Aaaannnnd…now I feel better. Thank you."

She laughed again, and as I crawled into bed, I closed my eyes and got lost in the musical sound.

"It must be nice to be able to look up everything you want to know about me. I want to be able to search your past."

"All right. Let's level out the playing field. If there were a computer in front of you right now, what would you type into the search bar?"

"Ummm, I don't know. When was your last relationship?"

"We broke up about two months ago, but we hadn't really been together since Anne died. She's a nice enough girl, even though my mom called her a bitch today." I chuckled at the memory.

"What?" she half gasped, half laughed.

"Yeah, so, apparently, Meg called and told Mom we were dating. She stopped by for an interrogation."

"Oh shit. Did you tell her the truth?"

"Uhhh…" I mumbled, trying to buy myself some more time. "She's my mom, Levee. I swear she won't tell anyone."

Hesitance colored her voice, but she didn't make a big deal out of it. "Well, what did she say about us seeing each other?"

"Nothing really. She's cool with it. Oh! She made me promise to ask if you know Lionel Richie."

"Actually, I kinda do. I did a collaboration with him at an awards show a couple years ago."

"Okay, well, I'm going to lie and tell her you don't."

"Why? I know his agent. I could probably get him to sign some stuff for her."

"Because my mother is an incredible woman and mom, but when it comes to Lionel, she loses her ever-loving mind. You do not want to be the only person standing between her and that man."

"Shut up. Are you serious?"

"Unfortunately, I am. When you get back, I'll have her break out the photo album. I was Lionel for Halloween every year until I was six. I'm pretty sure she would have named me after him if my dad hadn't stopped her."

"Oh. My. God. I need those pictures. ASAP."

"I'll see what I can do. Now, what else do you want to know?" I sucked a deep breath in through my teeth, anxiously awaiting her next question.

"Are you smoking?"

"No. I'm in bed, actually."

"Is it too soon for me to ask you to quit?"

"Too soon to ask? No. Too soon to expect me to follow through? Yes. But you'll be happy to know my mom also chewed my ass out today and made me swear that I'd quit."

"I'm gonna need your mom's address," she rushed out excitedly.

"For what?"

"Because, if she actually gets you to quit, I'm going to figure out a way to get Lionel Richie to personally deliver her flowers."

I barked a laugh. "Please don't do that. She'd either die of a heart attack or end up in jail for refusing to let him leave."

She giggled then sighed, "I wish I were with you right now."

"Me too," I breathed. God, did I wish that too. But harping on it wouldn't help her. So I changed the subject. "Well, at least you got your phone back. Did you get my beer picture earlier?"

"I did. It's my home screen now. It's also the reason I missed dinner because I was busy in the shower."

I practically choked on my tongue. She giggled as I coughed.

"Reallllly?" I drawled.

"Really," she whispered on a moan. "It wasn't as good as one of our showers. My hands were too soft, but they'll have to do for the next few weeks."

My cock swelled in my jeans at the idea of Levee's fingers playing between her legs while images of my body danced through her head. It guaranteed I'd probably miss dinner in lieu of a long shower tonight too. It also guaranteed that sit-ups and a new gym membership would be happening tomorrow.

"You have to stop," I growled. "Or keep going in a lot more detail. Your call."

She softly giggled. "Can I ask you something?"

I adjusted my cock and, much to my dismay, assumed she was stopping. "Anything."

"Why do you sometimes pick up your cigarette butts and sometimes you leave them on the ground?"

My stomach dropped, and I shifted to my side on the bed, staring into the blank space where Levee had spent only one night, though it would forever be her side.

"Anne," I answered shortly. I was going to need to elaborate, but it would take a second to speak around the lump in my throat.

"Oh," she breathed. "I'm sorry."

I swallowed hard. "After one of her episodes, she and my mom had a falling out, so Anne moved in with me."

"Sam, you really don't have to answer. I didn't know."

"No. It's okay. I don't mind. So…anyway…Anne moved in with me, and it was really nice, actually. I enjoyed having her around, and it gave my mom a much-needed break after having spent her life caring for people. It made me feel good that I was helping, and it gave me peace of mind that Anne was safe. Anyway, she hated that I smoked. So, one day, while we were at a thrift store, picking up a few pieces for the shop, she found one of those old skeletons that they use in health class. I should have known by the gleam in her eye that it wasn't going to be good for me, but I bought it anyway."

I shook my head and smiled at the memory. "When we got home, she took it to my shop and covered the chest cavity in mesh then dumped the contents of my ashtray inside it. She was so fucking proud of herself. She even went so far as to name that damn thing Herman." I chuckled, but Levee was so quiet that I had to pull the phone away from my ear to make sure I hadn't lost the call. "You still there?"

"Yeah. I'm here."

I heard her moving around. "Did you just get in bed?"

"Yeah, but like the shower, it's a poor excuse for yours." She sighed. "Keep going I want to hear the rest of this. I mean…if you still want to tell me."

"Levee, I'll tell you anything you want to know as long as it means you're with me to keep asking."

"I'll have my attorney send over the copyright release on that one too."

"When should I expect my royalties to hit the bank?" I teased.

"I pay in sexual favors."

I could almost envision the mischievous twinkle in her whiskey-colored eyes. God, I wanted to see her smile.

Suddenly, I got an idea. "Why are we talking on the phone?"

"Uhh…do you need to go?"

"No! That's not what I mean. Hang on." I pulled my phone away from my ear and pressed the button for FaceTime. It went unanswered. I put it back to my ear. "Are you gonna pick up?"

"Have you lost your mind!" she shrieked. "You can't spring a video chat on a girl! I look like shit."

"Answer the damn call, Levee."

"No! I'm serious. I didn't do my hair when I got out of the shower. I look like an ungroomed poodle. Plus, I can't even find half of my makeup. There is no way I'm giving you that visual of me while I'm gone for the next month."

"Levee, I've seen you crying with makeup running down your face, asleep and drooling in a car, and with sex mats covering your head. I still wanted to fuck you senseless. I don't care what the hell you look like right now. Answer the damn phone!"

"Nerp. Not happening. I'll fix myself up tomorrow."

"You're ridiculous," I bit out in frustration.

"Trust me, this isn't exactly easy on me. I can't even remember what you look like. I vaguely remember you being somewhat attractive, but I'm not completely sure. I don't even have a picture of you."

"And you're not going to get one, either," I lied. I was going to blow up her phone with pictures of me until she sent me one of her. Sure, I could have found a million images of Levee on the Internet, but I really just wanted one of my Designer Shoes.

"Can we please just get back to your story? I'm dying to know about this skeleton."

I let out a huff, grabbed my laptop off the nightstand, and pulled up Photoshop. "So, after she covered Herman in mesh, she rolled him onto my porch with a huge smile on her face. I couldn't even argue with her when she declared that, when the skeletons lungs were filled with cigarettes, so were mine. She made me promise to collect all of my butts and deposit them in Herman, and when his chest was full, I had to quit smoking. It was a big chest, so I agreed. I got into the habit of keeping all of my butts and giving them to her at the end of each night." My heart sped, and my hands, which had been furiously moving over my laptop, froze. "Sometimes I forget she's gone and I still collect them."

"Sam," Levee breathed. "I'm so sorry."

"It's okay. I like talking about her sometimes. I miss her a lot."

I heard her shifting again, and I tried to imagine her beside me as I worked on my laptop. I had it so fucking bad for this woman.

"I bet she was beautiful."

"She really was." I sucked in a deep breath and smiled through the pain. It wasn't so overwhelming with Levee. And, if I hadn't already been falling for this amazing woman, that fact alone would have had me jumping in headfirst. "Anyway…anything else you want to know?"

"What'd you have for dinner?" she asked randomly.

"Dinner?"

"Yeah. I'm starving. Someone, who shall remain nameless, forced me to miss dinner with his sexy stomach, remember?" She giggled.

And with that, the pain disappeared completely.

chapter nineteen

Levee

I was like a kid at summer camp, hiding with the covers over my head to sneak my phone. Mandatory lights out had been hours earlier, but I wasn't ready to let Sam go, even as my eyelids became heavy with sleep. Over the first few days, they had confiscated my phone while I'd been assessed. Doctor Post had tweaked my antidepressants and taken me off the antianxiety medication all together. I really was feeling better, but managing my life inside the stress-free environment of the center was completely different than managing it on the outside, where millions of people pulled me in different directions. However, I was committed to doing my absolute best, even if it meant drastically changing my life when I was able to go home.

I was supposed to be resting and relaxing while giving my mind and my body a chance to recover, but nothing healed me more than those hours I spent on the phone with Sam.

It was three in the morning before we were both so out of it that we decided to actually hang up. Even with as late as it was, I still felt the loss with a physical ache. I missed him more than ever. But, when my phone pinged with an incoming photo, it was all erased.

At some point during our six-hour phone call, Sam had been busy. On my screen was an image of Sam in a bathing suit, lounging on a beach and looking like a tattooed Greek god. Heat pooled between my legs as I got an eyeful of him for the first time in days. Then a loud laugh escaped my mouth when I noticed a picture of me behind him. I immediately recognized it. It was one of the numerous times I'd accidently made a fool of myself by falling at the most inopportune time. My mouth was hanging open, my hair flying out to the sides in the most unattractive way possible, and absolute fear covered my distorted face.

I was no longer on the red carpet where it had originally been snapped. I'd been edited out of my dress and into a bikini, but my heels still graced my feet. Only, now, they were covered in sand, and I was falling only a few feet from Sam. I'd forgotten that he was a graphic designer, and if this picture was any indication, he was really fucking good. It was a seamless rendering that definitely gave me a good laugh, but my heart soared when I read the caption at the bottom.

You could look like this every single day and I'd still want to see you. Pick up the phone tomorrow.

I looked at that picture for over an hour, until I fell asleep with my phone in my hand and a smile on my face.

Over the following weeks, Sam and I talked every single day. Yes, via FaceTime. He also sent me a new picture of us "together" each night when we hung up. They were all different, but he always looked like an Adonis and I always looked like shit. How he found that many terrible pictures of me was alarming. But there was always a funny message at the bottom that made the momentary embarrassment totally worth it. In Sam's nightly images, we were traveling the globe together. From the Eiffel Tower to the Grand Canyon, I'd fallen on my face all around the world.

My favorite picture of all was us in Thelma and Louise's green Thunderbird convertible. Sam had the signature scarf around his neck, which should have been humorous, but with those tattooed forearms resting on the steering wheel, he was still sexy as hell. For me, he had used a photo from when I had been riding a rollercoaster with a little girl from the Make-A-Wish Foundation. My mouth was wide open, and a terror-filled scream was being forced from my throat. He'd even gone so far as to add a bug flying into my mouth when he'd placed me in the car beside him. When I noticed that the front license plate read *Sam & Levee 4-eva*, I melted.

I was falling fast for that man, and I could only hope I was taking him with me.

A month ago, I had been standing on a bridge, contemplating jumping off, but with him at my side, even just in a Photoshopped car, I'd never been happier in my life. And it scared the hell out of me. I wasn't sure how I'd ever be able to cope if he didn't feel the same. Drugs might not have been my problem, but I was absolutely addicted to the quiet high he offered my mind.

For two full weeks, Sam and I lived in a bubble of new-relationship bliss.

It wasn't all laughs and smiles, but that was what made it feel real.

I loved bickering with him. We'd found a ton of trivial crap to disagree about. But that's all it was—meaningless crap. Slowly, it became obvious that Sam and I did in fact come from different worlds. But it also became blindingly obvious that that was exactly why I needed to hold on to him.

Sam: Umm…why did four $6,000 guitars just get delivered to my house?
Me: It was my subtle way of telling you I want some bookshelves.
Sam: With brand new custom Gibsons? Are you insane?! I could have gotten broken guitars

for fifty bucks at the music store.

Me: Slow down, cheapo. Those are my favorite. I use them exclusively.

Sam: No.

Me: No what?

Sam: No, I'm not destroying $24,000 worth of guitars.

Me: Why the hell not? You can't return them now.

Sam: The fuck I can't, princess.

Me: That was a low blow, asshole.

Me: Really? You're just gonna disappear now?

He didn't respond for three full unnerving hours. But, when he finally did, a photo of two guitar bookshelves leaning against his bedroom wall preceded it. They appeared to be generic acoustics—definitely not my Gibsons.

Sam: I'm sorry. You're right. I'm an asshole. It's just hard when your woman has Gibson taste and a thrift store man. I made these for you last week. I'll start on your guitars tonight.

Sam: P.S. I'm really sorry about the princess thing.

Sam: P.P.S. I'm a dick.

Sam: P.P.P.S. Here's a picture of my cock to make up for it.

Attached was a photo of a chicken.

Sam: P.P.P.P.S. I named him Curtis.

Sam: P.P.P.P.P.S. I can't wait for you to meet him.

I didn't respond for half an hour—because I was sobbing. Of course

I felt bad for having made him feel like he was my thrift store man, but that wasn't why I was crying.

He'd already made me bookshelves.

And implied that I was his woman. A fact I knew but had never actually been verified.

And he'd made me laugh when I should've still been pissed.

But, most of all, I was crying because I knew that that was the exact moment I'd fallen in love with Sam Rivers.

There was no going back now—not that I wanted to.

I also knew I couldn't make it two more weeks without him.

Me: Come see me.
Sam: Tell me when and where.
Me: Tomorrow. It's family day and Henry is supposed to fly up, but I really need to see you.
Sam: Then I'll be there, Levee.

I squealed like a teenager as my heart exploded in my chest.
He's coming.

Sam: I'll see if I can find someone to watch Curtis.

I burst into laughter with tears still sliding down my cheeks.
Yeah, I'm absolutely and hopelessly lost in this man.

chapter twenty

Sam

I was at the airport an hour after Levee had asked me to come see her. Before that moment, I hadn't even known visiting her was an option or I probably would have taken up residence in Maine weeks ago. The trip was long, and I flew standby the whole way, but finally, at seven the next morning, after having slept in the Philly Airport, I was back in the same state as my Designer Shoes. I grabbed my rental car and headed directly to the address she had texted me the night before.

At nine o'clock on the dot, I marched through the doors and up to the receptionist desk.

"Hi. I'm Sam Rivers. I'm here to see—"

The thin blonde sitting behind the desk immediately cut me off. "For privacy, we don't use guests' names."

"Oh, right," I said awkwardly, trying to figure out how to explain to her why I was there without using Levee's name. "Well, my name is

Sam—"

"Rivers. Yes, I got that. Please allow me a minute to look you up."
She smiled, but it came off as more of a grimace.

Well, isn't she a bitchy ray of sunshine.

I anxiously tapped the toe of my boot as I imagined Levee sitting
somewhere nearby. She was probably chewing her manicured thumbnail into submission. I dropped my gaze to my shoes in an attempt to
cover the shit-eating grin I was hopeless to hide.

A deep voice interrupted my thoughts. "Please come with us, sir."

Two men in dark suits, who might as well have stepped out of the
movie *Men in Black,* suddenly appeared at my side.

I nodded with a smile, my stomach bubbling with excitement as I
followed them through a set of double doors.

She's so close.

Only she wasn't close at all.

They led me to a set of glass doors that opened to the back parking
lot.

"Uhh…" I mumbled when Agent K shoved it wide.

"You're not permitted on the premises, Mr. Rivers. If you return,
the local authorities will be notified immediately. This is your first and
only warning."

"I'm sorry. There must be confusion." I lowered my voice to a whisper as I said, "Levee Williams is expecting me."

"There's no guest here by that name. Please don't make this difficult," Agent J bit out.

My anticipation quickly swung to anger as disappointment settled
like acid in my stomach. Stepping forward, I seethed, "She gave me the
address. I'm not leaving without seeing her."

"Get. Out." He snapped a finger to the parking lot and leveled me
with a menacing glare.

I didn't budge. *Fuck this asshole if he thinks he's keeping me from her.*
"Find. Levee."

"I won't ask you to leave again," Agent K declared as J slipped around behind me.

"Fuck you." I pulled my phone from my pocket and dialed Levee's number.

She answered on the first ring, and if my head hadn't been about to explode, I would have given her shit about it.

"Are you here yet?" she asked.

"Yes, and no. Security is kicking me out."

"What?" she shrieked so loud I had to pull the phone away from my ear.

"Goodbye, sir," Agent J growled, shoving me toward the doors.

I stood my ground as rage boiled in my veins. I poked a hard finger into his brick wall of a chest. "Don't fucking touch me again."

"Sam, what the hell is going on? Let me talk to them."

Gritting my teeth, I lifted the phone. "Levee wants to talk to you."

They glanced at each other in unspoken agreement.

Neither took the phone.

One did take my arm though—and twisted it behind my back. The other held the door open while he shoved me out of it. My phone skidded across the concrete as I stumbled forward, barely staying on my feet as the door shut and locked behind me.

What. The. Fuck. Just. Happened?

The muscle in my jaw twitched as I fought to regain some sort of composure that didn't have me shattering that fucking glass door and killing two men. Then I heard Levee's voice coming from my phone on the ground.

"Sam!"

Snatching it up, I was only able to grit out, "I'm going to jail. It may be for a long fucking time." I stomped toward the door and banged on the glass, but the MIB had already walked away.

"What? Sam, stop and tell me what's going on!"

"I just got fucking thrown out for trying to come visit you!" I shouted. I closed my eyes and sucked in a deep breath, fully aware that this wasn't her fault. "I'm sorry," I quickly apologized.

"Just calm down, okay? Let me go talk to them, and I'll call you back. Don't. Leave."

"Funny. That's not what they said as they tossed me on the street," I snapped then sighed. "Sorry. Again."

"It's okay. You want me to have them fired?" she asked in jest, and if I could have slowed the adrenaline pumping through my system, I probably would have smiled.

I raked a hand through my hair and huffed, "That would be fan-fucking-tastic."

"Consider it done. Now, chill out and I'll see you in a minute."

Chill out.

Yeah, that wasn't at all what I wanted to do, but with the promise of seeing her in a minute still ringing in my ears, I managed to pack it down.

I stomped around the side of the building to my rental car.

Then I waited.

And waited.

And fucking waited some more.

For over an hour, I sat in the car, staring at the entrance of the building. My phone wasn't ringing, and Levee's had started going straight to her voicemail. I was already tired from having traveled all night, and as the adrenaline drained from my body, I was suddenly exhausted.

Grabbing my phone, I shot out a quick text letting Levee know that I was going to grab some coffee but wouldn't be far.

She didn't respond.

Levee

"Who did this?" I screamed like the diva I prided myself in never becoming. But, then again, no one had ever meddled in my personal life before.

"Calm down, Miss Williams." Doctor Post and someone, whose name I'd promptly forgotten but had been introduced as the center's head administrator, were sitting in a small conference room, attempting to defuse me.

"I swear to God, you either show me those fucking papers or I will ruin you! You won't be able to pay someone to come to this place when I'm done with you."

"We are attempting to locate the physical copy of your sign-in papers. Our records are digital."

"Try harder!" I yelled as they both scurried from the room.

I snatched the telephone off the hook. My cell phone had died shortly after hanging up with Sam, but I'd been using the phone in the conference room to repeatedly call Henry. I knew he was traveling to see me, but his flight should've landed already. The really unnerving part was when I got the same radio silence from Devon as well. Something was going on, and clearly, I was the only one in the dark.

"Hey, beautiful!" Henry purred when he fucking finally answered.

"Swear to me you didn't know about this shit with Sam," I gritted out through clenched teeth.

Henry gasped. "What did my lover-boy do?"

"Sam didn't do anything. But *someone* put his name on my list of banned visitors. You filled out my paperwork, Henry. Please, please, *please*, tell me you didn't do this."

"Son of a bitch," he whispered then sighed.

My pulse raced for whatever answer he was about to give me.

"I didn't fill out your paperwork, Levee. I started chatting with the male orderly, so Devon filled out your papers."

My heart splintered. I almost wished it had been Henry instead. We could've had a huge-ass fight where he explained why he had done it, and I would have put him in his place for interfering. We wouldn't have spoken for a week, but we would have eventually gotten over it.

I couldn't say the same for Devon. While I considered him part of my family, I couldn't lose sight of the fact that he was also my employee who obviously didn't know his role. I was supposed to be able to trust this man with my life, and he was taking advantage of that trust for some reason that was lost on me completely. Fine, he didn't like Sam, but he wasn't required to. His only job was to make sure I was safe. And the way my stomach knotted at this little revelation made me feel anything but.

"Shit," I hissed into the phone.

"I'm sorry. Look, Carter and I will be there in about an hour. Devon's on the flight behind us. We'll all come together and figure this out. Just tell them to let Sam in. They can't keep you from seeing him."

I groaned. "Apparently, they can. They're refusing to let me see him until they speak to a member of my family. I'm not calling my parents to ask permission to see my boyfriend, Henry." Tears welled in my eyes.

It was too much.

All of it.

I was supposed to be relaxing and getting things under control. Instead, I felt like a prisoner inside not only these walls, but my entire fucking life as well.

And just like that, the familiar free fall engulfed me.

I closed my eyes and fought the ache in my lungs.

"Is Sam still there?" Henry asked.

"I think so," I managed to squeak.

"Just tell him to wait. I'll be there soon. We'll get this fixed, okay?"

But I didn't want to tell Sam to wait. I wanted to see him.

And go home with him.

And let him do exactly what he had unwittingly been doing since the day we met—healing me from the outside in.

Suddenly, my eyes popped open. Why couldn't I have that?

Yes, my life had spiraled out of control. But the only person who was stopping me from taking charge of my own future was *me*.

Levee Michelle Williams was a fighter. I hadn't gotten my success in the music industry by sitting around and letting people tell me how to run my life. I had done it by clawing my way to the top with nothing more than a guitar and head full of dreams.

Fuck this place. No one was going to tell me how to run my life—a life I suddenly realized I never wanted to leave. And that epiphany hadn't come from the bottom of a prescription bottle or inside those walls. It had come in the shape of a gorgeous man who'd saved me with nothing more than a quick wit and a simple conversation. And he was sitting only yards away in a parking lot because his name was on a magical fucking list.

I dropped the phone from my ear and pushed the conference room door open, then the hallway door, and finally, the front door of the entire building. I didn't stop until my high heels hit the asphalt of the parking lot.

Voices called my name behind me, but they were all muted by my newfound determination.

My feet kept moving in search of a pair of golden eyes that I soon realized were nowhere to be found. As I came up empty, nerves didn't take over. I didn't have a million thoughts of guilt and worry. I was no longer allowing the free fall to dictate my life.

I squared my shoulders and smiled proudly, feeling like myself for the first time in months.

"Levee!" Doctor Post called, but I quickly slipped behind a car, squatting low until the voices disappeared.

I wasn't going back, not even to explain that I wasn't going back. I wasn't in the mood for an argument. I was in the mood to start living.

Without my phone, I couldn't call Sam, but there was only one place I needed to go. So I started down the sidewalk and hailed a cab.

He'd know where to find me.

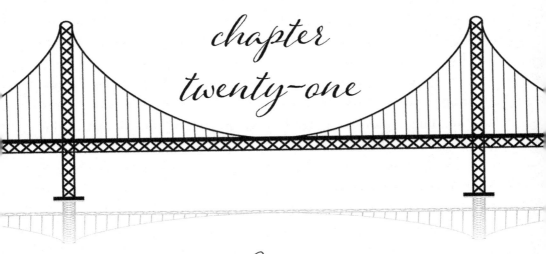

chapter twenty-one

Sam

After almost three hours of chugging coffee, smoking cigarettes, and talking myself off the ledge of rage, I decided to head back and see if I could charm my way in to see Levee. As I pulled into a parking spot, I was thrilled to see a familiar face. Carter, the barrel-chested bodyguard who had driven me home from Levee's house after our fight the first night together, was standing out front, barking into a phone. I threw my car in park then jogged up to him. Maybe he could get me inside.

His eyes grew wide as I approached. Using his hand to cover the phone, he asked, "She's not with you?"

"Levee? No. They won't let me in. I was hoping—"

He lifted the phone back to his ear. "Sam just arrived, Mr. Williams. She's not with him. We'll keep you updated."

Mr. Williams? Levee's dad?

He hung up. "Come with me, Sam." He walked toward the door.

I grabbed his arm. "What the hell is going on? Why would you think Levee was with me?"

"Follow me," was his only reply.

The receptionist glared at me as Carter escorted me past her and into a back office. I was already a bundle of nerves, but the moment I caught sight of Henry's hollow eyes, I realized something was terribly wrong. He stopped midpace, and hope filled his empty expression.

"Oh thank God!" He rushed in my direction and peered over my shoulder. "Where is she?"

"I have no idea." Bile rose in my throat.

He threw his hands over his mouth and spun in place to face Devon and the Men in Black conferring in the corner. Several other people lined the walls, all looking equally as devastated by this realization.

"Someone please tell me what the fuck is going on!" I barked as my gaze flashed around the room, pleading for some answers.

But no one so much as made eye contact.

"Damn it!" Henry screamed, swiping a hand out and dramatically clearing off the desk. He pointed an angry finger at Devon. "Find. Her. Right fucking now."

Find her.

Fuck.

Devon nodded and started to leave the room, but I caught his arm first. Someone was going to give me some answers.

"Fill me in."

He didn't. With furrowed brows, he snatched his arm from my grasp and headed out the door.

I approached Henry who looked like he was about to fall apart at any second, but so was I. "Talk to me. Now!" I roared, all patience gone.

"Devon put you on her banned visitors list. She lost her mind. She called me in tears and I told her to stay put, but she took off. We assumed she was with you."

I menacingly leaned into his face. "What the fuck do you mean she took off?"

He threw his hands out to his sides in frustration and yelled, "I mean we have no fucking clue where she went!"

My entire world stilled then flipped completely upside down. A whooshing noise filled my ears, and Anne's smile appeared behind my lids with every blink. Her words from the past echoed in my mind.

"I'm fine."

I knew exactly where Levee was headed.

And it was the most terrifying moment of my entire life.

Without another word spoken, I sprinted from the room like an Olympic athlete on fire. And, judging by the burn in my chest, I really might have been.

No. No. No. No.

There wasn't much this world could throw at me that I hadn't already experienced, but this…

Oh, God.

The pendulum of my anxiety swung epically high, sledgehammering my knees on the way up. They were shaking so badly that, if I hadn't needed them to find her, they would have buckled. Pure force of will kept me on my feet—well, that and a pair of Designer Shoes that I prayed were still securely on solid ground.

I slid behind the wheel of my car and pulled up the maps app on my phone. Then I peeled out of the parking lot, still zooming in and out, frantically searching for the closest bridge.

I tried to be rational and tell myself that she wouldn't do this to me. She'd been doing so much better. She was just upset and needed to blow off some steam. That didn't mean she was suicidal. However, when she was nowhere to be found on the first bridge, the overwhelming fear made it difficult to stay positive.

After the second bridge, it was damn near impossible.

And, after the third, I was lost in the pits of despair.

But I kept going with nothing more than her last words to me fueling my hope.

"I'll see you in a minute."

I would never forget as long as I lived the moment those brown curls came into view. There wasn't even a pedestrian lane on that small bridge overlooking what could only be described as a creek. But she was there, standing at the concrete railing—her heart still beating, her breath still filling her lungs. And, as my car came to a screeching halt in the middle of traffic, a smile covered her face.

I was so relieved that I couldn't have cared less when cars started honking as I jumped from my car and slid across the hood like Bo Duke.

"Jesus Christ, Levee," I breathed when I crashed into her, folding her securely in my arms.

"Well, that took you long enough," she teased.

I wanted to be pissed. I really did. But that could wait. I needed to figure out where her head was. She didn't seem upset or distressed, but she was definitely standing on the edge of a bridge for a reason. I just hoped it wasn't the reason I thought.

Horns continued to blare as cars drove around mine.

"What are you doing up here?" I asked.

She leaned away and smiled widely. "Waiting for you."

"On a bridge?" I asked, incredulously.

"It's a tiny bridge, Sam." She glanced down at the water below. "I'm not even sure if that fall would have broken my legs."

"I don't give a fuck if it's a log over a ditch. It's still a bridge," I snapped.

Her eyes narrowed at my outburst. "Well, you found me, didn't you? I'm fine."

I flinched at her word choice. "Yes, after searching every bridge in this city. I was scared to fucking death, Levee."

Her attitude slipped. "Shit, I'm sorry. I didn't think about that. Jumping isn't at all why I'm here. I swear. Actually, I've been doing a lot of thinking since I've been up here. I'm not sure I ever wanted to kill myself, Sam. It was just the idea of escaping all the chaos and overwhelming guilt I had in my life that sounded so appealing. But that doesn't mean jumping—it just means making some changes. Changes I'm officially ready to make now." She smiled proudly.

And, truth be told, I was proud of her too.

I was also frustrated.

"You couldn't call and tell me that? Maybe wait for me at Starbucks?"

She darted her gaze away, embarrassed. "See, funny thing about cell phones. I don't actually *know* your number by memory."

I rolled my eyes and started to give her more shit when a soda cup hit me in the back of the head. A motorist shouted from his car, "Move, asshole!"

"Son of a bitch!" I cursed, wiping the liquid off the back of my shirt.

I scowled when Levee began giggling.

The smile she tossed back at me immeasurably eased the vise on my chest.

She was…really and truly…*fine.*

And, as she flipped off the angry soda guy as he sped away, it didn't even pain me to admit it.

"Let's get out of here," I said, tugging on her arm. "No more fucking bridges. I'm officially making solid ground our *thing.*"

She nodded enthusiastically and followed me to the car.

"I'm sorry, Henry. I'm serious," Levee said into the phone as I put my cigarette out and headed back through the balcony door to join her on the bed.

We were in a budget hotel not far from the bridge where I'd found her.

I had attempted to take Levee back to the rehab center, but she quickly put that idea on the back burner by dropping her hand into my lap. I wasn't budging on the fact that we needed to talk about what had led her to bolt the way she had.

But I was a man, and I hadn't seen her in weeks.

A hotel room at least kept my options open for after that chat.

"Hey, my mom is beeping in again. I'll call you in a little while. Okay. I love you too."

She pulled the phone away from her ear long enough to switch calls.

"I'm fine!" Levee huffed into the phone without so much as a greeting. "No! Do not come to Maine, Mom." She groaned before copping an attitude. "Well, I guess you can, but I won't be here." She shot me an exasperated look then rolled her eyes. "Okay, I need to go. Yep. I'm great. Uh-huh. Okay. Talk to you later. Bye."

Her mom was still talking on the other end when she hung up.

She tossed my phone on the bed and sighed, flopping down beside me. "You would think that I was lost on the streets of Abu Dhabi for a month."

"They were worried, Levee."

She curled into my arms, tangling her legs with mine. "Oh bullshit. Dad's mistress was probably worried this would affect her new jewelry collection, and Mom was probably just concerned that she'd have to finally acknowledge her at my funeral. Ick!" Her shoulders shuddered in disgust. "There is a reason I don't talk to my parents. I'll sign a check any day of the week if it keeps them in Arizona and away from me."

I filed that little rant in the things-to-ask-Levee-about-when-we-didn't-have-a-million-other-things-to-talk-about folder in the back of my mind.

With a sigh, she shifted her head onto my pillow and placed a kiss on my lips. It started out as chaste, but it didn't take long before our tongues were gliding against each other and our bodies found a similar rhythm, grinding together.

"Why are you wearing so much clothes?" she asked, slinging a leg over my hips to rub her core over my cock, which was unfortunately still hidden within the denim.

"Because I want to talk to you about today." I grabbed her ass to still her movements.

"Ugh! I swear you are the most talkative man I've ever met. You're supposed to want to have sex all the time, and *I'm* supposed to want to talk. Which I don't. So let's skip to the sex part."

She went in for another kiss, but I placed my lips on her forehead instead.

"Tell me why you were on the bridge, Levee," I whispered.

"I already told you. I didn't have my phone, and I knew that was where you'd look for me."

"Not the one today. The one when we first met."

Her whole body stiffened in my arms. "I...uh...I guess was just exhausted and overwhelmed." She shrugged.

"That I know. You have to give me more though."

She rolled to her back and blew a breath out but didn't say a single word.

"Tell me why you were on the bridge, Levee," I urged again.

She finally lifted her head and bluntly said, "Because I was a walking disaster."

Her use of past tense encouraged me.

I brushed the hair off her neck and placed a gentle kiss on her lips. "No you weren't."

"I really was, Sam." She smiled tightly. "I couldn't shut down anymore. You know that feeling you get in your stomach from a sudden drop? Mine felt like that all the time. I couldn't sleep. I couldn't eat. I was just stressed about everything. Especially all the kids like Morgan dying at children's hospitals."

My head snapped back. "What?"

"I can't visit them all. I just can't. I do my best, but do you have any idea how many dying kids there are out there?" She pushed out of my arms and got to her feet. "It's so fucking unfair." Her chin quivered as she began to pace while chewing on her thumbnail.

I sat up on the bed. "Levee, Morgan isn't dying."

She stopped, and her eyes jumped to mine.

"She was released a few days ago, actually. She was only at the hospital because she kept getting sick during her treatments. So they moved her to a more sterile environment."

She swallowed hard, and tears filled her eyes. "Really?"

"Do you even ask about these *dying* kids you go see?"

"No. I'm not going to invade their privacy by asking a million questions. When I go, it's to offer them a diversion, not to remind them why they are there in the first place."

"Levee, you're killing yourself with guilt over sick kids who are fighting and *winning*."

"They aren't all winning, Sam." Her voice cracked at the end.

I kept my tone soft but firm. "But a lot of them *are*. Focus on the right part of that equation. No wonder you're depressed. You think every kid who visits a hospital is dying."

"I don't think they all are....but—"

I interrupted her again before she had the chance to muddle it back up in her head. "Hospitals are where kids go to get *better*. Yes, some lose their battles, but most do *not*."

"But some *do*," she snapped. Hanging her head, she whispered, "My sister, Lizzy, died *in a hospital* three weeks after she was diagnosed with leukemia."

And there it was.

Levee had a past of her own.

And just knowing that we shared something so similar gutted me.

"C'mere," I said, but I didn't wait for her to obey. I went to her.

Her arms were tucked between us, but she accepted my embrace, leaning her head into the base of my neck. I backed her toward the bed then turned at the last second and pulled her down on top of me.

"How old were you?" I asked as her stiff body relaxed.

"Eight," she squeaked.

"That's a long time ago. Have you ever seen someone...ya know... to talk about it?" I smoothed her curls down and kissed the top of her head.

"Yeah. I did when I was a kid."

"And recently?" I prompted.

"I don't really remember her all that well. I mean, I do. But it's not like she's haunting me or something. Most of what I remember of her was in the hospital for those three weeks. Then how lonely I felt when she died. She was two years older than me. I wanted to be just like Lizzy when I grew up. Then, one day, I was older than she was. That was really hard."

I nodded in understanding. It did suck. Anne was three years younger than me. I was older than she'd ever be.

"It's funny. I don't remember a ton about Lizzy, but one of my clearest memories of her was the day a celebrity visited the hospital she was at. She was so sick at that point, but the moment he walked in the room, bearing nothing more than a stuffed animal and a T-shirt, she perked up completely. She was laughing and smiling. We thought meeting someone famous was the coolest thing in the entire world. I swear she was a different person for at least a week. It was crazy how something so small meant so much to us back then."

"Who was the celebrity?" I asked, smoothing a hand down her back in understanding.

"Ric Flair."

I arched an eyebrow in question. "The wrestler, Ric Flair?"

She nodded with a smile creeping across her lips.

"The Nature Boy, Ric Flair?" I threw in his signature "woo" just so there was no confusion.

She nodded again, her smile stretching wide.

"I honestly have no idea if you're serious right now."

She laughed. "I'm completely serious."

I leaned away to get a full read on her face, still not believing her. "You were a wrestling fan?"

"No! And I think that's the part that stuck with me. Lizzy didn't have to know who he was. She just needed to feel special. I worked my ass off to fulfill my dreams of making a living out of music. The split second I got a song on the radio, I started spending my weekends with sick kids. Half of them didn't even know who I was at first, but they would still smile and laugh as I walked in the room. I saw Lizzy's face in every single one of them. Once I became more known, the pressure only built. I had to do more. Give more. Be there more." The words lodged in her throat, and I could feel her heart slamming wildly in her chest.

She was working herself into a panic attack from just talking about it. I couldn't imagine how she had dealt with it on a daily basis.

"Shhh. Relax." I squeezed her tight to my chest.

"Goddammit." She banged her fist against the mattress. "I promised myself I was taking my life back today. And look at me. I can't even talk about this without losing my shit."

"Your view on life is seriously warped," I told her matter-of-factly.

Her whole body flinched, making it clear that those words weren't the sugarcoating she had been expecting from me. But someone had to tell her.

"You're not Spiderman." I smirked.

"And you're not funny," she deadpanned.

"Yes, I am. But hear me out. You can't save everyone. I get it, Levee, because for so fucking long, I felt the same way. Hell, after the way I freaked out when you went missing today, I might still feel that way. But at least I can recognize it. For years, I beat myself up over the fact that I wasn't there sooner the day my dad killed himself. The guilt ate at me. Until one day, my mom sat me down and explained that I wasn't Spiderman." I laughed at the memory. "Keep in mind, I was sixteen when she told me this, not ten. But, God, it was the most freeing thing anyone ever said to me after he died. I was just one person. I couldn't be everywhere for everyone. Not for Dad. Not even for Anne."

"Sam, that wasn't—"

I didn't give her a chance to tell me what I already knew. "It wasn't my fault. I know. I just wish I could have done more. It's the struggle of decent people everywhere. Levee, that's not a bad feeling to have. It only becomes bad when those wishes consume you and when you get so wrapped up in helping people that you lose sight of the toll it's taking on you. I could have sat with Anne twenty-four-seven. My mom could have done the same for my dad. You could easily toss your career in the trash and go on a world tour of hospitals everywhere, but how would that affect *you*? At some point, you have to make your own life a priority. No one else can do that for you. Not a doctor or your family and friends. Hell, not even I can do it. That's on you, Levee."

Tears filled her eyes. "That's not true. You do that for me all the time. I don't feel so out of control when I'm with you."

I couldn't fault her there. She did *that* for me, too. She was just confused on what *it* was.

"No I don't."

"Yes, you do."

"No. I really don't."

"Yes, you *really* do!" she snapped, starting to get angry.

I couldn't help but laugh as she narrowed her eyes at me. I rubbed my fingers over the pinched skin between her brows. "You're going to give yourself wrinkles if you keep doing that. I need you to stay hot so I can show you off to my friends when you finally let me tell them."

She swatted my hand away. "You can't tell me how you make me feel. You're not in my head."

"I can tell you whatever I want," I said indignantly.

"No, you can't."

"Yes, I can."

"No. You. Can't." She got even more pissed, and I, once again, started laughing.

"I love you."

Levee sat straight up as if a bolt of lightning had just struck the bed.

Yep. That was my smooth move. I'd just blurted it out while we had been bickering, fully dressed, in a random hotel room in middle of Maine. That was going to be the story we told our kids about—the magical moment you only get once in a lifetime with someone. It was

Sam Rivers's romance at its finest—completely and utterly ridiculous, but also more honest than anything in the world.

"You what?" she half breathed, half accused.

"Designer shoes, I said, 'I love you.' I have for a while. Probably from the moment you used your body to shield the wind so I could light my cigarette. Maybe even before that. It was love at first stalk, Levee."

"Sam…"

"So, yeah, I can tell you whatever I want. And I'm telling you all I do is offer you a distraction from the rest of your crazy life. It's a really fucking good distraction, and I'm praying that you love the hell out of that distraction and want to keep it forever. But, at the end of the day, you have to be the one who wants to live. All I can do is be at your side while you do it." I shrugged simply.

Although, as I stared into her brown eyes, there was absolutely nothing simple about it.

I love her. Now, I had to sit and wait to see if she loved me too.

She held my gaze while a combination of emotions passed over her gorgeous face. Her cheeks pinked shyly. Her lips twitched with humor. Her eyes filled with love. But her mouth said, "You're a dumbass."

Well, okay, then.

chapter twenty-two

Levee

Sam barked out a laugh as he confidently folded his arms behind his head but eyed me warily. "Excuse me?"

"I said, 'You are a dumbass,'" I repeated, but a giant smile threatened to swallow my face.

He loved me. He was also a dumbass, hence why I felt the need to inform him of such information. But, really, I was too busy fighting to keep my feet on the ground while my heart was attempting to soar away. *He loves me.*

A matching grin formed on Sam's mouth. "Oh really? How's that?"

"First, I need you to retract your declaration of love."

He shook his head and curled his lip in disgust. "No way."

I turned toward him and crisscrossed my legs in front of me. "You have to! I can't talk about my ex-boyfriends after you tell me you love me! It's bad form."

He tipped his head to the side. "Why in the hell would you feel the need to talk about your ex-boyfriends right now?"

"Because it explains why you're a dumbass," I announced before bending forward to touch my lips to his. Pulling away just an inch, I whispered, "It's a really good story, too."

Sucking in a deep breath, he grabbed the back of my head and kissed me again. Holding me against his lips, he exhaled on a content sigh. "I'm not retracting anything, but if you absolutely must, I give you full permission to talk about your exes."

"Okay." I attempted to sit up, but Sam wasn't having it.

Instead, he grabbed my leg and pulled me to straddle his lap. Then he stripped my shirt over my head in one swift movement, which was quickly followed by his own. I stared at his mouth-watering, ink-covered chest, noticing for the first time that Anne's name was woven between the random designs. I reached out to trace my fingers over the black ink, but he caught my wrist and lifted my hand to his mouth.

Kissing the back of my hand, he said, "Now, why am I a dumbass?"

"Oh, right. Thomas Reigns, Chris Spears, Davis Long, and Lee Shultz were all distractions."

"Jesus, did you date anyone who wasn't in the NFL?"

"Lee plays baseball." I shrugged.

"Anyone else?"

"Johnny Depp. But he was so weird."

"And old," Sam scoffed, clearly not enjoying my parade of exes.

I giggled as he cussed under his breath. "Anyway, what I'm saying is I've had a lot of distractions in my life. So I can say without a single doubt that you, Sam Rivers, are not one of them."

"Levee—" he started, but I silenced him with a kiss.

"From the moment I first met you, you made the world lighter. You didn't even know you were doing it at first. But just knowing you would be on that bridge every night soothed the madness that was ricocheting around inside my head. You made me laugh, and like Ric Flair"—I paused while he chuckled—"you made me feel special. The relief I felt in your arms made the craziness manageable. You were never a distraction to me, Sam. You were always my reprieve."

I smiled, hoping to receive one in return, but as he traced a finger down my cleavage, concern covered the strong angles of his face.

"I fucking love that. I really do. But what if, one day, I'm not there for you? I'm worried that you won't have the right mindset about this. I can't fix your problems just by making you laugh."

"Maybe not. But I've been thinking a lot over the last few weeks and especially today. I don't want to learn how to cope with my old life. I want it to change. I dreamed for years about getting to where I am today, but I've lost myself in the spotlight. I miss writing songs, Sam. Did you know I only wrote four of the twelve on my last album?"

He shook his head and began sliding his callused hands up and down my sides. Chill bumps pebbled my skin in their wake.

"I swore I'd never be that artist. Writing music was always my passion, long before I ever even dreamed of taking to a stage myself. I started jotting down lyrics right after Lizzy died—I couldn't even play guitar yet. Maybe that's who I'm supposed to be, because I'm quickly realizing I might not be cracked up for the fast lane of fame."

His hands stilled. "Are you saying you want to quit?"

"No! But maybe taking a step back for a little while isn't a bad idea. I could write some music and remember why I wanted this life to begin with."

He skeptically arched an eyebrow. "Levee, I think a break is a brilliant idea. But, if I'm being honest, I'm concerned that, if you don't get some real help, you'll find yourself spending even more time at hospitals, killing yourself in a different way."

God, I loved the way he gave it to me straight. Which was exactly why I knew I could handle this transition with him at my side.

"I've always gone to the children's hospitals, Sam. But it wasn't until recently that it became some sort of addiction. I need someone who can help me keep that in perspective—to tell me when I start getting off-balance. I'm obsessive about stuff. It's who I am, but I'm not irrational. Henry used to be my voice of reason, but he has his own life now, and it's dragging us in different directions."

Bending down, I kissed him. Then I kissed him again. Then I kissed him as if it were the very last time, and as far as I was concerned, it was. Because, on the flipside of that kiss, I wanted something brand new with Sam.

And I wanted to start it right.

"I fell in love with you when I was at rock bottom. But I'll never be able to look back on those dark days with anything but a smile. I wanted to jump, Sam, but I never once expected the fall to go up."

"Jesus, Levee." He pulled me into a hug. He held me painfully tight and rained kisses over my neck and my shoulder. They weren't sensual the way I knew Sam's mouth was capable, but I felt every single one of them deep within my soul.

Gradually, his hands drifted to my breasts, but for the first time since we'd met, I was the one who wanted to talk.

"Wait. Listen." I leaned away but circled my legs around his waist to keep us connected. "I love you."

His entire face lit as his eyes smiled.

"And I need you to trust me here. I know you're still worried about me, but I'm not going back to that place."

His body tightened, and his eyes squinted suspiciously.

"I want to go home with you, Sam. I'll see a therapist if that's what it takes to make you feel comfortable, but I want to end every night with you. Your nightly phone calls and silly pictures have helped me more than any doctor ever could. Take me home and let me struggle with you."

His head lolled back as he stared up at the ceiling. "That's not fair. You can't use my words against me."

"I'm not using them against you." I grabbed both sides of his face and tipped his lips to mine. "I repurposed them." I winked.

He chuckled against my mouth. "Fine."

I smiled huge. "Fine?"

He let out a resigned growl. "Come home with me, Levee."

"Okay, okay. If you insist," I teased.

"I officially insist." He turned, tossing me off his lap and onto the bed.

His hard body followed, covering me completely. Holding his weight on his elbows at my sides, he lowered his mouth to mine in a hypnotizing kiss that sent heat pooling between my legs. I slid a hand down the back of his jeans and used his ass to grind against him.

"Fuck," he hissed, his dick thickening between us. "I'm also going to insist you start birth control as soon as fucking possible. I'm done with condoms." He pushed off the bed and, in one fluid movement, popped the button on my jeans open and dragged them off. His pants quickly joined them on the floor.

Lying in front of Sam in nothing but my bra and panties was more exhilarating than any stage I'd ever stepped foot on. His eyes turned dark and warmth washed over me as they swept up my body.

"You've gained weight," he said, removing my panties.

I wanted to be annoyed, but two of his fingers filled me, and just as quickly, his thumb found my clit. It had been too long without his touch, and my legs fell open, pleading for more.

"You'll always be beautiful, Levee. But you were too thin before. This"—he guided a hand over my stomach then up to my breasts—"is perfection."

Pushing up on my forearms, I caught his mouth before he had a chance to straighten back up. My hand cupped the back of his neck as I held his lips to mine, only releasing when his fingers suddenly twisted inside me.

"Oh, God," I breathed, falling back against the pillows.

Sam stood at the edge of the bed, watching me lose myself in his skilled hands. I opened my eyes long enough to find him working his thick shaft with his free hand while he stared at where his fingers were pumping inside me. He constantly licked his lips, and pure, unadulterated lust covered his face. As if he felt my gaze, his eyes flashed to mine.

Absolute love shined in his golden eyes, rendering me unable to look away.

He'd been wrong. *That* was perfection.

"I want you inside me," I breathed.

He didn't answer me, but his hand disappeared as he began searching the ground for his jeans.

I sat up and took his dick in my hand, stilling him by stroking it from base to tip. "No condom, Sam."

"We need to be safe—shiiiit." He groaned when I leaned down and laved my tongue over the metal barbell. He threaded his fingers into my hair as I swirled my tongue around the rim of his head and over the salty bead of pre-cum that had formed at the tip.

Peeking up through my lashes, I repeated, "No condom."

"We can't," he complained, but he did it while giving up on the search for his wallet and prowling after me as I scooted up the bed.

"I've been on birth control since I was seventeen," I said while he silently removed my bra. "I'm clean and I'm assuming you are too. Now, fuck me bare. Please."

His eyes flared wide, but that was the only warning I received. Kneeling between my legs, he slammed inside me. Sex with Sam was always that way.

Needy.

Fast.

Rough.

Incredible.

But, without a barrier between us and with love radiating from his eyes, it was so much more.

It was the end of uncertainty.

And the beginning of us.

For over an hour, Sam alternated between fast and hard, and slow and steady. Whispered "I love yous" echoed between us as he pushed me to the edge more times than I could count, but each time, just before I was able to step off, he'd shift gears. Finally, with a sheen of sweat covering both of our bodies, Sam planted himself to the hilt and emptied inside me as I came crying his name.

No matter how overwhelming my life was from that point forward, there was no way I'd ever be willing to give up those moments with Sam.

I couldn't change for him. I understood that.

I was making my life a priority for myself.

But, if I got to live it with him at my side, it was an easy choice to make.

chapter twenty-three

Sam

evee and I decided to leave that next morning to head back to San Francisco, and I was already having doubts about bringing her home. I definitely wanted her with me, but it felt all kinds of wrong to take her away from the help I so desperately wanted—needed—her to receive. But, as we drove to the airport with her smiling and laughing beside me, it was easy to pretend that I could handle it.

Maybe I was Spiderman for Levee.

Or maybe I was just setting myself up for my biggest failure yet.

With the exception of a few people stopping Levee for an autograph or a photo, we made it out of Maine virtually unnoticed. However, that wasn't at all the case when we landed in California. We had taken the same flight, snuggling in first class like newlyweds, but when our plane had landed, we'd gone our separate ways. Levee wasn't ready for the media attention yet, and as frustrating as it was, I was willing to do anything to keep her stress level as low as possible. Sucking in a deep breath, I begrudgingly walked past her as a large group of people started snapping pictures and calling her name the moment she exited the security area.

Henry's head of security, Carter, had arranged for two bodyguards to meet her when we landed. I'd only made it a few yards away before my attention was drawn back to the commotion. Nerves settled in my gut as my feet became rooted to the ground. I had yet to truly experience Levee's celebrity status up close, but my heart raced as a sea of people swarmed around the woman I was irrevocably in love with. It was an unbelievably miserable thirty seconds before she emerged sandwiched between the two giant men.

With a stoic expression and a pair of shades covering her amazing eyes, she looked more like the woman I'd first met than she had in a long time, but the oddest thing happened. Seeing her like that felt wrong. No matter how nostalgic it made me.

Deep down, she'd always be my Designer Shoes, but now, she was also my *Levee*—the strong and brave woman I was planning to never let go.

Even in a crowd full of people, her gaze instinctively found mine. Tipping her glasses up, she smiled and winked as they hustled her toward a waiting limo. I shouldn't have done it, but there wasn't a chance in hell I could have kept it in. Crossing my arms over my chest, I returned her smile, mouthing, "I love you."

She didn't respond with words, but her cheeks blushed, giving me all the answer I needed.

After pulling a pair of shades from my backpack, I dropped them over my eyes and walked anonymously to my Jeep in long-term parking.

The night before, Levee had spent two hours arguing on the phone with

Henry after she'd informed him that she wasn't going back to the rehab center. He was worried. And I couldn't say that I didn't share his fears, but he'd finally relented when Levee had assured us both that she could continue therapy at home. The idea of having her all to myself during her self-imposed break definitely made it easier for me to accept. It also didn't hurt that, the minute her bag hit the floor in my bedroom, she was on the phone, scheduling doctor appointments for the rest of the month.

I secretly texted Henry to let him know she was following through with her end of the arrangement. And I guessed he was relieved, even though his only reply was to ask for naked pictures. I sent him an image of a tribe of naked men I'd found on National Geographic online. It wasn't like he'd been specific or anything. He didn't find it nearly as funny as I did, responding with a picture of a puppy puking. An amazing and unlikely friendship was born out of those first few messages.

Levee had refused to speak to Devon in Maine. He'd called numerous times and had even gone so far as to show up at the hotel we had been staying at attempting to explain. Levee wouldn't even tell him our room number. She pretended to be mad, but when her eyes watered every time she ended his call, I could tell she was more hurt than anything else. I, on the other hand, was pissed enough for both of us. I figured she'd want to talk to him eventually, and I hoped that I'd have a chance to cool off by then. I couldn't imagine that a brawl with Devon would end well for me.

We'd barely been back at my house for two hours, but we had already broken my bed in —twice. Levee was still naked and curled into my side when my phone started ringing with an unidentified call. She hadn't gone back to pick up her belongings from the center, and until her new cell was delivered the following day, she was using mine as her sole source of communication. I didn't even bother answering before passing it in her direction.

"Hello?" she said, propping it against her ear so she could continue teasing her nails over my stomach.

I was gliding a hand over her ass when she suddenly sat upright.

"Uh, who is this?" Her gaze flipped down at mine accusingly as she said, "That's funny because I thought *I* was Sam's girlfriend."

I dove for the phone, but Levee jumped out of my reach, sending me crashing off the end of the bed. Only one woman would use a blocked number to call me, knowing good and damn well I wouldn't pick up if I saw her name pop up on my phone.

Confirming my suspicions, Levee said, "How long have you and Sam been together, Lexi?"

"Levee, give me the phone." I pushed up to my feet, but she ducked under my arm and headed to my kitchen.

Oh, this is going to be bad.

Lexi was in-fucking-sane, especially if she thought I was seeing someone new. I couldn't even imagine the amount of bullshit she was firing at Levee.

"What a prick!" Levee yelled from the other room as I hurriedly tugged a pair of boxers on and following her.

Shit shit shit.

"He told me he loved me," Levee whined as I cautiously made my way towards her.

Fuck my life.

The moment I rounded the corner, I found Levee in my discarded T-shirt that hadn't even made it to the bedroom when we'd gotten home. She was bent over, searching the refrigerator with the phone stuck to her ear. Placing her hand over the speaker, she whispered, "Do you have any beer?"

My mouth fell open as she casually went back to talking to Lexi, whimpering, "I can't believe he would do this to me."

"Ummm…bottom drawer," I mumbled, dumbstruck.

She tossed me a wink and pulled out two before passing me one. She clinked the neck of her beer against mine and then tipped it to her lips. I watched in a weird combination of astonishment and confusion.

Shit. Maybe Levee is insane too.

Placing my bottle on the counter, I closed the distance and attempted to take the phone from her hand. Levee laughed, backing away.

"Stop," she mouthed.

"She's not my girlfriend. I swear—" I explained, but she silenced me with a finger over my lips.

Pulling the phone from her ear, she pressed the speaker button and dropped it on the counter. Lexi was talking a million miles a minutes and using present tense in reference to our relationship.

I opened my mouth to object when Levee covered it with her palm and wrapped her other arm around my waist, sliding it down into the back of my boxers. Raking her teeth over my earlobe, she whispered, "Is she the one your mom called a bitch?"

A relieved breath rushed from my lungs. Levee was, in fact, insane, but at that moment, it was working in my favor. I nodded, and she leaned away long enough to taunt, "Wait, Lexi, was this before or after he got my name tattooed..." She trailed off while inspecting the ink on my torso. Finding an empty space, she finished with, "On his left side."

"What?" Lexi screamed.

I attempted to stifle a laugh, only barely keeping it packed down because Levee began dragging openmouthed kisses over my neck.

She paused to say, "Yeah, it's huge. You definitely would've noticed it. I can send you a picture later if you'd like?"

My eyebrows popped up in question before she whispered into my ear, "You can Photoshop that, right?"

I shook my head. Then I shrugged and nodded.

I wouldn't...but I totally could.

After lifting her to sit on the edge of the counter, I nabbed the phone and handed it to Levee. Whispering, I said, "You are an evil, evil woman. I wasn't sure I could fall in love with you more. But stop giving her more fuel to be a bitch and hang up." I gently glided my thumb over her peaked nipple, causing her to gasp.

She smiled, placing a lingering kiss on my lips as she took the phone from my hand and blindly pressed the end button. Locking her legs around my hips, she stated, "You really traded up for me. You know that, right?"

I laughed. "Yeah, I know. Although I figured you'd be serving up my balls as sashimi right about now."

She laughed. "Why? Because you have a crazy ex?" Wrapping her arms around my neck, she nuzzled her cheek against the scruff on my jaw.

"No, because most women would have bought into all of that shit she was spouting."

She sighed and leaned away to catch my eye. "I trust you, Sam. And, as hard as it may be, you're going to have to trust me too."

I twisted my lips in annoyance. "It's not hard to trust you."

"It will be when a magazine publishes pictures of me hugging some guy with the headline that he's my new boyfriend. You would be amazed at the shit they find to publish about me. Every picture snapped, no matter how innocent, is fair game for them to manipulate."

"Yeah, I heard you were pregnant with Henry's love child last month. I've been waiting for you to tell me," I teased, rubbing her stomach.

She slapped my hand away. "One baggy shirt and suddenly I'm knocked up by my best friend." She groaned and then whined, "It was my favorite shirt, too."

I chuckled, tucking a curl behind her ear. "I trust you, Levee."

"That's easy to say now—"

I cut her off by teetering her on the edge of the counter. "It's easy to say, period. Give me a little credit here."

Her shoulders fell as she dropped her forehead head against my chest. "I know. It's just that I've never dated someone who wasn't in the public eye before. I don't want to lose you over a tabloid headline you pick up at the grocery store."

"No, I'm not famous, but I'm not stupid either. Let's make a deal. You deal with my crazy ex for me, and I'll deal with the entire fucking world for you."

Her head popped up with a smile. "Wow! That makes me seem really high maintenance."

I exaggerated a sigh. "You really are. But I promise you, if the world ever becomes too much and I get jealous over pictures of you dry-humping small-cocked Thomas Reigns"—she laughed, slapping my chest—"I promise I'll talk to you first, okay?"

Her whole body melted into my arms. "I love you, even when TMZ says otherwise."

I kissed her neck and teased back, "I love you too, Lexi…I mean, Levee."

She barked a loud laugh. "Hilarious."

"I thought so."

"So, why'd you two lovebirds break up anyway? She seems like such a delightful young lady." Her voice was thick with sarcasm.

Shrugging, I replied, "She was sleeping with her personal trainer. Showed up two hours late to Anne's funeral because of it."

Levee's eyes flared wide, and her mouth gaped for only a second before she shrieked, "That bitch!"

"She's nice enough, just—"

"Nice enough?" she asked, incredulously. "I'm gonna put a hit out on her!"

"Okay, hold on there, Tony Soprano. No one's putting a hit on anyone." I paused. "Just to be clear, you don't have those kind of connections, right?"

"No, but I have money! I'm sure I can buy some connections," she answered in all seriousness.

I fucking love her.

Dipping down, I folded her over my shoulder.

"What kind of person does that? Your sister had just died!" She continued to rant as I carried her back to the bedroom.

"Let it go," I said, tossing her on the bed.

"I can't let that go!" she replied, lifting her arms so I could tear the shirt over her head.

"Okay, then don't. But can you open your legs so I can eat your pussy while you mentally defend my honor?" I smirked, crawling up the bed after her.

"Such a bitch," she mumbled, dropping her legs open wide.

They were the last audible words I heard from her before my mouth sealed over her clit. A long, garbled moan escaped her throat as her hand snaked into my hair. I'd fucked her twice already, but my cock instantly became hard beneath me.

She writhed against me as I dipped a finger inside her, curling it before twisting the way I'd learned set her ablaze. This time was no different. Circling her hips off the bed, she fisted the back of my hair.

"Roll over," she ordered.

Levee was like that. As much as I loved licking her pussy, she loved my cock. She was never able to wait long before pleading for it. And, more often than not, I was more than willing to give it to her.

But not this time.

After prying her hand from my hair, I pinned it to the bed at her side. I alternated between sucking and nipping at her clit and thrusting my tongue in and out of her wet opening. Her other hand found my hair as she continued to beg me to roll over. My only response was to pin her other hand to the bed as well.

"Wait, wait, wait." she said, sitting up even as she ground herself against my mouth. Then she sucked in a deep breath, which she held.

"You want me inside you?" I asked between licks as her whole body coiled in impending release.

"Yes," she squeaked, still not exhaling.

"Not until you come." I sucked hard on her swollen nub, flicking it with my tongue.

Falling back to the bed, she cried, "Oh, God!"

Her orgasm sprang to life as her cunt began to pulse against my mouth. That was my cue. Pushing up to my knees, I spread her legs wide and flipped her on her side. Straddling her thigh against the bed and pulling the other over my shoulder, I drove inside her harder than ever before. A string of cuss words flew from her mouth as she continued to pulse around me.

Levee and I were in love—there was no doubt about that. But we were still getting to know each other on so many levels.

Not our bodies though. They were sexual soulmates.

Levee ground her hips in a rhythm that she knew could snatch the orgasm from my balls. And I worked her deep, making sure the metal of my barbell found just the spot that would still her merciless hips.

It was a constant give and take of driving each other toward the brink, all while furiously fighting away our own releases.

At some point, one of the two of us would fail. This particular time, I wasn't too proud to admit that it was me.

"Fuck," I cursed as my cock shot off wrapped in her tight warmth.

Needing to take her over the edge with me, I dropped my thumb to her clit and rubbed a tight circle as I continued to pump inside her. My orgasm was already shredding me, but the moment her muscles began to clench around me, a whole new wave of ecstasy tightened my balls, leaving me utterly empty in its wake.

But, as my eyes opened and I watched Levee's lithe body trembling beneath me, I'd never felt more full in my life.

Yes, I was coming down from an unbelievable orgasm with an even-more-so unbelievable woman, but I had no doubt whatsoever that the feeling currently expanding in my chest was the *great* I'd always been searching for. It was by far the highest high of my life, and even as her body continued to milk me and I softened inside her, I couldn't even enjoy it.

In my life, after every high came the lowest of lows.

And, while looking down into her sated eyes, which were staring up at me so filled with love that it nearly ached, the fucking pendulum swung all over again.

chapter twenty-four

Levee

I spent two glorious days lost in Sam before I came back up for air. I wished I could've stayed tucked in his bed forever, but he had work to do, and unfortunately, I did too. Really, I didn't want to do any of it though.

Sure, I needed to return the hundreds of calls I'd ended from Stewart and let him know that I was taking an indefinite hiatus from music. I was positive it wasn't going to go over well.

I also needed to fire Devon. My heart broke at the idea, but no more than it had the day he had taken it upon himself to come between me and Sam—that killed.

And, after all of that was done, I needed to head up to my house, change all the locks and security codes, and then relocate half of my wardrobe to Sam's closet. There had never been a question of his place or mine when we'd gotten back. His shop was out back, and he had

Sampson to take care of, so his place was the obvious choice. But, above and beyond all that, I loved Sam's house. I'd only spent one night there before I'd left, but somehow, it felt like home. I wasn't necessarily moving in for good, but I wasn't planning to go back home any time soon, either.

Sam had been up for hours when I finally dragged myself out of bed long enough to do my hair and makeup. I took my sweet time, hoping another day would slip to night so I could avoid my to-do list, but an hour later, when I slid my heels on, the clock only read eleven in the morning.

Grabbing my new phone, I decided to procrastinate on Twitter for a while before starting my day.

It was the wrong decision.

So. So. So wrong.

The very first message to pop up on my feed was a video of a bald little boy no older than three, connected to more wires than I could count. He looked so weak, but as someone offscreen turned my song "Discovery" on, he started shimmying and shaking in his hospital bed. The song only lasted for a few seconds before it cut off, and the boy immediately broke into tears when it ended. It was turned back on and he started dancing all over again. My stomach wrenched as I pressed play repeatedly, only pausing long enough to read the tweet.

@LeveeWilliams You should come to Indiana and meet your biggest fan.

It was a harmless message that had been retweeted over three thousand times, but it was like a knife to my gut. *I really* should *do that.*

It would have cost me nothing to be on a plane that same night, but I knew the real price would be paid when I started the vicious cycle all over again.

I'm on a break.

Yet my fingers still typed out in response:

@SandyJoe176 Absolutely! I'd love to meet that handsome little guy. My manager will be in touch.

My finger hovered over the send button for entirely too long.

Visiting one sick kid wasn't the same as exhausting myself in hospitals every opportunity I got. *What would be the harm in just flying out for one day?* It wouldn't even have to be a full day. I could be back in time for dinner. Or, better yet, maybe Sam would go with me and we could make it a fun trip for both of us.

My finger inched closer to the send button.

Surely, he'd be on board with something like this. He knew how important visiting sick kids was for me. I mean, he couldn't expect me to give it up completely.

"You're not Spiderman."

Shit.

I pressed play on the video once more, my finger still hovering over send as I watched that little boy's eyes light when my song came through the speaker of my phone.

It's the right thing to do. No matter how it affects me.

But what about how it affected *Sam?*

Before I even realized it, I was on my feet and heading out to Sam's shop. I slung the door open and was instantly greeted by the loud grinding of a power tool. Sam was in the corner, hunched over a table, a cigarette dangling between his lips. The room fell silent as his gaze swung to mine. I must have looked panicked, because he immediately dropped the tool on the table and marched in my direction.

"What's wrong?"

"Can we go to Indiana?"

He spun to drop his cigarette into an ashtray before turning back to face me. "Depends on why you want to go, I guess."

"There's a sick little boy who sent me a video on Twitter. I think it would be a really nice thing to do. It's not like I have a lot going on right now. But I bet it would mean a lot if we showed up. I could have Stewart get in touch with his parents and make it a big surprise," I rushed out in one long breath until I ran out of air.

He arched an eyebrow.

I sucked in deeply before exclaiming, "We could both go! Make it a romantic getaway!"

He stared at me for a minute before silently flipping his palm up, requesting my phone. I sidled up beside him as he pressed play on the video.

My eyes bounced between his face and the phone as I watched him smile warmly at the child on the screen. When it ended, he tossed an arm around my shoulders, and just like I had, he pressed play again. I cuddled into his chest, wrapping my arms around his hips. Closing my eyes, I listened to his strong heartbeat as I awaited the verdict.

"What do you want to do, Levee?" he asked when the video ended.

I didn't open my eyes as I answered, "I want to go."

"And you think that will help him?"

"I don't know."

"But you think it might help *you* though, right?"

Yes. "I don't know."

Sam sucked in a hard breath, my head rising as his chest expanded. "You know I love you, right?" he said.

I didn't answer that question, nor did I release my hold around his waist even when his arms fell away from me. "You're going to tell me no, aren't you?"

"No. I'm not *telling* you anything. If you want to go, go."

I craned my neck back in surprise. "You want to go with me?"

"Nope," he answered shortly.

"Why…why not?" I stuttered.

"Because you're supposed to be on a break. You're supposed to be going to see your therapist tomorrow. You're supposed to be firing Devon, contacting Stewart, cleaning out your closet." He paused, raking an angry hand through his hair. "You're *supposed* to be fucking moving in with me."

Shit. Maybe I am moving in permanently.

I finally stepped away. "What do you expect me to do, Sam?"

"The things you promised!" he roared before collecting himself. "If you want to go, do it. But that's on you," he snapped, turning his back on me.

My guilt morphed to anger. "See, that's exactly the problem. It is on me!"

His back was still to me as he lit a cigarette. "Two days." He laughed without humor.

"What's that supposed to mean?"

I was more than ready for an icy gaze as he turned to face me, but I was nowhere near ready for the level of disappointment that showed on his angry face. "It means two days ago, I agreed to play Spiderman and bring you home with me. It means I love you so fucking much that I was willing to risk your life just to spend more time with you. And two fucking days later, I'm already failing."

My stomach sank, and the air between us became too thick to breathe. "You aren't failing. I just wanted to visit a kid!"

He lifted the cigarette to his lips for another drag. "Then what?"

I opened my mouth to reply, only I didn't have an answer at all. I had no fucking clue what came next. It was just an impulse to help someone. It wasn't the spiral down I was quickly realizing he was convinced I was going to take.

"That's what I thought," he whispered on a cloud of smoke. "Eventually, you'd end up back on that bridge." He wrenched his eyes shut.

"Sam, I won't let that happen again. I swear."

Scratching the back of his head, he announced, "I think you need to go back to Maine, Levee."

"No!" I cried, taking a giant step toward him. "Listen to me, please. I won't go to Indiana. It was just a gut reaction to seeing that video. I came out here to get your honest opinion."

He looked at the ground, shaking his head. "Well, you got it, didn't you?"

"Look at me," I ordered, and his eyes immediately lifted to mine. "I don't need to go back to Maine. I made the appointments with the doctor. I'm trying here."

"Are you?" He tipped his head in question. "I mean, are you *really*?"

"Yes, I *really* am."

He put his cigarette out and lit another. "Then why haven't you called Stewart? You've told no one about the break you so adamantly promised me you were gonna take. Henry didn't even know when I mentioned it last night."

"You were talking to Henry?"

"We're both worried about you, Levee."

I didn't know why I was so shocked by the fact that they were communicating without me, but even in the midst of an argument, it warmed me in all the right places.

"Oh. Well. I just haven't had a chance to tell him yet. That's all."

Sam's eyes flashed back to the door of his shop, which he stared at for entirely too long. I wasn't sure what was going on inside his head, and when I was about to ask, he whispered, "I'm scared."

"What?" I asked, walking closer so I could hear him better.

He cleared his throat but kept his eyes on the door. "I said, 'I'm scared.'" Then his empty eyes lifted to mine. "I think you want to take your life back. I really fucking do. But I'll be honest here: I'm not equipped for this. I thought I could do it, but I was wrong. Remember when you told me about that feeling you had in your stomach—like you were falling?"

I nodded as tears welled in my eyes.

"That's exactly how I felt when you walked in here. My stomach dropped the moment I saw the anxiety in your eyes. I feel it every night when I watch you fall asleep."

Oh, God. "The free fall," I whispered.

"It's terrible, but I was so fucking relieved when I realized it was just a sick kid you were upset about."

I inhaled deeply then closed my eyes. "I'm sorry." I jumped in surprise when his arms suddenly folded around me.

"No. I'm sorry. I should have pushed harder for you to stay in Maine. Levee, I love having you here. I'm just terrified that I'm going to fail you too." He squeezed me painfully tight, burying his face in my hair. "I can't lose you too."

I hated the idea of leaving more than I could ever adequately express, but when I closed my eyes and put myself in his shoes, I understood why he needed me to go. And, above and beyond all the stuff about his past, there was absolutely nothing in the world I wouldn't do to extinguish the free fall for him.

He had, after all, done it for me.

I squeezed him tight and breathed in a lungful of the smoky sweetness that was Sam's scent. "I'll go back."

His body sagged in relief.

"But not to Maine. They were idiots."

"Okay. Somewhere new. I'm good with that. Maybe somewhere closer this time." He kissed the top of my head while gliding his hands up and down my back.

"But, if I do this, I expect something in return."

He chuckled. "Whatever you want, baby. Just name it."

I laughed, because with that one phrase, I knew I had him cornered. "Quit smoking while I'm gone."

"You're such a funny girl," he said patronizingly.

"I'm not joking. You're not the only one who's scared. Struggling through lung cancer with you isn't exactly my idea of a good time. You quit smoking and we *both* get healthy."

"Fuck. It was sexy when you showed this evil side to Lexi. Me…not so much."

"Sam—"

He groaned loudly. "Fiiiine. I promised my mom I'd quit anyway. I guess this is two birds, one stone and all."

I cuddled even closer into his chest. "I love it when you call me a bird and threaten to throw stones at me."

He smoothed a hand down my back. "I figured. You always have been kinkier than I am."

"So we're really going to do this?" I asked, peeking up at him.

"I'm in if you are, Levee. There's nothing I wouldn't do for the peace of mind that your getting some help will give me."

I bit my lip and glanced away. I hated knowing that he worried about me like that, almost as much I loved knowing he cared enough to worry like that. He was such a good guy.

My guy. A smile grew on my lips.

"Does that include finally dicing up twenty-four thousand dollars in guitars?" I asked as my eyes landed on my four Gibsons leaning, untouched, against the far wall.

"Whoa! Now, you're just getting crazy." A devilish smile formed on his plump lips, and all of his earlier anger and anxiety disappeared completely.

My breath caught in my chest. God, he was gorgeous.

I cupped his strong jaw. "There must be a million women throwing themselves at you. How are you not married with a boatload of kids by now?"

His smile spread impossibly wide. "I hadn't met you yet." He shrugged before taking my mouth in a reverent kiss.

Well, for Sam, it might have been just a kiss. But, for me, it was definitely reverent, because the whole time his lips were on mine, I thanked whatever God that ruled our crazy universe for guiding him to me on that bridge all of those nights before.

chapter
twenty-five

Sam

"And you're sure? You're going to need to install a security gate and everything. It's going to totally fuck up the homey feel when you pull into your driveway!" Levee yelled over the wind as we drove in my Jeep up to her house.

"I swear to God, if you ask me that again, I'm going to change my mind!" I shouted back. "Yes, Levee. Move in with me. Bring all seven billion pairs of your shoes and clutter up my spare bedroom until I'm forced to convert it into a new closet for you." I tossed her a smile without taking my eyes off the road—or my hand off her thigh.

"I feel bad though." She tucked a leg underneath her as she turned to face me. "At least let me pay for all the security stuff."

I slowed at a stoplight and squeezed her thigh. "If it will make you stop freaking out about living with me, I'll put the entire fucking mortgage in your name. Now, chill!"

She narrowed her eyes at my outburst. "I'm not buying you a house, Sam."

"Then remind me what the point in dating you is again?" I flinched as her hand shot out and twisted my nipple.

Immediately crossing her arms over her chest, she attempted to protect herself from my retaliation, but I just pinched the side of her ass instead.

"Ouch!" she screamed before bursting into a fit of laughter.

I was going to miss the hell out of that crazy woman.

It had been three days since Levee had agreed to go back into a treatment program. She still hadn't dealt with Devon. Nor had she told anyone that she was stepping away from the music industry for a while. I kept my mouth shut though, because she had found an inpatient program on the outskirts of San Francisco. It wasn't the luxury resort she had been staying at in Maine, but it was still a nice place. After a long conversation with the director of the facility, we'd both felt comfortable that they would be able to handle her issues as well as protect her privacy while she was there. They'd never had a high-profile patient like Levee before, but they assured us that it wouldn't be a problem.

Levee was adamant that I be involved in the process this time. I couldn't say that I minded. It did wonders for my anxiety to know step by step what kind of help she would be receiving. Given our situation, Levee's new doctor made a house call in order to meet us. Doctor Spellman was an older lady who was professional to the core. She told it exactly like it was and didn't even do it with a smile. I fucking loved that about her. She didn't blow smoke up our asses by saying that everything would be fine. Instead, she laid out a solid treatment plan, outlining exactly what she hoped Levee would take from her time spent under her care. She also recommended Levee spend a full thirty days in inpatient then switch to six months of outpatient therapy.

Levee was still hesitant about the whole thing as we watched Doctor Spellman drive away

I, however, was not.

I was damn near ecstatic.

And, for that reason alone, I lost my ever-loving mind for a full ten seconds.

Levee's eyes were huge as I pulled the pack of cigarettes from my pocket and, one by one, crumbled them on the floor.

Five minutes later, I all but cried as I cleaned them up.

And that was how I found myself riding in my Jeep without a cigarette for the very first time. I did, however, have a nicotine patch on my arm, a mouth full of mango gum, and a beautiful woman I loved fiercely at my side. I could live with that.

As we pulled up to the security gate in front of Levee's mansion, she prattled off a mouthful of codes I'd need to get back in later that afternoon. I had to head up to rePURPOSEd and sign off on some paperwork I'd been ignoring since she'd gotten back, but Levee was staying at her place to get things ready for the little get-together for my family and friends she'd insisted on throwing before she left the following morning.

Levee still wasn't keen on announcing our relationship to the press yet, mainly because we'd been so successful at staying under the radar. San Francisco wasn't LA. Paparazzi weren't lurking around every corner. Just the night before, we had managed to sneak into a movie undetected. We were just a normal couple who'd gotten there late, made out in the top row like teenagers, then left early to have sex in the back seat of my car—granted, it was securely inside my garage when we'd done it, but she'd definitely ended the night with her ass naked on my back seat all the same. I wasn't in any more of a hurry to give up the small things like that than she was.

However, she was full steam ahead about meeting my mom and Ryan. And, with Ryan, came Meg, her husband Ty, and, of course, Morgan.

And, because Morgan was going to be there, Levee had guilted Henry into coming too.

"I love you," Levee whispered against my lips as I prepared to leave.

"I love you too. I'll be back with the crew at four. We're all meeting at my place then caravanning back up here."

She smiled and nodded absently.

"You nervous?" I asked.

She nodded again.

"Don't be. My mom loves you already."

She picked invisible lint off my shirt. "Did you tell her that I know Lionel?"

"Um, if I had, I wouldn't tell you not to be nervous. I'd tell you to run and hide."

She giggled then kissed me again.

"I did tell her to bring the photo album though."

Levee drew in a sharp breath. "Yesssss!" she hissed.

"That's right. I'll sacrifice my own manhood by allowing my mother to show you photos of me with a Jheri curl just to make sure you're comfortable. You should know I expect you to express your appreciation with your mouth around my cock tonight."

Sliding her hand to my ass, she replied with a quick, "Deal."

After running at least a dozen errands, which included picking up a cooler full of beer for later that night, I was chilling on my couch, working on a new Photoshopped picture for Levee, when Ryan suddenly flew through my front door. Sampson started raising hell only to settle when he recognized who it was.

"What the fuck?" I yelled as the door slammed behind Ryan.

He propped himself against it as if a pack of zombies were hot on his heels. "Say yes," he panted.

"What?" I asked, closing my laptop and setting it beside me.

"You're my best friend. I'd do anything in the entire world for you. I love you like a brother. Just say fucking yes!"

"What are you talking about?" I snapped, pushing to my feet.

"Okay, I didn't want to have to do this, but do you remember that time in high school when I did your *Great Gatsby* book report for you?"

"Uhhhh, you only did my report because you broke the dishwasher by filling it with laundry detergent and you needed me to fix it before your mom found out," I quickly corrected.

He huffed. "That is *not* the point. You had a need and I took care of it."

I rolled my eyes. "What do you need?"

He drew in a deep breath and straightened the collar on his button-down. "I need to get in Jen Jensen's pants, and the way you can take care of this is by allowing me to bring her to meet your famous girlfriend."

"No fucking way! Family only!"

Suddenly, there was a soft knock at the door.

Ryan smiled sheepishly. "Oh, and by the way, I already invited her. We just had a fantastic lunch and a very romantic stroll around the park."

My mouth gaped as I blinked in utter shock. "I made out with Jen. And you want me to take her to my girlfriend's house for a barbeque?"

"Why must you always remind me that you made out with my future wife? It was one kiss over a year ago."

I stepped into his face. "She grabbed my junk, dude."

He stepped right back into mine and snarled, "Awesome. Now, say yes so she'll be grabbing mine tonight."

I backed away, shaking my head and pinching the bridge of my nose. I couldn't believe that I was going to agree to this. "Just make sure she keeps her mouth shut, yeah? Levee and I aren't telling people we're together yet."

"Not a problem. I had her sign a nondisclosure agreement." He smiled proudly.

I arched an eyebrow, incredulous. "Who the fuck are you? Christian Grey?"

He curled his lip in disgust. "Who the fuck are *you?* A post-menopausal woman? Why do you know anything about Christian Grey?

I screwed my lips tight. No fucking way was I telling him that that was the movie Levee and I had watched together. So, instead, I sighed and said, "Yes. Bring Jen."

His hand shot up in the air in victory. "My dick appreciates this. A lot." He patted my shoulder enthusiastically.

Just then, the door opened and my mom came walking in carrying a dish full of pasta salad with Jen following behind her. "Ryan, honey, I think you forgot someone outside."

Tossing his arm around Jen's shoulders, he replied, "Of course not, Mrs. Rivers. How could I forget about a woman this beautiful?" He glanced down at Jen and spoke in the most ridiculous baby voice I had ever heard. "Sorry, baby. Sam and I had some business to talk about."

How that woman didn't roll her eyes, I'd never know, because mine threatened to roll out of my head.

Ten minutes later, everyone had arrived, and we began our ascent to Levee's place.

I knew that something was wrong the moment we arrived.

"Dear God," I breathed as I took in the sight in front of me.

"Wow," "Shit," "No way," and "Holy cow" all echoed behind me.

It had been just over six hours since I'd dropped Levee off, and somehow, during that time, her yard had been transformed into a weird combination of an extravagant white wedding mixed with the state fair—complete with a small Ferris wheel and every carnival game imaginable. Pearl-colored balloons decorated the corners of each booth, while large, pink floral arrangements covered all eight of the tables under the huge, white canopy.

My mom elbowed me in the ribs. "Perhaps I should have brought something a little fancier than pasta salad…and maybe worn a cocktail dress." She lifted her chin to a man in a tux pushing open the front door for us.

"I think our idea of a get-together might be a little different than Levee's," I replied.

"You think?" Meg snapped. "I'm in jeans!"

"Levee!" Morgan cried when she suddenly appeared in the doorway looking every bit like the A-list celebrity she was—perfectly styled hair, tight, white dress, designer heels, a face full of makeup, and the fakest smile I'd ever seen that woman wear.

I started laughing as her eyes found mine.

"Give me a second," I told the group as I headed in her direction.

"Hi," she squeaked when I wrapped her in a tight hug, lifting her off her feet.

Setting her back on the ground, I asked, "What did you do?"

Her eyes flashed away. "Well, I burnt the cake I was trying to make, and then I got nervous, so I called a party planner, and I...well, I may have gone a bit overboard."

Henry walked up behind her. "A bit?"

"Shut up and go hit on one of the waiters," she barked before shyly looking back up at me.

Cupping my hand to my ear, I asked for clarification, "*One* of the waiters?"

Henry lifted his hand and wiggled four fingers, quickly extending it for a shake when Levee turned to glare at him.

I reached out and took his hand. "What's up, man?"

"You know, just drinking your girlfriend's Cristal and trying to convince her that red shoes would've looked better with that dress. But what do I know?" He shrugged, tipping a champagne glass to his lips.

My eyes once again found Levee's. "Cristal?"

She huffed. "I already said I overdid it. Don't give me shit. I was nervous, and that party planner was wicked pushy. I told her kids were coming, and before I knew what happened, carnies were setting up."

I grabbed the back of her neck and bent to touch my lips to hers. "I'm not going to give you shit. It's really nice. *Completely unnecessary.* But sweet nonetheless. Is there cake?"

Her body melted as she wrapped her arms around my neck. "Red velvet *and* chocolate."

"Good! Morgan's birthday is next week. I'm telling her this is her party. Save Meg and Ty some cash." I winked. Releasing her, I tossed my arms out to my sides and spun to face my family. "Happy birthday, Morgan!"

Her eyes lit as she threw her hands over her mouth.

As if on cue, Henry bustled out the door. "Wait. Morgan's here?"

At the sight of him, Morgan burst into tears.

Meg and Ty laughed.

My mom clutched her heart.

Jen's cheeks pinked as she gasped.

Ryan looked down at her and cursed, shooting an angry glare in Henry's direction.

Levee's arm looped around my waist.

And I smiled for what felt like the very first time.

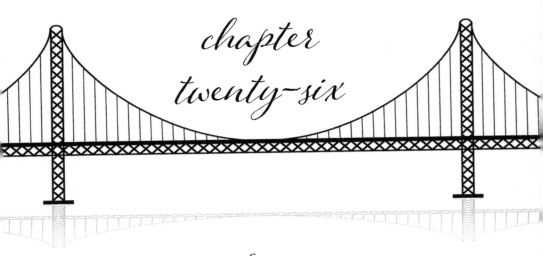

chapter twenty-six

Levee

"**A**nd here is Sam at four. We went for 'All Night Long' Lionel that year. I think it turned out pretty great," Sam's mom said as she turned the page of a huge photo album.

For over an hour, the two of us had sat at one of the corner tables flipping through page after page of Sam's childhood. There were numerous pictures of Anne and Sam's dad too. It was easy to see where Sam got his good looks, but after talking to his mom, it was easy to see how he'd turned out to be such an amazing man as well.

"All right. Enough is enough," Sam said as he strolled up beside us with a beer in one hand and a gift bag in his other.

"Whatcha got there, hot stuff?" I asked as he placed the gift bag in front of me.

"Well, I figured we should show Mom our photo album too?" He tossed me a mischievous grin.

"We have a photo album?" I asked.

"Yep," he answered as his smile grew. "Hey, Henry. Wanna see how Levee and I met?"

I immediately pushed to my feet as my eyes nervously flashed down to his mom. I did *not* want her to know how Sam and I had met. Hell, I wished Sam didn't even remember how we'd met.

"Umm, maybe we shouldn't do this here?"

Looping an arm around my waist, he tugged me against his chest and whispered, "It's not what you think."

I swallowed hard and searched his eyes, finding them dancing with humor. "Okay," I breathed, sitting back down as everyone gathered around us.

After reaching into the bag, I pulled out a rectangular book. It was the shape of a license plate, and on the front, in an airbrushed font, was *Sam & Levee 4-eva.*

I started laughing, but as I opened the book, my vision began to swim.

Yeah, Sam had been busy.

Once upon a time… was written in script across the top of the page. The image was one of Sam's composites where he'd cropped us together. And, for once, I wasn't falling on my face. We appeared to be on a street corner, and Sam was sitting on the ground in filthy clothes, holding a cup for change, with Sampson sleeping at his side. His mouth was hanging open in awe as he looked up at me.

For me, he had used a still from one of my music videos where I was dressed from head to toe like the princess America viewed me as. My expression was fierce, and my curls were blown back away from my face while my leg peeked from the high slit in my sexy version of a ball gown.

"Oh my God," I laughed.

The next page read: *The princess met a pauper and gave him a job building her bookshelves.*

The image was of me standing over him with my arms crossed

while he looked like he was yelling at me, but in his hand was the un-mistakable hollowed-out body of one of my Gibsons.

I sucked in a sharp breath, looking up at him in question.

"I only made you *two* of them," he explained. "I figure you can sign the other two and we can donate them to a charity auction or some-thing. Make us both feel better about destroying twenty-four grand."

At that, my vision did more than just swim. A tear rolled down my cheek as a huge smile spread across my lips.

Sam used his thumb to wipe it away, whispering, "I'm glad you approve."

I went back to the book, turning the page to find the caption: *The princess didn't realize how much she would like the pauper's beer and chicken.*

I burst into laughter at the picture of Sam in a pair of jeans that were riding low on his hips. He was shirtless and his abs were flexed impossibly tight, and if I wasn't mistaken, they were airbrushed a good bit too. Even from behind the beer bottle that was tipped to his lips, I could see the smirk on his mouth.

I had no idea how he'd found a picture of me on my hands and knees, but somehow, he had, and he'd placed me directly in front of him. If it hadn't been for the rooster I appeared to be chasing from be-tween his feet, it would have most definitely been X-rated.

Henry suddenly piped up behind me. "I'm going to need a copy of this book."

"Consider it done," Sam answered without hesitation.

The next page read: *And that was when the princess began falling for the pauper.*

I immediately recognized the picture as the first one he had ever sent me. Everyone around us began laughing, but warmth washed over me at the memory.

The following pages were the rest of the pictures he'd sent me while I had been in Maine. Each one was captioned with: *And falling...*

With each page, the group would laugh louder, pausing to point out something funny, like the random chickens Sam had hidden in background. I, however, couldn't tear my eyes off him—in person or in the pictures. In Sam's little story, I was the princess and he was the pauper, but in that moment, with his friends and family huddled around us, I realized he was the wealthy one. I was most definitely the pauper in our real story. I didn't care though. I'd never been more proud to call someone mine in my entire life.

After several pages, the caption changed to: *But the good news is he was falling for her too.*

The following pages were brand-new images I'd never seen before.

And they were stunning. Not because I really looked great, but because they were pictures of *us*. *Real pictures*. It started with the selfie of us that had been taken outside the theater before we'd gone to see *Fifty Shades of Grey* just a few nights earlier, only Sam had transported us to the red carpet at what looked like the premiere, and he'd added a pair of handcuffs dangling off the wrist he had slung over my shoulder.

Ryan burst out laughing, throwing Sam a high five that got left hanging.

The next page read: *And falling…*

It was a picture of me sleeping, cuddled up in a ball on Sam's bed. Only the side of his face was visible as he kissed my nose. My heart began to melt at something so sweet, but a laugh bubbled from my throat as I leaned in close, realizing he had added a trickle of drool coming from my mouth and a wet spot on my pillow.

My hand immediately snaked up and tweaked his nipple. I figured mine were safe since his mother was sitting beside me. But Sam didn't hesitate before reaching down to pinch mine as well.

"Sam!" His mom swatted his arm, but he just shrugged, completely unfazed.

Laughing, I turned to the last page in the book, only to freeze when I took in the image in front of me. My heart began to race, and frenzied butterflies stampeded in my stomach.

I wasn't in the last picture at all. It was just a picture of Sam in those same filthy clothes from the beginning, and he was standing in a jewelry store, handing over Sampson's leash and a crate full of chickens in exchange for a huge diamond engagement ring.

His mom gasped.

But I had absolutely no air in my lungs. Was he proposing? It was way, *way* too soon, but the word *yes* wasn't even teetering on the tip of my tongue. It was in the starting block, ready to fire from my lips the moment I opened my mouth.

The caption read: *And, eventually, that pauper sold all of his meager possessions just to be able to afford to keep that princess forever.*

As I slowly tipped my head up to look at him, another traitorous tear escaped my eye, giving Sam my answer to his unspoken question.

Smiling warmly, he lifted his thumb to my cheek, wiping the damp trail away before pressing it to my lips. Whispering, he said, "That's what I thought. But I just wanted to check. Turn the page, Levee."

I didn't want to turn the page at all.

But, at the same time, I'd never in my life wanted something more.

I was terrified that he was just being rash. We had so much going on. So much more to overcome. He didn't even know what it was like to really be with me. So far, we'd been living in a perfect little bubble of solitude. What if Sam didn't like life in the limelight? What if he couldn't trust me when the tabloids attempted to ruin us with rumors? We needed more time.

It's too soon.

I was unquestionably going to say yes though.

And, for as long as I lived, I would never regret that yes.

I knew, from the depths of my soul, that Sam was the rest of my life. Everything else would fall into place.

We'd fall up together.

So, sucking in a deep breath, I turned the page.

Then I burst into full-on tears.

Jumping to my feet, I threw my arms around Sam's neck as he held me tight against his body.

There was no proposal.

But there was definitely a promise.

And, in that moment, it was better than any ring he could have put on my finger.

There was no picture. It was only a white page with the words: *To be continued. (In thirty days.)*

"Well, that was anticlimactic," Henry deadpanned.

I was still holding Sam impossibly tight when Meg's hand slap his shoulder as she said, "That was mean!"

It wasn't mean.

It was us.

And, more than that, it added a whole other gear to my drive to get myself together over the next month.

It was the best gift he could have ever given me.

"I love you so much," I murmured into his neck.

He chuckled. "I can tell."

"Thank you for not proposing."

He laughed a little louder. "You're welcome, Levee."

"Please don't sell Sampson to buy me a ring. And, just so you know, I'm not sure I'd marry you without the cock. So please keep that too."

"Noted." He squeezed me hard before releasing his grip.

I stepped away, suddenly aware of our audience and my makeup probably siding down my face. "So, who wants to eat?"

"Me!" Morgan yelled.

After picking up my new prized possession off the table, I snagged her hand. "Let's go, pretty girl."

As we walked away I could hear Sam's mom scolding him for the non-proposal.

He just laughed. "Stop, Ma. She loved it."

I really, really did.

The party was winding down, and Morgan had just finished blowing out the candles on her makeshift birthday cake. Henry and I were huddled around her, taking pictures so she could show her friends, when there was an angry knock at the front door. Initially, I assumed it was someone else Sam had invited, since they'd clearly gotten through the security gate, but the moment it swung open, I realized I should have made changing my codes and keys a priority.

Devon stormed in, leveling me with a murderous glare before I even had the chance to utter a hello. Or, more likely, a get-the-fuck-out.

"You fucking married him!" he roared, raking his eyes over my dress and getting the completely wrong idea about what kind of party we were having.

And, because I was still hurt from the little stunt he'd pulled in Maine, not even to mention his showing up and screaming at me in front of a room full of people, I answered, "Yep. And you were not invited. Leave."

"You ungrateful bitch," he snapped before stumbling off-balance, barely keeping himself upright by leaning back on the wall.

Is he drunk? I'd never even seen him have a drink.

Henry and Sam both rushed forward.

"Hey! Watch your mouth," Sam growled.

Devon's eyes flashed to Sam just seconds before his fist clumsily sailed through the air. Sam was able to move out of the way. Henry wasn't so lucky.

"Oh, God!" the whole room gasped as Henry stumbled back, cupping his jaw.

Ryan and Ty both jumped in their direction. Thankfully, from out of nowhere, Carter came barreling into the room, wrapping Devon in a bear hug from behind before slamming him to the ground.

"How could you do this to me?" Devon screamed from the ground as Carter held him in place with a knee in this back. "I love you!"

"You what?" I shrieked back at him, more confused than ever.

"Oh, fuck," Henry mumbled, still rubbing his jaw.

"I've given up my life for you, Levee. I've spent every waking minute at your side. I'm a fucking bodyguard, not your servant. Or even your driver or butler. But I sucked it up and did it for you because *I love you.*"

My head was spinning, but he continued before I had a chance to catch up. *Devon loves me?*

"I sat back and watched you parade dumbass after dumbass around for three goddamn years, but I knew eventually you'd see me as more. I was *always* there for you. And you fall in love with some suicidal asshole you met while trying to jump off a bridge. What is wrong with you?"

The free fall didn't just find me—it swallowed the entire room.

"Oh my God!" Sam's mom cried, throwing her hand over her heart.

Sam's face paled as he quickly said, "It's not what you are thinking, Ma." Rushing toward her, he folded her into his chest. "I swear to God it's *not* what you are thinking."

"Come on. Let's go outside." Meg took Morgan's hand. "Ty. Ryan. Jen. Let's go."

Ryan eyed Sam carefully. "Swear to God you didn't lie to me," he pleaded, crossing his arms over his chest as the rest of them filed from the room.

Sam just tilted his head at him and impatiently flared his eyes.

Ryan nodded, throwing his hands up in surrender before backing away.

"He's lying, Ma. None of that happened." Sam looked up at me with wide eyes while holding his mother in his arms.

I could see it in his eyes that he wanted to tell her the truth and assure her that she wasn't going to lose her only remaining child the same way she had her husband and her daughter. I could also see that he didn't want to reveal my secret in the process.

"Bullshit," Devon slurred.

And that's when it hit me.

It *really* was bullshit.

All of it.

The fact that it had happened.

The fact that I was hiding it.

The fact that Devon was trying to use it as an excuse for why I had fallen in love with Sam.

It was *all* bullshit.

"Devon, you're an idiot. Because I love you too."

Sam's head snapped to me. "Excuse me?"

I waved him off and kept talking. "Maybe not the way you want me to love you, but it was still love. You and Henry were the only two people I could depend on without question. I wish you would've been a man and said something instead of acting like a little boy pulling the pigtails of your crush. You know why I haven't returned any of your phone calls or even confronted you about the crap you pulled in Maine? Because I was scared it would mean that I'd have to say goodbye. I was hoping I could cool off and discuss things with you on a personal level, but then, tonight, you come into my home...drunk... hurling lies and insults?" I shook my head in disgust. "Thank you. You embarrassed the hell out of me in front of some really amazing people, but you made my life so much easier. Devon, you're fired." I squared my shoulders and looked at Carter. "Get him out of here."

"Levee, wait," Devon pleaded as Carter pulled him to his feet.

"Henry, you want to press any charges?" I asked as he made his way over me.

"Nope," he replied, draping his arm around my shoulders in a show of solidarity.

"Okay, then. Devon, if you ever show your face on my property again, I *will* call the police. I *will* have you arrested. And I *will* press charges." I held his gaze for several seconds to reinforce how serious I really was.

My heart was still absolutely breaking, but I sucked it up, because I had to.

I wasn't Spiderman.

I couldn't fix the way Devon felt for me.

I couldn't keep him employed just because I felt guilty.

I could, however, do what was best for *me*.

"You did good," Henry whispered as Carter led Devon out of my front door.

My shoulders slacked, but my stomach rolled. I had so much more good to do.

"Mrs. Rivers, I'm sorry you had to witness that, but what he said was the truth...kinda."

"Levee, leave it alone," Sam warned.

"No. First of all, with the way that went down, I give it until the morning before Devon airs all of my dirty laundry to the press. Secondly, don't lie to your mom on my account. Mrs. Rivers, Sam and I met on the top of a bridge. He was there mourning Anne. I was there to kill myself...I think. I don't really know for sure because I never made it that far. Sam has saved my life in more ways than I can count, and tomorrow morning, I'm heading out to a treatment facility in a desperate attempt to get my life back under control. I've been drowning for a long time, and your son not only breathed air into my lungs, but he dragged me from the water altogether. You raised an amazing man, and I'm doing everything in my power to get to a place where I can be the woman he deserves. You should be really proud."

"Wow," his mom breathed, looking up at Sam.

I smiled tightly, following her gaze up to his eyes.

Pure adoration was etched over every inch of his handsome face. "I'm so fucking proud of you," he praised.

"Don't speak too soon. I think we need to do some sort of press release before Devon has the chance to sell all of this information. I'd like you there so at least he can't use you as some sort of leverage against me."

Sam's smile grew. "Levee Williams, are you asking me to be your public boyfriend and not just your secret lover?"

"Eww," his mom said, stepping out of his arms.

"I think I am." I smiled. "I think I'm ready for the world to try to steal you from me."

Sam's lips lifted even higher as he sauntered in my direction. Using my chin to tip my head back, he placed a kiss on my lips then arrogantly said, "I dare them to try."

chapter twenty-seven

Sam

After a million apologies from Levee, my family decided to call it a night. Before my mom left, she pulled Levee aside and had a little chat with her. They both ended up crying and hugging before Mom finally walked out the door.

As we watched them all drive away, Levee leaned her head on my shoulder and declared that I was never allowed to meet her parents. I laughed then tossed her over my shoulder and headed up the winding staircase to her bedroom.

I would love to say that I stripped her naked and we blocked out the world while tangled between the sheets. However, when I deposited her on the bed, Henry was lounging next to her. And, as I collapsed on the other side of her, I knew things were bad when Henry didn't even crack a threesome joke.

"So, are you sure about this? I mean, do you really think Devon would sell you out like that?" he asked the ceiling.

"I don't know. Two hours ago, no. But now…I'm not sure. How the hell did I not know he was in love with me?"

Sliding my arm under her head, I said, "I told you he was your Kevin Costner."

"Oh, hush," she teased, rolling to my side.

"For what it's worth, I think you're doing the right thing. Hiding doesn't help anyone," Henry said, climbing off the bed and moving to the chair in the corner. "You still planning to step away for a little while?"

Levee's head tilted back to look at me. While holding my gaze, she responded to Henry. "Yeah. I really think I need to."

"Good. Then call Stewart. Make an official statement. Blast it everywhere, and then get better so I can stop spending my weekends alone with you two. It's making me horny. I can't even remember the last time I got laid."

"Tuesday. The photographer," she informed him. "I got the play-by-play on Wednesday."

Henry smiled fondly. "Ah, yes. I should call him."

She turned her attention back to me. "Are you sure you're ready for all of this? I'll totally understand if you want to stay out of it."

"What do I have to lose, Levee? I'm in this with you one hundred percent, and if it means you get to stop hiding and we get to live a life… together, I'm ready for it all with you." I smiled, kissing the tip of her nose. "And yes, I'll sign the copyright release on that too."

With a groan, she lifted her phone to dial. "Nah. You can keep that one. It wasn't that great."

"What!" I exclaimed.

"Yeah, not your best work. You really should have tried harder."

"Seriously?"

"Oh, come on. Don't look at me like that. That wasn't anywhere close to as good as 'I want to struggle with you.' Sorry, Sam. I think you were a one-hit wonder."

"Well, we can't all be Levee Williams, I guess." I tickled her until she rolled off the bed with the phone to her ear.

"Stewart? We need to talk."

For over an hour, Levee paced the room, talking on the phone. Henry sat in the corner, alternating between listening to her and whispering his opinion. I sat silently on the bed, wondering what the hell they were talking about. I was a smart guy. But I swear they were speaking a different language. From what I gathered, they were debating the pros and cons on what details Levee should release in her official statement.

Finally, when she hung up, she dropped her chin to her chest and announced, "And now, we wait."

"That's it?" I asked, rising to pull her into a hug.

"Yep. My publicist will do the rest."

"Let me know if you need anything. I'm going to see if the sexy photog sends dirty pictures." Henry rubbed his palms together before heading down the hall to his rooms—plural.

When Levee had originally said that we needed to do a press release, I hadn't been quite sure what to expect, but it sure as hell wasn't lying in bed while staring at our social media accounts.

"Oh, oh, oh. It's up," she said, sitting up in bed.

When I refreshed my rePURPOSEd Instagram account, a notification appeared that I had been tagged in a photo.

It was a picture of Levee and me from earlier that night. I was pretty sure Meg had taken it on her cell phone, but it was utterly breathtaking. We were huddled together while talking to Henry. I was holding a beer and laughing, and Levee was pressed up on her toes, kissing my cheek, her smile visible even from the side. My arm was anchored around her waist, and her hand sat lovingly on my stomach.

The post read: *Once upon a time...I fell in love with Spiderman. #TrueStory*

I knew that Levee hadn't posted that picture. Some publicist or assistant somewhere had pressed the magical button, sharing our intimate moment with the world.

But I knew with absolute certainty that Levee had penned the message, and even though it was a load of shit, it meant the world to me.

Grabbing my hand, she intertwined our fingers. "Don't let go. No matter what, okay?"

Staring into whiskey-brown eyes that represented the rest of my life, I knew there was only one answer. "Never."

My life changed that night.

She was right.

Everything *was* different.

But, even as pictures of us flashed on the screen while news stations reported that Levee Williams was checking into a mental health treatment program for depression and a possible suicide attempt, one thing remained the same.

Us.

She drew circles on my chest as we stayed up into the wee hours of the morning, laughing and talking like two people madly in love.

And, at the end of the day, that was all we really were.

Our relationship had absolutely nothing to do with Levee's celebrity status or my lack thereof.

She wasn't the princess.

And I wasn't the pauper.

She was just a sad girl who liked to write songs.

And I was nothing more than a simple guy who was lucky enough to have made her fall in love with him.

chapter twenty-eight

Sam

Levee had been gone for thirty days.

Thirty unbelievably chaotic days.

The first week had been hard. Just like in Maine, Levee had gone into a black-out period where she didn't have her cell phone. It was probably for the best though, because the world was aflutter with all things Levee…and Sam.

I was just aflutter for a smoke. An urge I resisted…barely. Quitting smoking was the hardest thing I'd ever done. And I, even one month later, wasn't sure I'd really done it. But I kept going. I'd made a promise to every single woman in my life, and come nuclear warfare or the zombie apocalypse, I was keeping up my end of the bargain.

World-ending disaster seemed easier though. *God, it's hard.*

But back to my new celebrity status…even if it was a miserable, smoke free one.

With the exception of rePURPOSEd's online orders, nothing exploded after Levee had released the truth about her sudden departure from music. If anything, the public had rallied around her. There was a massive outpouring of support, and while, yes, a ton of critics were predicting that this was all a big publicity stunt, for the most part, everyone was supportive. Even the fans who hated my guts. But especially the ones who thought I created unicorns.

Reporters weren't camping out on my doorstep the way Levee had feared, but there was no shortage of people grilling me for information about her. I'd had to change my phone number three times, and more than once, I'd been followed by a photographer while walking Sampson at the park. I just smiled and kept going.

I'd gotten the girl. It was going to take more than a few pictures to bring me down.

I landed my first tabloid cover on week two. It was a completely fabricated story about how I was really Levee's stalker who she'd fallen in love with after I'd held her captive for a weekend. I was relatively sure they didn't know about our stalker joke, but Levee and I got a big laugh out of that article. It was a delightful little piece of horseshit that I promptly framed and hung over our bed.

As far as we could tell, Devon never went to the press about anything. All of our true secrets remained our own. There were a million speculations about how Levee and I had met, especially once the reporters had started digging into my past, but not a single person ever came up with the magical formula that ended with us standing on the top of that bridge together. I guessed Devon really did love her—or, at the very least, he loved the ability to earn a paycheck. Despite my urging otherwise, Levee gave him a glowing recommendation. She stated that their issues were personal and not professional. While I was against it at first, I was happy to hear he'd landed a job with a large security firm two thousand miles away in Chicago. I didn't have to worry about him randomly showing up at our door, stressing Levee out.

Unfortunately, there were plenty of others to more than fill that role.

The third weekend Levee was gone, I finally got to meet her parents. Bianca and Kyle Williams decided to pop up for a surprise visit.

Levee all but burst into tears, and I couldn't say that I blamed her. They were...awful.

Don't get me wrong. They loved Levee, and I was pretty sure Levee loved them too, but they were unbelievably exhausting to be around. Her mother paced, whined, complained, and nagged the entire time she was there. She lectured Doctor Spellman on the importance of accessorizing even while on the job. And the minute I removed my jacket, her lips curled in disgust. Levee lost her mind when Bianca asked how many of my tattoos I'd gotten while in prison. The woman was miserable, and to hear Levee tell it, she just liked to make sure everyone else felt as bad as she did.

Kyle Williams sat in the corner, quietly texting on his phone, only pausing long enough to jab insults at Bianca, which, in turn, set her off even more. No one could even get a word in edgewise because they argued the entirety of the two-hour visit.

At one point, they were arguing so loudly that there was absolutely nothing left to do but laugh. Levee scowled at me from across the room, where she was attempting to keep the peace.

After I'd made an exaggerated cross over my heart, I mouthed, "We will never be them."

Her whole body sagged, but her lips curved into a smile. She gave up on trying to intervene and joined me on the couch. While they continued to bicker, Levee and I engaged in a very serious thumb-war tournament. She won even though I believed she cheated. Somehow.

Over those weeks of separation, I fell even more in love with Levee than I'd thought possible. Every night, we spent at least an hour on the phone, talking about everything under the sun. It was during that time that I realized just how much I didn't know about her. There was probably a herd of her fans that could beat me in a game of trivia about the woman I had every intention of marrying one day.

I was okay with that. I knew all the important things.

I had to ask how she liked her eggs and what clique she'd belonged to in high school, but I knew how to make her laugh with a stupid joke and how to make her cheeks pink with a simple touch.

I knew her heart.

And I knew it belonged to me.

Thirty days, almost to the hour, after I'd dropped her off, I arrived to pick her up.

"Ohmygodohmygodohmygod," Levee nervously rushed out the moment I walked into Doctor Spellman's office.

I froze and eyed her warily.

Her gaze cut to Doctor Spellman before jumping back to me.

"I'm in trouble, aren't I?" I asked.

She shook her head. "I got an idea." If the timid inflection of her voice was any indication, it wasn't a good one—even if her eyes were dancing with excitement.

Doctor Spellman stood up and headed to the door. "I'm going to leave you two alone to discuss this." She stopped right before she reached the door and gave me a pointed glare. "Hear her out, okay?"

Oh fuck. This is not good. Even the doctor is in on it.

"Sit down." Levee reached up to take my hand.

"You're making me nervous."

She smiled, pulling me down on to the couch.

Then I knew that it was way worse than bad. She didn't settle next to me. She slung her leg over my hips and settled *on top of me.*

"Don't be nervous." She leaned in and pressed a lingering kiss to my lips.

Gripping her hips, I gave her an encouraging squeeze. "Spill it."

And spill it, she did. "I want to put out an album next year."

I closed my eyes and dropped my head against the back of the couch. "What happened to a break, Levee?"

"I'm getting to that part." She playfully pinched my nipple.

However, I wasn't feeling playful in the least.

I was anxious and frustrated.

"Then get to it," I growled, opening my eyes and pinching her nipple back.

"Ten songs. No deadlines. When it's done, it's done. No publicity. Not even a photo shoot for the album cover. Surprise release. No tour. No interviews. The album will speak for itself."

While they were all really great selling points for me—but maybe not for an album—they didn't answer my main concern.

"Why? Why now? Why not in six months after you finish with the outpatient stuff?"

She rested her forehead on mine. "Because I think it will be more therapeutic for me than anything else. Doctor Spellman agrees."

I laughed without humor. "What kind of voodoo did you have to do to get her approval?"

"None. I told her my ideas. She asked a few questions. Then said okay."

I blew out a breath. "And what are these ideas, Levee? Convince me, because right now, I'm not so sure I agree with the good doctor."

"You will." She smiled confidently. "Did you know that our bridge is one of the only ones left in the country without a suicide prevention barrier?"

Unfortunately, I did know this. It was one of the facts I'd obsessed about after Anne died.

I nodded.

"Did you know the city has approved a plan to put one in place? But it's ridiculously expensive and the state hasn't been able to fund it yet?"

Now that I didn't know.

I shook my head.

"*The Fall Up.*"

"What?"

"*The Fall Up.* That's the name of my album. I'm going to write ten songs about my journey to the top of that bridge. Then my journey back down. I want to tell it all. I started writing a few nights ago, and at this rate, I'll be done in a few weeks." She suddenly pushed out of my lap and onto her feet and began pacing the length of the couch. "God, it felt liberating, Sam. Molding all of that pain and darkness into something positive." Her eyes lit as she stopped. "I want to help people, but you're right. I have to make my life a priority. But why can't I do both? Those two things don't have to be mutually exclusive. So, with *The Fall Up*, I'm proposing I get the therapeutic relief of telling my story through music, and I donate every single penny I make so that no one can ever use that bridge as a weapon again."

A lump of emotions suddenly formed in my throat. I couldn't pinpoint what emotions they were, exactly, because never in my life had I felt anything like it before.

In that moment, even as the memories of Anne ravaged me, I fell even more in love with Levee Williams. I shouldn't have been surprised by this idea of hers.

It was thoughtful.

Smart.

Beautiful.

Kind.

Brave.

Exactly like Levee.

I swallowed hard, fighting to keep my manhood intact and the asshole tears at bay. But shit, I was overwhelmed.

I shouldn't have been surprised by that, either.

It was definitely Levee.

Standing up, I hugged her tight, tucking her head into the crook of my neck. She didn't even have a choice in the matter. She didn't exactly fight me though.

"I can handle it, Sam. I swear to God. This will be a really, really good thing for me. And if, at any point, I'm taking it too far, I know you'll be there to reel me back in. Please say yes."

After clearing my throat, I said the only thing that possibly made sense. "Marry me."

Her head popped up in surprise. "What?"

Cupping each side of her jaw, I repeated, "Marry me."

"Wha… Why?"

"Because I love you. Because you love me. Because every second that you aren't my wife, from this moment on, will be agonizing. Because I'm ready to start our lives together. Because I have absolutely no concept of romance and just blurt shit like this out, but I swear to God I've never, in my entire life, meant something more. Levee, marry me."

Her bright eyes filled with tears. A single one spilled from the corner, giving me the answer I knew I would receive, easing my entire world.

Her voice was thick with emotion as she attempted to tease, "But where's the other half of my photo album?"

Smiling, I wiped the tear away from her cheek. "I'll finish it this weekend. I'll sell my liver to buy you a proper ring too. I'm sorry I did this a little out of order, but I couldn't wait. *The Fall Up*, Levee? It's fucking brilliant. Of course I support you." Placing my tear-soaked thumb over her lips, I whispered, "Say yes."

She held my gaze and, in a very serious tone, spoke around my thumb, "I've made worse life decisions, I suppose."

I gave her an unimpressed glare then replied, "I can attest to that. I listened to your performance with Lionel the other night with my mom."

She returned my glare, but a smile crept from under my thumb.

"Say it," I implored.

Taking my wrist, she guided my hand away from her lips. While wrapping her arms around my neck, she took my mouth in a slow kiss that said even more than the tear, but it still wasn't the one word I needed to hear.

"Say it," I urged as she forced me on to the couch.

She didn't follow me down. Instead, she made her way to the door, twisting the lock on the handle before very sensually removing her jeans.

"Fuck. We should go home," I growled when she mounted my lap and immediately went for the button on my jeans.

Nipping at my neck, she murmured, "Can't wait that long."

"Jesus." My eyes flashed to the door as she stripped her shirt and her bra over her head in one swift movement.

"I love you," she breathed, finding my cock and dragging it through her folds before aligning us.

"Does this mean you'll marry me?" I asked, leaning forward to suck her peaked nipple into my mouth. Then I raked my teeth over the sensitive flesh before releasing it.

Slowly sinking down onto my cock, she stared deep into my eyes and hissed, "Yessss."

Close enough.

epilogue

Levee

It was raining. Isn't that the way all great love stories start? And also usually end? The cool breeze whipped through my curls as I stared off the side of that bridge.

Sam's hand folded over mine, taking the umbrella from my grasp. "How you feeling?" he asked, brushing his hand against my swollen, but still hidden, stomach before gripping my hip.

"Like shit," I answered through a smile as dozens of cameras flashed around us.

"I would like to use this moment to once again remind you that it wasn't a blow job that got you in this situation. Swallowing is, and always will be, safe."

I exaggerated a laugh for the crowd then wrapped him in a tight hug, sneaking a hand between us to secretly pinch his nipple. "I'm not sucking your dick. I almost puked just brushing my teeth this morning," I whispered into his ear.

He leaned away and lovingly held my gaze. "That explains your breath. You want some gum?" He winked, and a genuine laugh bubbled from my throat as he pulled a pack of mango-flavored gum from his pocket.

One year after Sam had proposed, we said, "I do," in front of three hundred guests in an over-the-top ceremony in San Francisco. News helicopters flew overhead making it virtually impossible to hear a single word Sam said, but I couldn't have cared less. I knew those vows by heart—it was, after all, the second time I'd heard them.

The truth was Sam and I had been secretly married on our bridge not even five hours after I'd said yes. We were both in jeans, and our ceremony was officiated by an ordained minister Henry had once slept with, but all we cared about were the promises we were making each other, even if they were sealed with plain, silver bands we'd picked up at a department store ten minutes before they'd closed.

An expensive, world-renowned photographer made us an extravagant wedding album after our public ceremony, but I didn't cherish it nearly as much as I did the one Sam had surprised me with on our real one-month anniversary. It consisted of a few selfies we'd taken to show off our new rings on the top of the bridge and funny composite images Sam had made, complete with beer and chickens strewn across the bar floor of our hillbilly wedding. Sam claimed that he wasn't good at romance, but as I sobbed while flipping each page of that album, I begged to differ.

He was good at everything.

And, together, we were unstoppable.

The Fall Up was released the month after our lavish wedding. The project had gotten away from me more than once, and it wasn't nearly as low stress as I'd hoped. But, each and every time I hit a snag, Sam bluntly became my voice of reason. Especially when my record label attempted to pick off a few of the tracks on the album. But, with my husband at my side and my head and heart finally aligned, I stood my ground. I threatened to hold the album and leave when my contract expired only a few months later. They were none too happy about the stand I was taking against them, but we both knew they needed me more than I needed them.

They backed down.

I held the album anyway.

Then I left them.

Then Henry and I started a record label of our own.

Then Sam's head exploded when I told him that I'd taken on a new project.

Eventually, he got over it. I had more than proven I wasn't the same girl he'd met on the top of that bridge. I wasn't drowning anymore. To be honest, I was truly living, maybe for the first time ever.

Upon release of *The Fall Up*, I hadn't been sure what to expect, seeing as no one had even known I'd been working on a new project. However, it shattered every single album I'd ever released, soaring to the top of the charts and selling millions the first week alone. Between the record sales and donations from other musicians wanting to help after hearing my story, we raised over one hundred and eight million dollars.

Being famous is a funny thing. For some reason, people think you're the special one. But, in reality, I wouldn't even be a blip on the radar without *them*. Yet, somehow, hundreds of people reached out to me to say that *The Fall Up* had changed their life.

And that changed mine.

I still visited children's hospitals when time permitted, and it still felt incredible to bring a smile to those tiny faces, but suicide prevention quickly became my personal calling. Sam and I even filmed a series of PSAs that would be aired during the Super Bowl.

The world took to Sam much the same way I did—in utter awe.

He was a natural in front of the camera, and I swear to God he signed just as many autographs as I did when we went out in public. We were both amazed at the amount of offers he had rolling in. Calvin Klein actually offered him a hefty sum to be the new face of their rugged wear line. Sam declined every offer except for one: Popular Wood.

rePURPOSEd took off with all of the new exposure, and Sam opened storefronts in Miami, Seattle, and New York within two years. He also decided to take a step back and hire a CEO to run things.

His business was booming.

So was my career.

We were crazy in love.

It seemed like the perfect time to flip our lives upside down.

Three years after we were married, I went off birth control. Five months later, I was hanging my head in the toilet, cursing the pregnancy gods for having lied to me that morning sickness went away after the fifteenth week.

Several hours later, I found myself once again standing on the top of a bridge, wrapped in Sam's arms, this time at the formal ceremony unveiling the brand-new Anne Rivers Suicide Prevention Barriers.

"My breath doesn't stink," I finally shot back at Sam before forcing him into another kiss.

"My nose disagrees," he joked then pushed a piece of gum into his mouth.

Sam had never once picked up a cigarette again. But, judging by the fact that he'd just devoured his tenth piece of gum since we'd arrived on the bridge, his memories were testing him.

"So, have you given any more thought to Sander?" he asked, turning to face the podium, where the governor had stepped up to give his speech.

"Sanders? Maybe. Sander? No. That end 's' makes all the difference."

He groaned even though he was still skillfully smiling for the camera. "Sanders Rivers is a terrible name. Don't set our son up for failure."

"I'm not setting our son up for anything. We're having a girl."

"Fine, but we aren't naming her Bridget."

I gasped, slinging my head to face him. "We met on a bridge!"

"That doesn't mean she has to suffer for it," he replied out of the corner of his mouth. "Thank God we didn't meet at Taco Bell."

"Her name could be Bella."

He rolled his eyes. "Fine. McDonalds."

"Donna Rivers is a beautiful name!" I exclaimed, interrupting the governor and causing every eye on the bridge to swing in our direction.

Sam laughed and dropped the umbrella forward to shield us from the cameras. Looping his arm around my shoulders, he pulled me in for a hard kiss. "Okay. Okay. Bridget it is. But, for the record, we're calling her Bree, not Bridge."

"Deal," I mumbled against his mouth as photographers worked their way behind us, furiously snapping pictures.

I should have cared that they were stealing that moment from us just to sell it to some magazine or website. But that was our life. It was hard to get worked up about that while safely cradled in Sam's strong arms.

So, instead of ending the moment in an effort to protect our privacy, I sucked in a deep breath and got lost in the golden-brown eyes that had saved my life in nearly the exact same spot all those years before. "I love you."

Sam smiled one of his award-winning grins then used the toe of his boot to tap my high heel. "I love you too, Designer Shoes."

The End

Coming in 2016
The Spiral Down
Henry Alexander's story

Other Books by Aly Martinez

The Wrecked and Ruined Series
Changing Course
Stolen Course
Broken Course

On the Ropes
Fighting Silence
Fighting Shadows

Savor Me

acknowledgements

Bianca and Bianca: Yes, I named a character after y'all. She was a bitch. You two are NOT! I love you both so hard. Thank you for sticking with me since the very beginning.

Megan: Thank you for all the black, but especially for the purple! I love you so hard.

Natasha: Calm down! No, seriously. You are the best. We have established this. Don't let it go to your head, because you are also a twat. HA! I love you! P.S. I need another 100 Kinder Eggs.

Amie and Miranda: What can I possibly say? You ladies rocked this hard! Thank you for the numerous pep talks when I wanted to quit. Sam appreciates you pushing for more dirty too. He told me so.

Mara: I'm still laughing at the gifs in your emails. HAHA! Thank you so much for all of your feedback.

Tracey: You have your own books now, and you still make time for me. You are amazing!

Lakrysa: I absolutely love your "I got nothing," emails. I squeal every time you write it. Thank you for being such an amazing friend, and yes…even telling me when you do have something. HAHA!

Gina and MJ: As usual, you two ladies rocked the proofread. My eye twitches when I think about what I would do with out y'all. HA!

Danielle: First Flinted and now, only three months later, Samted. I'm keeping you forever. I don't care if Ashley did call dibs first. BAHAHA!

Ashley: I owe you way more than this little section in the back of a book. You want a kid? No? A dog? No? A husband? No? Hmm… Okay, so a little section it is! Thank you for everything. No, like, seriously…. EVERYTHING! I have no idea what I would do without you.

Jessica Prince: You kept my ass in gear. Which is a task that can be pretty hard especially when there are m/m books to be read! HA! Thank you so much for all of your help on this one!

Erin Noelle: Thank you so much for reading every agonizingly unedited word of this book. I can honestly say this book is better because of you. Thank you so much for that!

The Rock Stars of Romance PR: Lisa, you rocked this so hard and I can't even begin to explain the peace of mind I have just knowing you are taking care of things. Thank you for being awesome.

Mo Mabie: I don't even know what to say. You know I love you even when I argue with you about…well, everything. HA! Thank you for being my middle school boyfriend and staying up late, talking on the phone for five hours until we've both plotted more books than we will ever write. I don't know that I'd be able to do this without you. But more than that, I don't want to try. You're stuck with me.

Jammy Jean Lovers: There are no words for how much I love y'all. This writing thing wouldn't be nearly as much fun without the three of you. You keep me sane in this world that can often get crazy. No drama. No judgment. Nothing but 100% support. (That's the sign of a good bra too!)

FTN Ladies: I'm so lucky to have found a group of talented, smart, and funny ladies. I love each and every one of you. You ladies make me want to be a better writer.

Stacey Blake: I've said it all before. You are the most priceless jewel I have met during this crazy indie author thing.

Mickey Reed: Had had had had had had had had had. Hopefully that makes up for the billion you HAD to add while editing this. HAHA! Sorry.

Alissa Smith: Thank you for keeping me in line. Without you, I'd be lost. No. Seriously. I still don't know how to find my Google docs. HA!

And last but not least....

The readers and bloggers: I would be nowhere without all of you. This book is for you!

about the author

Born and raised in Savannah, Georgia, Aly Martinez is a stay-at-home mom to four crazy kids under the age of five, including a set of twins. Currently living in South Carolina, she passes what little free time she has reading anything and everything she can get her hands on, preferably with a glass of wine at her side.

After some encouragement from her friends, Aly decided to add "Author" to her ever-growing list of job titles. So grab a glass of Chardonnay, or a bottle if you're hanging out with Aly, and join her aboard the crazy train she calls life.

Facebook: https://www.facebook.com/AuthorAlyMartinez
Twitter: https://twitter.com/AlyMartinezAuth
Goodreads: https://www.goodreads.com/AlyMartinez

CPSIA information can be obtained
at www.ICGtesting.com
Printed in the USA
LVOW04s1834021116
511368LV00010B/1285/P

9 781518 711398